Thursday's Child

Andrew Grey

Dreamspinner Press

Published by
Dreamspinner Press
4760 Preston Road
Suite 244-149
Frisco, TX 75034
http://www.dreamspinnerpress.com/

Thursday's Child
Copyright © 2009 by Andrew Grey

Cover Art by Dan Skinner/Cerberus Inc. cerberusinc@hotmail.com
Cover Design by Mara McKennen

ISBN: 978-1-935192-96-1

Printed in the United States of America
First Edition
May, 2009

eBook edition available
eBook ISBN: 978-1-935192-97-8

Dedicated to Elizabeth N., Mara M., Lynn W., Anne R., and Kim G. Your efforts and talents are greatly appreciated.

Monday's child is fair of face,

Tuesday's child is full of grace,

Wednesday's child is full of woe

Thursday's child has far to go,

Friday's child is loving and giving,

Saturday's child must work for a living,

But the child that's born on the Sabbath day

Is fair and wise and good and gay.

—Mother Goose

Part One
Rebirth

Chapter One

"Cembran!" Travis rushed inside, slamming the door behind him. "Cembran!" No answer. Travis hurried back outside and down the path to the goat barn, ignoring the calm, pastoral scene that was part of his home. "Cembran!"

"I'm in here!"

Travis heard Cembran call from the far side of the barn. He'd forgotten it was milking time. Travis slowed his pace as he walked through the barn to the milking station. Cembran sat on a stool, a goat in a raised stall. Cembran's head with his ringlet curls rested against the goat while he gently and efficiently milked her as she munched on hay.

"There's a carnival in town, and I was wondering if you'd like to go."

Cembran looked up from his task, smiling broadly as he looked at Travis. "Sometimes, you're just like a little kid." He shook his head but stilled it as Travis leaned forward to kiss him.

Their lips moved together, and Cembran moaned softly as Travis's tongue gently pressed for entrance. Cembran's lips parted, and he felt Travis's fingers card through his hair as the pressure on his lips, and the urgency of the kiss increased. Without breaking their kiss, Travis knelt in front of Cembran, pulling their bodies together, their satyr instincts taking over as the rest of the world faded away.

A stomp and a gentle nuzzle from the goat brought them back to the present, and Cembran snickered against Travis lips. "Guess she wanted a kiss too."

Travis laughed gently as he patted the goat's nose. "He's mine, girl. Sorry."

Cembran returned to his milking. "If you'd like to go to the carnival, we can go. Just don't make me go on any woofy rides."

"Deal! I wonder if the boys would like to go as well?" The "boys" were Dovino, Phillip, and Jeremy—three young satyrs, rather than boys—who helped them work the farm. The three boys had been together for almost two years now and were best friends as well as lovers, and the arrangement seemed to be really working for them.

Cembran finished his milking and released the goat from the pen. "They finished their chores a few minutes ago, and I think they were heading toward the lake." Travis rolled his eyes, and Cembran tittered to himself. During the summer, the boys usually went swimming after work, and quite often their swimming turned into the three of them making love on the beach. "They're satyrs, Travis...." Cembran's voice had his "what do you expect" tone.

Travis leaned close. "I know, but sometimes I want to take you down to the beach. Remember our first bacchanal?" Travis raised his eyebrows invitingly at Cembran as he saw a shiver ripple through his lover.

"They just went down to the lake a few minutes ago. You're probably safe."

"Thanks, Lamb. Are you almost finished here?"

"Yes, Lemmle. I have one more goat to finish, and I need to put the milk away."

"Good. I'll meet you at the lake in half an hour. Don't bring a bathing suit; you won't need it." Cembran's eyes smoldered as Travis leered at him before turning around, walking out of the barn, and down the path.

Approaching the lake, Travis could hear the sound of the boys playing in the cool water. Travis made plenty of noise as he approached the lake. Travis was not born a satyr, but had been made a satyr by Bacchus himself as a reward, and as with most satyrs, sex was a very important part of his life. But Travis felt very deeply that each expression of Cembran's and his love was private, very special, and wasn't to be shared with others. Consequently, he extended that same belief and courtesy to others.

Fortunately, the three young men were just swimming and hadn't progressed to their usual satyr-like diversion. "Hey, guys!" Travis waved as he called out.

The three young men stopped their frolicking and waved back. Dovino, the oldest and usual spokesman for the three, called back, "Are you and Cembran coming swimming?"

"Well, Cembran and I were planning on coming to the lake...." Travis kept the rest of this thought to himself.

The young men looked at one another knowingly, "We'll be out in a few minutes." There were no snickers or snide looks of any kind. Travis was their boss, and he owned the land, but more importantly they cared for and deeply respected the relationship between Travis and Cembran.

"Say, we're going to the carnival in town after dinner. Would you three like to ride along?"

Heads swiveled, and they arrived at a silent group decision. "Sure. We'll be ready." The three of them started for the shore as Travis headed down the path through the woods that led toward the farm. As Travis crested the small rise at the edge of the farm, he couldn't help looking over the bucolic scene in front of him. The sheep and goat barns surrounded by their pastures and pens, their sturdy, rustic-looking house, the orchard and vegetable gardens, as well as the hay fields and woods beyond. Their land; their home. Cembran had built the original farm himself, and together they'd enlarged it with the addition of pastures, the orchard, and the huge vegetable garden. Travis smiled to himself as he strode down the now well-worn path toward the comfortable house. Cembran had built the original portion of the house, consisting of the kitchen, living room, and a single bedroom and small bath. Together, Travis and Cembran had enlarged the house, adding a master bedroom and bath, as well as an office for Travis. All of the lumber to build the addition had come from trees that they'd felled to enlarge the pastures. Both Travis and Cembran felt very strongly that no materials harvested from their property should be wasted.

Once inside, Travis grabbed their beach blanket as well as towels, a bottle of Champagne, and two glasses and then headed outside and back down the path to the lake.

The clearing around the lake was quiet and utterly peaceful as Travis spread out the blanket on the small beach beneath the shade of a huge oak. Slipping off his shirt, shoes, and socks, Travis settled in the shade, waiting for his mate to make an appearance. He didn't have long to wait.

Cembran stepped from the trees surrounding the lake a few minutes later, looking around. Travis could instantly tell when Cembran saw him: his eyes sparkled, and a bright smile lit his face. Cembran walked to Travis and settled next to him on the blanket, accepting a deep kiss from his lover and mate.

Travis's hand carded through Cembran's ringlets as his lips slid against Cembran's hot mouth. Cembran's lips parted in invitation, and Travis accepted with gusto, settling Cembran back onto the blanket as he continued to pummel the man's mouth with his tongue and lips. "God, Cembran, you are beautiful." Travis's voice was soft, the words whispered reverently as he let the cloak that hid his satyr features fall.

Cembran's eyes met Travis's intense gaze as he allowed his own satyr features to appear. "And you are the sexiest man I've ever seen." His voice was soft, rough, and filled with passion. Like most satyrs who live among humans, Travis and Cembran had the ability to mask their satyr features and did so out of habit. But when making love, they show their true selves to each other as a sign of their trust, love, and their bond as life mates.

Travis smiled as he buried his face in the base of Cembran's neck, sucking gently on the hot skin. Slowly, deliberately, their passion built. Clothes fell from their limbs; lips explored hot skin. Reclining back on the blanket, Travis pulled Cembran on top of him, their chests pressing together, lips opening to each other, tongues exploring, soft murmurs of pleasure escaping. "I love you, Lamb."

Lifting his head, Cembran peered into Travis's eyes, gazing into his mate's heart to glimpse the love that he knew filled it. "And I love you, Lemmle." Their words were special, just for each other, but completely unnecessary. Their hearts were joined, and they could feel their love for each other every day in everything they did. They were part of each other. "You're the best part of me."

"And you me, Lamb." Travis locked his legs around Cembran's waist, pulling their bodies together, while he brought Cembran's lips to his. Slowly, exquisitely, he felt Cembran enter him, joining them physically, as their hearts and souls were bound together emotionally. Their bodies moved together rhythmically, eyes locked together, soft words and the sounds of passion uttered softly for each other's ears and hearts only. Hands stroked soft, smooth skin covering hard, strong muscle; lips pulled on lips, bodies undulating together, desire building slowly and steadily.

Travis felt Cembran's rhythm become irregular, both of them reaching the heights of passion. Throwing his head back, Travis tightened his body around Cembran, triggering his release as Travis experienced his own body-shaking orgasm.

Cembran was still shaking as their bodies separated and Travis pulled him close. "Shhh. Relax, I have you." His hands glided along Cembran's back, soothing him, allowing him to come down slowly. "You were incredible, Lamb…," he said, kissing him softly. "My love… my heart."

Still breathing heavily, Cembran allowed Travis to take charge and gave himself to his mate's trusted embrace, burying his face against Travis's shoulder, his chest heaving with the release of spent passion.

Travis continued cooing and whispering tender words of love while his hands stroked Cembran's back and his fingers carded through soft ringlets.

Slowly, Cembran lifted himself off Travis, settling onto the blanket next to him.

Travis reached next to him, retrieving the bottle of Champagne and the glasses. Cembran smiled as Travis popped the cork and poured two glasses. "Do you know what today is, Lamb?"

Cembran squinched his eyes, looking confused. "I don't think so. It's not our anniversary or one of our birthdays."

Travis leaned close and smiled softly. "I was sixteen and up here to go swimming. I swam across the lake and, when I reached this side, I saw a small lamb stuck in the mud. Right over there." Travis pointed to where the stream entered the lake. "That was the first time I saw you up close and the first time we ever spoke." Travis clinked against Cembran's glass and they each took a sip. "I thought you were a god, the most handsome man I'd ever seen. When I close my eyes I can still see you wearing only a pair of rough shorts and this." Travis ran his fingers over the chain and the sun-shaped amulet that rested against his chest, while he gently pressed his lips to Cembran's, tasting the Champagne on his lips.

Setting his glass on the sand, Travis rose and took Cembran's hand, helping him to his feet. "Come on, Lamb. I'll race you to the center of the lake and back."

Cembran grinned. "You're on!" He raced into the water without waiting for Travis.

"That's cheating!" Travis took off after him, splashing in the water until it was deep enough for him to dive and swim.

Cembran reached the center of the lake first, but Travis overtook him, turning and getting back to the shore first. Cembran was grinning as he walked out of the water into Travis's waiting arms. "It won't be long and you'll be able to beat me." Travis was a very strong swimmer, and he'd taught Cembran to swim early in their relationship.

Cembran laughed, his body pressed to Travis, his head resting on his shoulder. "Not likely." Cembran gave Travis's bare butt a gentle, playful squeeze. "We should get back and finish the chores so we can be ready to go."

"I know." Travis pulled his mate into a deep kiss. "I just like holding you."

Cembran's fingers squeezed Travis's firm butt cheeks. "I like you holding me."

Travis raised an eyebrow. "Feels like you like holding something else too."

Cembran chuckled lightly and released his grip on Travis, slowly moving away. After drying themselves, they quietly dressed, picked up their glasses and the bottle, as well as their blankets and towels, linked their hands together, and walked contentedly down the path back toward the farm.

At the rise, Cembran kissed Travis lightly before heading to the barn, while Travis, carrying the remains of their interlude, headed toward the house to make dinner.

After a light dinner, Travis called the boys and told them to meet him and Cembran at the house and they'd head into town. The boys were ready and waiting when Cembran and Travis were, and they all piled into Travis's car and headed to town for an evening of fun at the carnival.

Everyone chatted noisily as Travis drove through the countryside, particularly the three boys in the backseat. Travis chuckled to himself as he listened to their chatter.

"So, Travis, which rides are you going to make me go on with you?" Cembran had gone with Travis the last time the carnival had come to town.

"I don't know." Travis gently squeezed Cembran's leg. "I promised I wouldn't take you on any woofy rides and I meant it." The last time, Cembran had turned the tilt-a-whirl into the tilt a hurl, and he wasn't eager to repeat that experience. "Just being with you is enough. We can go on anything you want." Cembran leaned closer to Travis, kissing him lightly on the neck, while a collective "Awww" arose from the backseat, followed by good-hearted laughter from all the occupants of the car.

Arriving in town, Travis parked the car and everyone got out. "Have fun, guys. We'll meet back here at ten." They had no need for money on the farm, so Travis always deposited their pay directly into each of their bank accounts. Travis handed each of them some cash. "Find me if you need more. Enjoy yourselves." Travis watched as the three of them headed off. "Let's go have some fun."

The carnival was a cacophony of lights, music, and people. They wandered down the main street of town watching the rides as they twisted and turned, past food stands and game stalls. Cembran played a few games, but was asked to leave because he kept winning, the rigged carnival games no match for his superior eyesight and reflexes.

At each stall or attraction, there was someone out front, trying to draw everyone's attention. One of the attractions advertised the world's biggest rats and had a drawing that showed them as big as large dogs. Cembran snickered softly as Travis shuddered. "I hate regular rats, let alone the world's biggest ones."

"Then I shouldn't ask to go in?"

"Only if you want to go alone." Travis shivered again.

Cembran smiled mischievously. "That's okay. I just wanted to see you squirm… again."

Travis leaned close, his lips close to Cembran's ears. "You already know what makes me squirm and writhe, and shout, and even beg." Now it was Cembran's turn to shiver.

As they continued through the carnival, an attraction caught Travis's eye and he pointed it out to Cembran. "Does that look familiar to you?"

Cembran looked where Travis was pointing, and stopped. "I… I…. It can't be."

Travis shook his head slowly. "God, I sure hope not."

The barker out front was yelling that the next show was in five minutes. Without thinking, Travis handed him the money for two admissions and they entered the brightly colored tent.

Inside, they found themselves in an area big enough for twenty people with canvas on three sides and a curtain at the far end that covered what appeared to be the side of a trailer. As they waited, a few other people filed in and, just before the show started, Travis saw Dovino, Phillip, and Jeremy enter the tent. The three of them saw Travis and Cembran and stood quietly next to them, dread and curiosity plain on their faces. The five of them stood together, waiting for the show to begin.

"Before we begin, I caution you… no loud noises or sudden movements. Ladies and gentlemen, we are pleased to present 'Manimal,' half man and half animal." The curtain in front parted.

Travis was speechless as he stared, while he heard Cembran whisper, "Oh my god… oh my god…."

Chapter Two

Travis could feel Cembran shaking against him as his soft words of disbelief washed over him. Gently, he slipped his arm around Cembran, pulling him close as he stared in disbelief at the scene in front of him.

The curtain retracted fully to reveal a small stage. Standing on the stage were two huge men each holding the end of a heavy chain and carrying tasers. In between the two men was what looked to be a satyr with a collar around his neck, with the chain the two men were holding attached to it. As Travis looked, he realized that this wasn't some faked carnival act; this was a real, live satyr complete with long horns, strong hairy chest, and hair-covered legs. He did, however, appear to have human-like feet, indicating to Travis that while he was probably mostly satyr, he did have some human blood. Travis looked into the eyes of what appeared to be a very strong satyr, but saw only resignation, despair, and confusion. Travis turned to Cembran, whispering into his ear, "He appears almost drugged."

Cembran shook his head slowly. "He's been broken." Moving slowly, Cembran edged closer to the stage and Travis heard him speak very softly: "Trau va aided."

Travis heard Cembran, but he didn't understand what he said. However, he did see the satyr raise his head and look into Cembran's eyes before lowering his gaze back to the floor.

Cembran stepped back to Travis and motioned for Dovino. "Do you speak Old Satyr?" Dovino nodded his head slowly. "Then follow my lead."

Cembran smiled and started to speak to Dovino. Back and forth they talked. Their speech was slow and deliberate, their attention focused on each other.

Travis watched as the gaze of the satyr on stage zeroed in on their conversation and his body went rigid. The two handlers reacted to his change in posture and got their tasers ready. Travis gently put his hand on Cembran's shoulder, their conversation tapered off, and the satyr on stage seemed to relax. The curtain began to close and everyone in the tent began to file toward the exit.

The five of them exited the tent in silence, stunned by what they'd seen. The fun of the carnival was forgotten as their thoughts focused on the captured satyr. Slowly, and without thought, they walked back to the car and headed back to the farm. The ride was silent, the only noise the sound of the engine and the tires on the pavement.

Arriving back at the farm, they walked silently down the path to the farm, each separating as the path diverged toward their homes. At the fork in the path, Travis broke the silence. "Come for breakfast in the morning; we need to talk."

Everyone nodded slowly and without another word stepped down their respective paths.

Near the house, Cembran spoke, his voice unsteady. "I need to make sure the animals are bedded down for the night."

"I'll help you."

Together they checked on the sheep and goats before heading back to the house and getting ready for bed.

Travis got cleaned up and joined Cembran in their bed. "Lamb, are you...?"

Cembran turned toward Travis, a tear streaking his face. "How can they do that to him?"

Travis pulled Cembran to him, hugging him close. "To them he's an animal, not a person with thoughts and feelings."

"They've broken his spirit. No satyr would ever voluntarily allow himself to be collared like that. It goes against everything in our nature. Parts of him should be screaming for release, but he seems so resigned."

More tears flowed down Cembran's face as he spoke, his emotions very close to the surface.

"I think he understood at least part of what you were saying." Travis's hand stroked down Cembran's back, trying to soothe his mate.

"I hope so. I tried not to look at him while we were speaking so I wouldn't alert…" Cembran screwed up his face with a look of distaste, "the guards."

Travis could finally feel Cembran starting to relax. "What did you say, Lamb?"

"Initially I asked if he needed help, and that seemed to get a slight reaction, so I thought he might have understood me." Travis nodded and kissed Cembran's forehead, silently urging him to continue. "When I was talking to Dovino, I told him our names and that we were satyrs, and that we could try to help him." Cembran gazed into Travis's eyes, looking for reassurance. "I said we lived nearby, and that was when you touched my shoulder."

Travis hugged Cembran close, nuzzling his neck softly, "He got tense, and the guards looked like they might use their tasers. I'm glad you understood my signal." Travis smiled. "You did good, Lamb, really good. That was quick thinking, conversing with Dovino like that. To the guards, you looked like tourists speaking a foreign language."

Cembran took a deep breath and let it out. "What do we do now?"

"I don't know, but we'll figure it out in the morning." Cembran nodded against Travis's chest as he curled close.

"Are we going to try to help him?" For Cembran the question was more a matter of form than anything else. He knew without a doubt that Travis was going to try to help. When Travis was made a satyr by Bacchus himself, he was charged with taking care of Bacchus's children, and that was a charge Travis took very seriously.

"Of course we are." Travis voice was firm, without any doubt. "Try to sleep, Lamb." Travis lifted Cembran's chin, kissing him softly. "I love you."

"I love you too." Cembran held Travis tight as he tried to fall asleep.

Travis woke early to something that had become very unusual: an empty bed. Both Travis and Cembran woke early to complete their farm chores, usually together, having a few quiet moments together before starting their day. Travis slipped out of bed and padded into the kitchen. The room smelled of fresh coffee, but the house appeared otherwise empty and quiet. Pouring himself a cup, he sipped the hot liquid as he padded back into the bedroom to get dressed.

Travis had just finished dressing when he heard the door open and close. "Travis, are you up yet?" Gathod's voice boomed through the house.

Stepping out of the bedroom, Travis smiled as he met Gathod around the table, "Hell yes, I'm up, and I've even had my first cup of coffee."

Gathod returned the smile and then got serious. "Cembran called me this morning and told me about the carnival last night."

Travis sat at the table and sighed. "Yeah. It was definitely a shock to see a satyr in a collar and chains being paraded around like some sort of freak."

Cembran called from the kitchen as he made breakfast. "You know, I think he understood what Dovino and I were saying, or at least part of what we were saying in Old Satyr."

Gathod shifted in his chair, looking at Cembran. "Do you think he could be a wild satyr?"

Cembran shrugged. "I suppose it's possible. But where could he have come from? There haven't been any wild satyrs since before I was born."

Travis sipped his coffee. "What's a wild satyr?"

Gathod returned his gaze back to the table, staring into his coffee mug before looking at Travis. "A wild satyr is one whose animal characteristics rule his personality. They may be wild all their lives or...," Gathod thought for a second, "some event may have triggered the animal portion of his personality to take over."

Travis set down his coffee. "You mean, some traumatic event, like being held captive with a collar around his neck and controlled by men with chains and tasers?"

"Yeah, that's exactly what I mean. I don't know for sure, but it's a good possibility that, as a survival mechanism, his animal nature has taken over in order to help him cope with being a captive." Gathod shuddered involuntarily. "So what are we going to do?"

"I don't really know yet. But I do know that we need more information and we need it fast. The carnival is only in town for two more days and then they pack up and head for god knows where." Cembran had just finished making breakfast when the door opened and Dovino, Phillip, and Jeremy strode inside, their noses leading the way. Travis grinned. "I knew they wouldn't miss breakfast."

A chorus of good-mornings and hugs followed as greetings were exchanged and the newcomers took places around the table. Dovino sipped his coffee. "Were we interrupting anything?"

Travis smiled. "No, actually, you're right on time. We were just saying that we need more information."

The three young satyrs looked at one another, silent messages traveling between them. "After our chores, the three of us will head back into town and scope out the carnival. We'll try to find out what we can. Hopefully we can figure out where they're keeping him," Dovino again spoke for the group.

All three of the young satyrs nodded, but it was Jeremy who spoke this time. "I can't imagine being caged up like that. Did you see the look in his eyes? He looked so sad and defeated. Like he'd been broken."

"He must have been broken." The anger was plain in Phillip's voice, which startled Travis a little. "No satyr would ever voluntarily allow himself to be collared like that... not even as part of sex."

All five heads in the room nodded in agreement. They all knew that being collared was a sign of slavery and that no satyr would ever allow it. No way, no how... it went against every satyr instinct. Even light bondage during sex was only done under conditions of strict trust, and even then it was quite rare. Travis and Cembran, while they trusted each other implicitly, had tried it only a very few times and found that it wasn't something they could add to their regular sex life. While they found it pleasurable, their instincts kept rebelling against the captivity.

Breakfast was ready, and Cembran put steaming plates of pancakes with homemade maple syrup, bacon, and sausage in front of each of them before taking his own chair next to Travis. "I think Travis and I need to see the Manimal show again."

"Are you sure, Lamb?" Travis set down his fork, looking into his lover's eyes.

"Yes. I think we need to try to get a message to him. I think we need to find out for sure if he truly wants to be rescued." Forks clinked against plates as utensils were dropped. Cembran looked around the table at expressions that ranged from shock to disbelief. Cembran continued eating, ignoring their shock. "What if it's just a show and he's really happy with the carnival?" His words were still met with expressions of disbelief. Cembran shook his head. "I'm just saying, we need to be sure."

Travis slipped an arm around Cembran's back. "You're right. We do need to be certain. We'll go into town this afternoon and see the show again. You'll have to think of a way that he'll be able to answer you without letting anyone know."

Cembran nodded slowly. "I'll have to give that some thought." Cembran looked around the table, scolding the other men lightly. "Eat up before it gets cold."

After breakfast, the three youngsters headed down to the barns to complete their chores, followed shortly by Cembran, while Travis cleaned up the breakfast dishes, and Gathod lingered over another cup of coffee. "So, what do you want me to do?"

"I need you to research wild satyrs. Call whoever you need. Brock, Steven…." Travis let his voice trail off as a thought took hold. "Say, you might contact Dovino's father back in Switzerland. I bet there are people in the satyr village who'll know and can tell us something about wild satyrs."

"Okay, I can do that. When should we meet to compare notes?"

"Let's meet here for dinner and to decide on a plan, if we need one, depending on what information Cembran and I can gather."

Gathod finished his coffee. "Good deal. Do you want me to tell Doug what's going on? He may have some information."

"Okay, but be careful. We can't put him in a difficult position."

"Yeah, I know, and I wouldn't want to." Gathod and Doug had been together for almost three years and Travis knew that they had few secrets from each other. "But I really hate keeping secrets from him."

"I know. Tell him what you need to tell him. I trust that you and he will know what to do."

Chapter Three

"Travis, everyone will be here in a little while." Cembran slipped his arms over Travis's shoulders as he sat quietly staring at the fireplace mantel in their living room.

"Thank you, Lamb." Travis's attention didn't waver from the delicate carvings that graced the mantel. Most of them had been carved over the years by Cembran, and they depicted their family of a sort. One side of the mantel housed a grouping of gentle animals that Cembran had carved during the years that he was alone on the farm. The other side of the mantel had groupings of the people who made up Travis and Cembran's family. Whenever Travis needed to think, he'd sit and stare at the figures that Cembran had carved with such love. "I'm just thinking how to best keep your promise."

Cembran rested his chin on Travis's shoulder while his cheek gently caressed Travis's. "I know and I'm sorry I put you in this situation."

Startled, Travis turned toward his mate, meeting his loving, caring eyes. "Don't be sorry at all. I'm not. I probably would have done the same thing." Travis raised his arms around Cembran, shifting him for better access to his lips. "You did the right thing... we have to help. I'm just not certain exactly how... yet." Travis kissed Cembran gently; Cembran returned the gesture, adding a touch of heat and passion.

Their lips pressed together, tongues exploring mouths they knew intimately and yet found new with each kiss. Slowly, Cembran shifted in front of Travis, their mouths and tongues caressing, nibbling, definitely signaling more.... Cembran moaned softly as Travis pulled him onto his lap, an arm circling around his waist while fingers carded through soft ringlet curls. Cembran gasped softly, "Lemmle, I don't know if we…."

His thought was cut off by a soft knock and a laughing call. "Are you decent?"

Travis gave Cembran another kiss before answering. "Yes. Come in, Gathod. As usual, your timing is perfect."

Travis's familiar sarcasm made Gathod smile. "You never know with you two lovebirds."

Cembran smiled and started to get up, but Travis pulled him gently back onto his lap, holding him close, not ready to give up the closeness and warmth of Cembran's body next to his.

Gathod smiled to himself and made himself at home, pouring a cup of coffee while Travis and Cembran talked quietly to each other. Travis and Cembran were very demonstrative in their love and they weren't shy or slight with their affection for each other when they were in the company of trusted friends. Their simple displays of true affection and the love for each other those acts demonstrated were an inspiration to many of the people in their lives. "Lemmle, I need to start dinner."

Travis reluctantly released Cembran with a kiss and offered Gathod a chair. "Did you find out anything from Dovino's father?"

"Yes. Darifo was as helpful as he could be, but he only had limited information." Gathod looked around. "Are the boys joining us?"

"Yes, they should be here in a few minutes. You might as well wait and tell everyone at the same time." No sooner had the words escaped his lips than he heard a knock on the door. "Come in, boys." The three young satyrs strode into the room, talking animatedly between themselves. "Sit down. Cembran is fixing dinner, and Gathod was just about to tell us what he learned from Darifo."

Dovino leaned forward. "What did my father say, Gathod?"

Gathod settled in his chair. "He didn't know a great deal about 'wild satyrs.' But he did tell me that true wild satyrs were very rare and probably wouldn't have understood what Cembran was saying." Gathod had everyone's undivided attention.

"So what's the deal with him?" Cembran asked from the kitchen. "He clearly understood me."

"Darifo said it was very possible that the satyr in the carnival was probably a regular satyr who had been captured." Travis furrowed his brow but remained silent, not wanting to interrupt Gathod. "Darifo told me that if a satyr had been captured some time ago, and if he'd been caged and treated like an animal, then the animalistic side of his nature might take hold of his personality. In short, he could almost revert to being an animal."

Travis leaned forward. "That makes sense. From what we've seen, he was being treated like an animal with the chains, collar, and tasers. But if we rescue him, will his animalistic nature remain in control or will his human-like tendencies come to the front?"

Gathod shrugged his shoulders. "I don't know, and neither did Darifo. I think the best we can do is hope."

Phillip had remained quiet through the conversation. Now he spoke. "Regardless, I think we have to help him." Dovino and Jeremy nodded vehemently in agreement.

"This afternoon when Cembran and I attended the show, Cembran was able to ask him if he wanted help. According to Cembran, he indicated that he did. And Cembran promised that we'd help him. So, the question is not if we'll help, but what are we going to do? We don't have much time. The carnival packs up in two days."

Cembran brought the food to the table. "Then it looks like we have some planning to do, which will be easier on full stomachs." Everyone took that as their cue that dinner was ready and headed to the table. As they ate, everyone threw out ideas and suggestions, while relating the information they'd been able to gather at the carnival that afternoon. By the end of the evening, they'd developed a basic plan.

After everyone had left and the house was quiet, Cembran took a thoughtful Travis by the hand and, after turning out the lights, quietly led him into their bedroom and closed the door with a hushed click.

Travis sat on the edge of their bed, deep in thought. Cembran sat next to him. "Lemmle, what's bothering you?"

"I don't really know, Lamb. I think I'm nervous about bringing a wild satyr into our home."

Cembran shifted his weight on top of Travis, gently pressing him back onto the bed. "Trav... remember, he is a satyr and he won't do anything to harm us."

"How do you know? How can you be so sure?" The doubt in Travis's voice was unsettling for Cembran. He was used to a confident, assured Travis, not someone who doubted what he had to do, what he knew was right.

"I just know, Lemmle. I don't think he's particularly violent, just lost and confused. Besides, he's a satyr, we're satyrs, and we're probably the only ones who can help him."

Travis pulled Cembran close, the weight on top of him familiar, reassuring. "I know, and I know we're doing the right thing. It's just hard...." Travis smiled as he looked into Cembran's loving eyes. "I know, Lamb... who said doing the right thing was easy?" Travis took a deep breath. "I just don't want anything or anyone to threaten the ones I love."

"That's part of why I love you so much." Cembran kissed Travis hard, his passion rising along with his almost instinctive need to comfort his mate. "You take care of everyone." Cembran scooted Travis back onto the bed until his head rested against the pillows before turning off the light. He whispered softly in the nearly dark room, his words wrapping around Travis like a blanket., "Tonight, let me take care of you."

Travis smiled against Cembran's lips as he nodded slowly to avoid breaking contact, while Cembran's fingers carded through his hair, adding pressure to their kiss. After a few seconds, Cembran's lips pulled back from his, only to reappear at the nape of his neck, nibbling and sucking against his skin, while long fingers opened his shirt before peeling it away from his body. Travis felt rather than saw Cembran lift his body just before his hot lips and tongue attached to a now-hard nipple. "Lamb...," Travis half-moaned, half-whined. Cembran smiled as he nibbled gently against the hard bud, listening to Travis's short, panting breath. Cembran released Travis's nipple only to repeat the same treatment on the other. His fingers unfastened Travis's belt before opening his pants and slipping a hand inside, sliding his palm along Travis's hard length. "Fuck... Lamb...."

Cembran brought his lips to Travis's ear. "Not yet. That comes later."

"Oh... god...." Travis was panting deeply as Cembran cupped his balls in the palm of his hot hand. "I'm getting close...."

"Not yet." Cembran's tongue flicked along Travis's ear as his hand slowly withdrew from Travis's pants. Travis then felt Cembran's weight lift off the bed and he watched as Cembran stepped into the soft moonlight from the window. Slowly, deliberately, Cembran slipped off his shirt before opening his pants and letting them rustle to the floor.

Travis watched with rapt attention as Cembran climbed back onto the bed, straddling his legs. Deft fingers slipped Travis's shirt off his shoulders. Then his pants were slipped off his hips and down his legs. "Lamb...." Travis was throbbing with anticipation and need.

A finger settled against Travis's lips, quieting him. "Just relax, Lemmle."

"I'm trying, Lamb, honest."

Cembran again straddled Travis's hips, his cock rubbing against Travis's stomach as he leaned forward, kissing Travis hard. Reaching to the bedside table, Cembran lubed his fingers and stroked along Travis's length.

Travis hissed softly as Cembran's fingers glided along his length. Then he felt Cembran shift and he hissed again as Cembran sank onto him, taking him inside his hot, tight body.

"Don't move, Lemmle. This is for you." Slowly Cembran rose off Travis and then dropped back down. Travis thrust his hips forward, but Cembran stilled him by placing his hands on Travis's lower stomach. "Let me...." Cembran set a steady pace, raising and lowering himself onto Travis.

The sensations and pleasure washed over Travis in waves. Giving control to Cembran was driving him out of his mind with desire. Cembran's hot passage gripped Travis tightly as he watched as Cembran stroked himself. Every time he tried to move, Cembran stilled him, so now his fists clawed at the bedding as he watched Cembran descend into bliss. "Lamb... sweet Lamb...." Travis felt Cembran's love reach out to him, and his love for his mate responded. Their hearts joined together, their love adding to their passion. Since giving each other their Triuwes years before, their mate bond had grown stronger, and sometimes when they made love, particularly when one of them needed to feel the other most, their hearts would reach out to each other—and tonight Travis needed to feel that special connection with Cembran. "Lamb, I can't last... much... longer."

"Neither... can... I." Cembran was panting loudly as he brought their bodies together, and their climaxes crashed over them. Travis felt Cembran's release on his stomach as he emptied himself deep inside his beloved.

Travis pulled a trembling Cembran to him, wrapping his arms around his back as he brought their lips together. "You're incredible, Lamb."

Cembran smiled as he took another kiss before letting Travis slip from his body, and settled on the bed next to his mate. Reluctant to break contact with Travis, Cembran grudgingly got up from the bed and fetched a warm cloth from the bathroom. After cleaning them both, he put the cloth away and rejoined Travis in their bed. "We need to sleep, Lemmle. We have a long day ahead of us." Cembran settled next to Travis, his head resting on his shoulder, an arm around his waist.

"And an even longer night." Travis cradled Cembran in his arms as they fell asleep.

Travis woke first, the worry and concern from the night before a thing of the past, washed away with his mate's loving. Cembran was still asleep as the morning sun peeked through their bedroom window. Reluctantly, Travis carefully got out of bed, kissed Cembran gently on the forehead, and padded off to the bathroom. When he returned, Cembran was stretching, his long, lean body laid out for Travis's delight. "Damn... you make me want to go back to bed, Lamb."

Cembran's eyes sparkled as they raked over Travis's nakedness. "I could say the same about you, Lemmle, but we have chores to do." Cembran climbed out of bed, stepping to where Travis stood. "But maybe this afternoon we can go swimming and nap in the shade." The wicked twinkle in Cembran's eye was enough to get Travis moving.

The sun was just over the trees and they were both outside. Travis kissed Cembran softly as he headed to the vegetable garden while Cembran took the path to the goat barn. As he started working, Travis saw Dovino, Phillip, and Jeremy heading down to the barns to start their chores. All three of them waved to Travis as they walked, and Travis settled into his normal daily routine. There was work to be done and it wasn't going to get done on its own.

The rest of the day passed quietly, and at dinner, Travis and Cembran reviewed the plan for the evening, making sure they hadn't forgotten anything. In an unusual turn of events, it was Cembran who seemed nervous. "When do we need to leave?"

Travis ran his hand along Cembran's back. "The carnival closes at midnight, so we'll leave then. We need to give them time to close up and settle for the night. I've already got the tools we think we'll need in the car. We both need to wear dark clothes—jeans and a black T-shirt should work. We don't want to look suspicious, and that's how I saw a lot of the carnival workers dressed." Cembran nodded. He knew all this, but it was good to hear it again. "With any luck we'll look like the other workers and we can get close enough to the trailer to open it and get him out."

"What I don't understand is how are we going to disguise him once he's outside?"

"I'm counting on darkness and a quick trip to the car." Cembran looked worried. "I know it's not the best plan, but it's all we can do on short notice and I'm not exactly an expert on breaking satyrs out of cages."

"I know, and I think if we're quiet, we can get away with it. After all, the carnival is in a public place, so they can't really stop us from being there."

"That's the one thing in our favor. By putting the carnival on the main street of town, it means that there will be people on the street most of the night—not many, granted, but that should help distract from us." Travis could tell Cembran was nervous; heck, he was nervous too. "Let's finish dinner so we can get a nap before we need to leave. We'll need to be alert. Gathod, Dovino, Jeremy, and Phillip should be here in a few hours."

"Yeah, I think I could use one." After finishing the dishes, Travis led Cembran to their bedroom, where they held each other and dozed until they heard a knock on the door and a familiar "Are you decent?" called from the living room.

Getting out of bed, Cembran changed while Travis met Gathod in the living room and went to start a pot of coffee. Cembran joined them as the other members of their group arrived. After a final discussion and review of the plans, the six of them walked to Travis's car and Gathod's truck for the ride into town. The three occupants of Travis's car were quiet as they rode along the country roads. Arriving in town, they parked in a public lot and waited for Gathod's truck, which pulled into the spot a few minutes later. Once everyone was out, Travis motioned for the group to gather between the vehicles. "Okay, this is your last chance. Is everybody ready? If you want to back out, say so now." Travis held his hand over his heart. "There's no shame in it." The other five met Travis's eyes and said nothing. "Okay. Let's rescue a satyr."

Chapter Four

" **J**eremy and Phillip, you stay with the vehicles as planned." Travis watched as both young men nodded silently. Travis handed Phillip his keys, and Gathod gave Jeremy the keys to his truck. "Stay out of sight and stay ready."

"We will. Don't worry."

Travis nodded, and then retrieved the bolt cutters from the trunk, slipping them beneath his clothes, and the four remaining satyrs headed away from the cars and toward the main street of town.

Rounding the corner nearest the Manimal tent, Travis was surprised how quiet the carnival was now. The rides were silent and hulking, their lights dark. The game trailers stood closed in shadows. The only sound came from the few people wandering the sidewalk and from the small trailers where the carneys lived. The streetlights cast unreal shadows. It was weird how eerie the place felt, where hours before there had been laughter, bright lights, and merry activity.

"Dovino," Travis motioned and whispered very softly. "Stand in the doorway over there and keep watch. Cough if you see someone coming." Damn, he wished he'd thought to bring a pack of cigarettes to make Dovino more inconspicuous.

Dovino nodded slowly and took up a station in the dark doorway, leaning his body against the doorframe. Travis signaled the other two and they walked purposefully toward the trailer behind the Manimal tent. When they'd scouted out the trailer earlier, Travis had noticed the door was latched, but not locked. Now, however, Travis was grateful he'd brought a set of bolt cutters, because the trailer was secured with a large padlock.

Travis leaned close to Gathod. "Do you see anyone close by?" Gathod peeked around the corner of the trailer while Travis extracted the bolt cutters. Seeing Gathod shake his head, Travis opened the cutters and placed the blades on the bolt of the lock.

The snap of the lock cutting sounded to them like a shot going off. They stood very still, waiting to see if anyone reacted to the sound. A few seconds later, Gathod motioned that someone was coming, and they heard Dovino cough like he had a cold. Travis shoved the cutters into his pants while Cembran positioned the lock to look as whole as possible. The three of them retreated into the shadows between the tent and the trailer and waited.

A pair of carnival workers strode up the street looking around. "I know I heard something."

"I did too." Damn. Travis figured they were done for, until he heard a banging from inside the trailer. "Pipe down in there." One of the men banged on the far side of the trailer, stilling the noise from inside. "Must have been him. Let's get back inside... I need a fucking beer. I can still hear the damn screaming kids!" The rescuers waited until they thought it was safe and then emerged from their hiding place, hearts still pounding in their ears.

Travis removed the now useless lock and opened the door latch. Gathod slowly pulled back the door so the hinges didn't make noise, whispering, "Jesus, this is heavy."

Travis gazed into the now open trailer and heard Cembran involuntarily gasp next to him. He turned to see the look of horror on Cembran's face. Travis thought Cembran was going to cry. Travis followed Cembran's gaze and he understood Cembran's reaction. The sides of the trailer were reinforced with metal that connected to bars that ran about five feet off the floor. Cembran whimpered very softly. "He can't even stand up." The floor of the trailer was covered with straw and Travis saw a dish of what appeared to be raw meat and heavy plastic water bottles like those used to water cattle.

Travis couldn't stop himself. "Jesus...." Staring at them from the back of the trailer/cage was the crouched form of a large, naked satyr.

The only thing he was wearing was a thick, black collar around his neck. Cembran stepped forward and slowly held out his hand, speaking soft, reassuring words. Travis watched as the satyr crawled toward him, taking the proffered hand in his before stepping out of the trailer and onto the pavement. Travis looked around, but he could see no clothing of any kind in the trailer. Great, how do I get a naked satyr back to the car with nobody seeing, much less screaming if they do? Travis could read the same concern on Cembran's and Gathod's faces.

"Trav." Gathod leaned close. "Wipe off anything we've touched, leave the door slightly ajar, and bring the lock with you. Cembran and I will get him back to the car. I have an idea." Gathod whispered something to Cembran, and Travis picked up the lock, putting it into a pocket, wiped down the door, latch, and anything else they'd touched with the tail of his shirt, and pushed the door nearly closed.

"What's going on here? What do you think you're doing?" Travis turned around and found himself staring into the face of one of Manimal's handlers. Before Travis could answer, he saw the man crumple to the ground, his face replaced by the view of a large, smiling satyr. Damn, this guy is strong.

"Crap, he saw us." Travis looked to Gathod for any ideas.

"Cembran and I will get him back to the car." Gathod pointed to the prone body on the ground. "You make him think what he saw was a dream and that he escaped." Travis looked at Gathod with concern. "I know you feel strongly about this and I know why," Gathod whispered, "but it's the only way." Travis sighed to himself and nodded.

Travis had only done this once before when he and Cembran had incorporated this into their lovemaking, and he'd never tried it on a stranger, but he put his doubts aside and concentrated. The man was definitely out, but not truly harmed. Travis shivered as he entered the man's dreamy mind. The images he saw were ghastly. This guy liked to inflict pain; he got off on it. Blocking out everything else, Travis found the fresh images of the conspirators and rearranged them to look like the satyr was escaping. He made that image play over and over, reinforcing the altered truth. Then Travis disconnected from the man's warped mind, finding himself kneeling back on the pavement.

Slowly, Travis got back up, said a silent prayer that it worked, and strode down the street. As he passed the doorway, he noticed it was empty, and he hoped Dovino had gone with Gathod and Cembran. Walking briskly, Travis arrived at the vehicles to find that everyone was present. Cembran and the satyr were in the backseat of his car, Gathod waiting for him, and the three youngsters were in Gathod's truck, which was already moving.

Travis pulled the bolt cutters out, stuck them partway under the passenger seat, and climbed into the car. Gathod got into the passenger seat while Travis started the car, and, once all the doors were closed, Travis pulled the car out of the parking space and headed out onto the quiet street. Travis's hands were still shaking as he drove out of town and toward the farm. "How did you get him to the car without being seen?" Travis could hear Cembran in the backseat, speaking softly, and he knew he was trying to keep the satyr calm and reassured.

Gathod replied in a soft voice, "Cembran and I extended our cloaks to include him." Travis glanced at Gathod and noticed he looked pale. "It worked well enough to get us to the car in the dark, but I don't want to try that again. It really wore us out." Travis glanced at his mate in the backseat and he saw the same paleness in him as in Gathod.

"Are you all right, Lamb?" Cembran nodded softly, doing his best to keep the large satyr calm. "Do you know his name?"

Cembran relayed the question, and for the first time the satyr spoke. "Vauk." Travis heard Cembran say their names, so he figured introductions were being made. Travis continued driving while Gathod kept an eye on the backseat.

About halfway home, Travis stopped the car where a small stream flowed near the road. Travis handed the cut lock to Gathod, who threw it onto the flowing water. After hearing the plunk, Travis pulled the car back onto the road.

After what felt like the longest trip from town possible, Travis pulled the car into his usual parking place. Gathod's truck was already there with the boys waiting. Travis and Gathod got out of the truck. Travis opened the door to the backseat and helped Vauk out of the car while Gathod grabbed the bolt cutters from the floor.

Vauk's gaze darted around, his eyes dancing, and he looked slightly panicked, like he was going to bolt. Travis took his hand in a firm, but not tight grip. "Vauk." The satyr's magnificent head and piercing eyes searched Travis's face and then he seemed to relax. Travis indicated the path, and they all headed toward the farm. Steadily, they made their way away from the road and through the woods to the clearing that contained the farm. The moon cast enough light to make the farm and buildings glow. Vauk stopped at the edge of the clearing, taking in the view. "Come, Vauk." Travis gently motioned him forward, and the small group headed toward the house.

"Dovino, Phillip, and Jeremy," Travis hugged each of them in turn, "thank you for your help. You might as well go home."

"Okay, Travis." Each of them said good night, nodded respectfully to Vauk, turned, and headed down the path toward their small home on the property.

"Do you need me to stay?"

"No. Go home to Doug. He'll be worried."

"What do I tell him?" This was the sticky issue for Gathod, after all Doug was the county sheriff.

Travis thought for a minute. "Tell him whatever you want." Travis squeezed their friend's shoulder. "Don't let this have an effect on you and Doug. Tell him whatever he asks." Travis knew Doug wouldn't ask about things he didn't want to know.

"Okay. I'll see you in the morning." Gathod handed Travis the bolt cutters.

Cembran stepped forward and hugged Gathod tightly. "Good night… and thank you." Gathod returned the hug and headed back to his truck.

Cembran took Vauk's hand and led him inside, with Travis following behind them. Vauk stood just inside the door, unsure of where to go or what to do. Travis motioned for Vauk to bend over, and, after what seemed like careful deliberation, he complied. Travis turned the leather collar that Vauk still wore, found the lock that held it, and used the bolt cutters to snap it. Travis then removed the collar and, with Vauk watching, threw it in the trash. Vauk rubbed his now bare neck and Travis thought he saw a small smile. He put the bolt cutters down., "Cembran, I'll see if I can find him something to wear. Why don't you see if he needs anything to eat or drink?" Cembran nodded and started talking to Vauk, while Travis went into their bedroom to rummage for some clothes. It took him awhile, but he was able to find a pair of loose pants and a shirt that he thought would fit. When he returned to the living room, Cembran had Vauk settled into a chair and covered with a blanket, but as soon as Travis entered Vauk stood up and hung his head. Travis looked at Cembran, puzzled.

"Travis, Vauk recognizes that you're the Baccharist and that you've rescued him, and he's showing you respect." Travis smiled and bowed his head in recognition of mutual respect before handing Vauk the clothes.

Vauk took the small pile of clothing when it was offered but made no move. After additional conversation on Cembran's part and a few nods on Vauk's part, Cembran took the clothes and helped Vauk put them on.

"Travis, he doesn't appear to be hungry. All he wanted was water. I think we need to get him to bed." Cembran helped Vauk into the guest room and got him into bed before rejoining Travis in the living room awhile later. "He's a little restless and not used to sleeping in a bed. Should one of us sleep in here tonight?"

"No, Lamb. I don't want him to think he's being guarded. Let's go to bed. We'll hear him if he gets up." Cembran nodded and together they headed into their room, cleaned up, and got into bed, unsure of how well they'd sleep.

A few hours later, Travis woke to Cembran shaking him. "Travis, he's gone."

Still groggy, Travis mumbled, "Gone...."

"Yeah, the guest room is empty and the front door was open." Travis threw back the covers and pulled on his pants, unsure of what he and Cembran could do. If Vauk decided to run, there wasn't much they could do to stop him.

"If he's gone...." Travis didn't know what to do.

"He took a pillow and one of the blankets." Strange.

Quietly, Travis and Cembran checked the house and barns. Travis found Vauk in the sheep barn, asleep on a bed of fresh straw, blanket over his legs, clutching the pillow to his chest like a lover. Cembran joined him a few minutes later and they silently left the barn and went back to bed.

At first light, Travis and Cembran walked together to the sheep barn. They found the stall empty, and the blanket folded neatly with the pillow stacked on top of it. "Where is he, Travis?"

Travis shrugged resignedly and pulled Cembran close, holding his mate to him. "I don't know. I think we may need to give him some space." Travis kissed Cembran gently. "Let's get some breakfast." Cembran nodded, and they walked arm in arm back to the house. As they approached the house, they saw Doug heading down the path. Travis waved in greeting, and they met Doug at the door and went inside.

"What happened last night?" Doug's eyes were flashing. "Gathod came home late and crawled into bed."

Travis remained calm and sat at the dining table. "Did you ask him?" Doug reluctantly sat as well.

"He said that there was some business that needed to be taken care of and that it was best that I didn't know. This morning, we got a call from the carnival asking for help locating one of their animal exhibits that seems to have escaped, and I'll bet the escape was aided in some way." Cembran silently put a cup of coffee in front of Doug and went back to making breakfast.

"Doug, let me speak hypothetically for a while." Doug nodded, his anger dialing down a notch, though he was still skeptical. "Suppose we went to see this animal attraction." Doug nodded. "And suppose this attraction wasn't an animal at all." Doug set down his cup, his eyes locking on Travis's. "Suppose, just suppose, that this attraction was really one of us," Travis's eyes shifted to Cembran and then back to Doug.

Doug's eyes widened. "Travis, you're kidding, right?" While Doug wasn't a satyr, he loved Gathod with everything he had and he was a staunch defender of their privacy.

"I'm speaking hypothetically here." Doug nodded again and Travis took another sip of his coffee. "So, being one of us… we might have arranged for him to escape his captivity."

Doug held up his hand. "Say no more. I don't want to know. The carnival people swear their attraction escaped somehow and I'm going to leave it at that. They have to leave tomorrow anyway…." Doug winked. "So I hope the attraction lays low and stays out of sight." The now mirthful look in Doug's eyes was priceless. Doug finished his coffee and got up to leave.

"Don't be hard on Gathod, Doug."

"I know. He was protecting me." Travis nodded and as he opened the door, a loud, exuberant rumble echoed over the farm.

Doug looked at Travis in alarm. "What the hell was that?"

Travis looked at Cembran and saw him smile, and he turned back to Doug, grinning. "That's the sound of freedom."

Part Two
Reawakening

Chapter Five

rent glanced at the clock on the back wall of the classroom and sighed softly to himself. Ten after two—less than an hour until school was out for the day. Graduation was on Sunday, and in another week school was out for the summer. Trent returned his attention to the papers he was grading. Usually, grading essays was a chore, but these were an exception. These were for his humanities honor students and this was the first time he'd taught the class. The previous instructor had retired at the end of the last school year. Trent had set his expectations high and so far he hadn't been disappointed. These students were the brightest and best. Trent smiled as he wrote the score on the essay and placed it on the stack of finished papers. He glanced around the room, the only sound the scrape of pencils on paper as his honor students completed their final exams prior to graduation. As he watched his students, he saw Arthur Kraus, probably the brightest student he'd ever taught, quietly get up from his seat and walk to his desk.

"Mr. Walters, I don't understand this question." Arthur pointed to the final question on the exam. "Do you want us to discuss the characters in-depth first, or only compare and contrast the Greek and Roman versions and views of the god of the sea?"

Trent smiled as he looked into Arthur's eager face, whispering, "Brevity is appreciated, Arthur."

The young man nodded at receiving his answer. "Okay. I'll try." Arthur quietly turned around, walked back down the aisle to his seat, and returned to work. Trent did the same, reading through the last of the essays and recording the scores.

Five minutes before the bell, all of the exams had been returned and the students were talking quietly. Trent stood up and walked to the front of the class. "I've finished reading through your essays and I'm extremely pleased. You can pick up your papers on your way out of class. I know tomorrow is senior skip day, but I'll have your exams graded for you if you want to pick them up." Trent glanced at the clock one last time. "Enjoy graduation, and I'll see you tonight at the honors convocation." The bell sounded just as he was finishing and the students rose and headed into the halls, talking excitedly. Trent gathered up the exams and added them to the other papers he needed to grade, putting them in his briefcase. Luckily this was his only senior class, so he'd have the weekend to finish grading the other papers.

"Mr. Walters." Trent looked up, surprised—he hadn't heard anyone approach his desk.

"Yes, Arthur, what's up?"

"I was wondering if there were any extra tickets for the honors convocation. I was told in the office that you were organizing it and that you might have extra tickets."

Seating was limited and each student graduating with honors had been given three tickets: one for themselves and two for their parents. "As it happens, I do have a few extra tickets." Arthur's grin was priceless. "How many do you need?"

"If I can get four more tickets, that would be great. I can pay for them." Arthur reached into his back pocket to get his wallet. "Mom gave me money for the extra tickets."

"Put your wallet away, Arthur." Trent reached into his desk drawer and got four tickets, handing them to Arthur. "If anyone asks, tell them it's because you're the class valedictorian. They won't question it."

Arthur smiled brightly. "Thanks, Mr. Walters. I'll see you tonight." He headed out of the classroom and into the hallway.

Trent finished packing up and straightened the desks and chairs in the room before grabbing his case and heading to the teacher's lounge. A few other teachers said hello and he briefly stopped to chat before continuing on his way. In the lounge, Trent settled into a quiet corner and got out a few of the exams he needed to grade. The teachers weren't supposed to leave until four, so Trent figured he'd use the time to get some work done.

He was almost through finishing the first exam. "Hi, Trent." A high, familiar, feminine voice interrupted him, and he cringed inwardly.

Trent smiled as pleasantly as he could. "Hi, Sherry." He didn't offer her a chair, but she sat with him anyway.

"Is everything ready for tonight?" Sherry Newhouse, as the teacher for honors mathematics, had been assigned, along with Trent, to coordinate the honors convocation. She was a brilliant woman who could make numbers sing. She'd even had a number of papers published, which was unusual for a high school math teacher. Sherry knew her numbers, loved the kids, and knew how to make math interesting. She was able to add elements of fun to her classes. But, to Trent's dismay, she'd decided to pursue Trent with the tenacity of a bulldog with a bone, and she wouldn't take a hint no matter what.

"Yes, everything is all set." Trent kept his voice light and his annoyance at bay. "The cafeteria is being rearranged for the convocation and all of the tickets have been distributed. I even got a few members of the school orchestra who've formed a small ensemble group to play during dinner. Is everything ready from your end?"

"The food will be delivered a little before six and we should be ready to eat on time." While she was talking, Trent packed up his papers again. He wouldn't get any work done while Sherry was there. The woman would talk a blue streak. "I was wondering." Trent got nervous—what could she be up to? "Since we live just a few blocks away from each other, could I ride in with you?"

Trent almost agreed, to be polite, but then he stopped. Sherry would probably try to construe the ride as a date of some kind. "I'd be happy to, but I already have plans with Bryce for after the convocation and I won't be heading right home." Trent knew that would stop her. She hated Bryce—probably saw him as a rival—because while she was a superb teacher, she was also as competitive as they come.

Sherry shrugged and got up. "Okay, well, I'll see you tonight, then." Sherry walked away, swinging her hips and behind for all it was worth. Trent chuckled to himself. *If you think that will work with me, you're using the wrong bait.*

Trent picked up his case off the table and headed out as well, pulling his phone out of his pocket and making a call. "Bryce, it's Trent."

"Hey, Trent, what's going on?" Bryce was a ball of energy and always seemed upbeat.

"I need a favor. If you see Sherry, you and I are going for a drink after the convocation tonight."

Bryce chuckled. "Tried to corner you again, huh?"

"Yeah, and she just won't take a hint." Trent signed lightly to himself. The truth was that neither Trent nor Bryce had interest in Sherry, or women in general. When Trent first joined the faculty, he and Bryce had had a brief romantic fling, but they quickly found out that they made much better friends than lovers.

"Thank god, she sees me as some sort of rival; why I'm not sure. But at least she leaves me alone. Anyway, I'll cover for you, no problem."

"Thanks. I'll see you tonight." Trent hung up the phone with a sigh and headed out of the lounge and through the now quiet halls to his car. He needed to get home so he could relax and get ready for the evening.

The short drive to his small bungalow was uneventful. Pulling up in front of his house, he got out of his car and waved to his neighbors as he walked to his door. Trent liked his house. He'd bought it a few years earlier and he'd spent his weekends and summers fixing it up. Trent unlocked the door, set his case on the table, and headed to his bedroom. Stripping off his clothes, he stepped into the bathroom and started the shower before running a razor over his face. As he was shaving, he let himself relax and the small horns just above his forehead appeared in the mirror. Trent knew what they meant: his father was satyr. He could still hear his mother telling him how she'd fallen in love with a tall, dark, handsome man when she was, in her words, "young and stupid." According to her, it was only after she was pregnant that he'd told her what he was, and then he'd left town, leaving her pregnant and alone. He could still hear his mother's words in his mind. "I didn't know what to do. I thought about ending the pregnancy, but I just couldn't. Then I was so relieved when you were born and you looked normal." That normalcy had ended when, in his late teens, he'd started to develop horns and a tail. All he'd wanted was to be normal like the other kids. Trent could still remember going into the bathroom, closing his eyes, imaging what he'd look like without the horns and tail, and praying that they would go away. Miraculously, when he'd opened his eyes they were gone. It took him less than a week to master the ability to hide his physical satyr characteristics from the world. Even his mother hadn't seen them since they'd first appeared. After he finished shaving, his horns once again hidden, Trent finished cleaning up and got dressed for the evening.

The honors convocation was going according to plan. Trent had arrived early to make sure all was ready. There were a few issues, but he'd quickly ironed them out. Now everyone was finishing their dinner and the presentation of the awards was about to begin. The principal stepped onto the small stage that had been erected. "I'd like to thank everyone for being here this evening to support our school's best and brightest. But, before we get started I'd like to thank Mr. Walters and Ms. Newhouse for putting this convocation together." There was polite applause from throughout the room and then the program moved on to the academic awards.

Once all the awards had been distributed, dessert and refreshments were circulated throughout the room and the faculty and students used this as an opportunity to mingle. Trent saw Sherry weaving through the groups of people, obviously heading in his direction, and stifled a cringe.

Looking for an escape, he smiled when he saw Arthur Kraus heading in his direction. "Mr. Walters, my family is here and I'd really like you to meet them."

"Absolutely." Trent followed Arthur to where a group of six people were standing together.

"Mr. Walters, I'd like you to meet my parents, Jim and Sue Kraus. Mom and Dad, this is Mr. Walters." Trent shook hands with both of them. Arthur waited and then continued with the introductions, indicating each person in turn. "This is my brother, Brock, and his partner, Steven, and these are my uncles, Travis and Cembran." Hands were shaken and greetings exchanged.

Once introductions were complete, Sue picked up the conversation. "We're so proud of Arthur."

"You have every right to be. I remember when he first walked into my class as a freshman. He was so shy. He'd only speak if I called on him, and even then, his answers were as short as possible." Trent smiled. "And usually correct."

"Yes… he's blossomed in so many ways over these past few years." Sue smiled the bright smile of an extremely proud parent.

Trent looked at the faces around him and he could see that each and every one of them was bursting with pride. "Have you decided where you're going to go to college?"

Travis spoke up. "Yes, Arthur, where are you going to go?"

"Well, I got accepted to a number of schools. I talked it over with Mom and Dad and I've decided to go to Michigan State." Arthur looked at his parents, a little unsure.

"That's incredible, Arthur. I know you'll do well." The rest of the family was beaming and Trent felt he might be interfering with what was becoming an impromptu family celebration, so he excused himself and stepped away.

As soon as he turned he felt a tap on his shoulder, and the handsome uncles Arthur had introduced as Travis and Cembran were standing behind him. "We were wondering if we could speak to you before you left for the evening."

"Certainly." Trent smiled, a little curious.

Travis's smile was reassuring and warm. "Good. We'll look for you before we go." They headed back to where Arthur was standing with the rest of his family and Trent smiled as he saw both Cembran and Travis each embrace Arthur in a fierce hug. A sense of longing overwhelmed Trent, but he pushed it aside, plastered a smile to his face, and mingled with the other parents and students.

As the crowd began to thin, Trent felt, rather than saw, someone approach him. "Mr. WaltersWalters, do you have a few minutes?" Trent turned toward the voice.

"Yes." Curiosity colored Trent's voice.

Travis looked around at the other people in the room. "Is there a place we can speak privately?" The serious look on Travis's face made Trent cautious. "It's important… for you," Travis added cryptically.

"Okay. We can speak in my classroom." Trent led the way down the halls to his now dark classroom. Turning on the light, he stepped inside, followed by Travis and Cembran. Trent's apprehension grew as Travis shut the door.

Travis began. "Trent, I want to begin by telling you that we mean you no harm, so you can relax. We wanted to speak with you because we know what you are." Fear flashed through Trent's eyes. "Trent, we know you're a satyr."

"But... how could you?" Trent stammered, unsure how to react or what they meant to do. This told Travis a lot about Trent.

"I knew as soon as I shook your hand tonight. You see, Trent, we're satyrs too." Travis let his cloak fall, displaying his horns. "You have nothing to fear from us." Cembran nodded and moved close to Travis. "Arthur has spoken of you so highly that we wanted to be sure to meet you, and as soon as we shook hands, I knew you were one of us."

"But... how could you? I've never told anyone. The only person who knows is my mother, and she died a few years ago."

"Trent, it's one of my gifts." Travis sighed softly. "I know that being a satyr has caused you confusion, worry, and pain over the years, and we're here to help you. The Saturday after graduation, we're having a party for Arthur at our farm. We'd be honored for you to join us, and we'll have time to answer all your questions."

"I... I... don't know." Trent was so confused, scared, and a little relieved all at the same time.

Travis stepped forward, placing his hand on the teacher's shoulder. "Let me leave you with this: We know what you've been through, we understand who you are, and all we want to do is help." Travis looked at Trent's desk and took a blank piece of paper. After writing for a minute, he handed Trent the page. "Here are directions to the farm. The party starts at two. If you'd like to come early, you'd be welcome to join us for lunch."

Trent watched as Travis and Cembran said goodbye and quietly left the room. He heard their footsteps get softer and softer as they walked down the hall. Taking a few minutes to compose himself, Trent shoved the paper in his pocket and left the room as well, heading back toward the cafeteria and the convocation.

The evening was breaking up rapidly as Trent rejoined the few remaining people. The tables were being cleared and reset. Trent was relieved that Sherry was nowhere in sight, so after spending a few minutes making sure no one needed his help, he left the building, walked to his car, and drove home.

Entering his house, Trent flopped down on the sofa, but didn't turn on the television. He needed time to think. All his life he'd wondered about his father, who he was and where he came from. Maybe these people could provide him with some answers. Trent continued thinking and mulling over what Travis had said and what he'd offered. *Damn it, I owe this to myself. I've studied mythology for years trying to find answers to my questions.* A new thought occurred to Trent: *There are other people like me; I'm not alone.* Trent actually smiled as he lifted himself off the sofa and went into the kitchen. After making himself a snack, he settled at the table to start grading exams. *Maybe I'll be able to meet someone like me....* Trent let that thought linger until he picked up the first exam and immersed himself in essays covering Greek and Roman mythology.

Chapter Six

Trent followed Travis's directions closely. He really didn't want to get lost. The farm really seemed to him to be in the middle of nowhere. He'd debated with himself the entire week about whether he should come at all, but his curiosity won out in the end. Hell, if he were honest with himself, he had to admit that there wasn't really any decision to make. The opportunity that Travis had offered him to meet other satyrs and to have some of his lifelong questions answered was too good to pass up.

Luckily for Trent, the week had been busy with final exams for underclassmen, graduation, and final grades due yesterday. Thank god. He had just a few more days to tidy things up and he was free for the summer. Trent had thought about getting a summer job to earn extra money, but as of yet he hadn't decided. He took his teaching salary over twelve months, so he still had a regular paycheck through the summer. He just needed something to keep himself busy. Trent figured he had plenty of time to decide, so he wasn't worried. For now he was going to enjoy the end of the school year as much as his students did.

Arriving at the spot along the road where Travis indicated he should park, Trent was grateful Travis's directions were so detailed and specific. He was relieved to see another car already in place where the directions indicated; otherwise he'd have missed it for sure. Reaching into the backseat, Trent retrieved the bottle of wine he'd brought to contribute as well as a card for Arthur, locked the car out of habit, and followed Travis's directions down the path through the woods. The forest was peaceful, the leaves rustling in the breeze, the sun dappling through the canopy, lighting patches of flowers flourishing in the broken sunlight.

Trent stopped to admire a patch of delicate white trillium before moving down the path.

Breaking into the clearing, Trent followed the path to the door of the farmhouse as instructed. The door opened just as he was raising his hand to knock.

"I'm going to the lake to—" Travis bumped into Trent as he came out the door. "Excuse me, Mr. WaltersWalters, I didn't see you there." Travis extended his hand in greeting. "Glad you decided to come." Travis's smile appeared warm and genuine, helping Trent to relax a little.

Taking the offered hand, he said, "Please, call me Trent."

Travis returned the young teacher's smile. "I have to complete some arrangements down by the lake. Please go inside and make yourself comfortable. Cembran will have lunch ready soon and then we can talk."

"Thank you." Trent stepped inside the house. He wasn't sure what he expected, but it wasn't this. The inside of the house was incredible— elegant rusticity, and it was all real. The stone fireplace, wood-paneled walls, and handmade furniture worn smooth by use all combined to create one of the warmest, most hospitable places he'd ever seen. Trent craned his neck around the small interior, not wanting to miss a single detail. "This is extraordinary."

Cembran looked up from where he was working and smiled. "I built this portion of the house and the single bedroom," Cembran indicated a door off the living room, "decades ago. The office and master suite were added after Travis moved here with me." Trent peeked into the adjacent room. "Go ahead; look around." Trent went inside, his mind not quite believing what he saw. "The lumber for the addition came from the property. We had to fell some trees to enlarge the pastures and we used the lumber to build the addition." Trent saw Cembran standing in the doorway.

"Did you make the furniture?" Trent slid his finders across the surface of the desk, letting the warm wood caress his fingertips.

Cembran nodded and smiled, obviously proud of his craftsmanship. "Yes, most of it. There are a few pieces that we made together and a few family pieces." Trent's eye roved to a small hallway and his feet followed. "It's all right."

Trent poked his head into the master bedroom and glanced back at Cembran, unsure what he was feeling. His skin tingled a little and Trent gasped involuntarily. The room radiated sex, love, and passion, like the very walls had been steeped in it and soaked it up. "I...." Trent felt like an intruder, almost a voyeur, and yet never before in his life had he felt so alone. Shaking off the feeling, Trent was able to look around the room dominated by a large bed made of rough logs and branches and covered with rich, handmade bedding.

Cembran answered Trent's unasked question. "Our sheep have some of the softest wool possible."

Slowly, Trent stepped away from the door and followed Cembran back into the living area of the house. "Is there anything I can do to help?"

"I don't think so. Lunch is almost ready, and Travis is down at the lake taking care of the preparations for Arthur's graduation party. Would you like anything? Coffee? Water?"

"Coffee would be nice. Thank you." Trent sat in one of the chairs and Cembran brought him a cup of coffee and then returned to the kitchen area. Trent watched Cembran as he started dishing up lunch. Travis walked in a few minutes later, looking tired, and sat at the table. Without a word, Cembran brought him coffee and kissed him gently on the lips. The tired look in Travis's eyes faded, replaced by a gleam and a smile that only came from true contented happiness. Cembran moved away and returned to the table with heaping lunch plates.

Trent moved to the table and sat in the place Travis indicated. "I know you must have a million questions...."

Trent smiled. "I do, but I don't know where to start. I mean, I've been studying mythology from many cultures ever since I started to develop...."

Travis understood and nodded. "Well, you know that satyrs mature more slowly than humans." Trent nodded; he hadn't reached puberty until he was almost sixteen. "And you know that we don't reach sexual maturity until we're twenty-one." Again, Trent nodded. "What I bet you don't know is that satyrs can live for a very long time." Trent looked confused as Travis continued. "Let me ask you a question. How old do you think Cembran is?"

Trent looked at the beautiful man sitting next to Travis with his radiant blond curls and angelic face. "About thirty-one or thirty-two."

Cembran set down his fork and looked Trent in the eyes. "I'm approximately three hundred fourteen years old." Trent's mouth flew open in disbelief as Cembran went on to explain. "Once we reach maturity, our physical appearance ages based upon life events, such as mating, having children and grandchildren, the mating of our children, etcetera." Cembran took a bite and swallowed. "Travis and I mated a few years ago and in that time I've aged slightly for the first time in almost three hundred years. Since we'll never have children of our own, our appearance will probably remain as it is until we get close to death or if we decide to adopt a satyr child and bind him to us the way Jim and Sue have adopted Arthur."

Trent sat quietly while Travis explained other things about satyr life. "We can only conceive children beneath the full moon." Travis watched Trent closely. "So each month at the time of the full moon, satyrs gather together for the bacchanal, traditionally a night of wine, women, and song. Each month most of us are drawn to the bacchanal."

A smile lit Trent's face. "Is that why each month, I feel...." Trent lowered his eyes, slightly embarrassed.

Travis touched Trent's arm. "There's no need to be embarrassed or shy. We're satyrs. Sex is a part of who we are as much as eating, drinking, and breathing. So yes, that's why you feel horny as hell each month and that's the reason for the bacchanal—to provide a controlled outlet for those hedonistic tendencies. The lack of an outlet in your father's case is probably the reason you're here today."

"I always thought that he didn't want me or didn't like my mother." There was pain in his eyes.

"Do you know how long your mother and father were together?" Travis picked up his coffee, watching Trent as he sipped.

"My mother said that they were together for about a year. She really loved him and was heartbroken when he left." Trent's voice recalled the pain that his mother had expressed when she'd explained about his father. "She raised me herself as though I was a precious gift. Once my father left, she never dated again."

"Did your mother ever tell you his name?"

Trent nodded. "She said his name was Kadje." Trent thought a minute. "Years later, Mom said that he always seemed to be looking for something, but it still devastated her when he left."

Travis knew it was time to change the subject to something lighter. "Trent, each satyr is given a special gift from the gods. Cembran's is his gift with animals; our friend Gathod has the ability to heal."

"I don't know what my gift is. I've never done anything special. What's your gift?"

Cembran leaned forward. "Travis has many gifts." Cembran took Travis's hand and kissed it softly before returning his attention to Trent. "Travis wasn't born a satyr, but was made a satyr by Bacchus himself, and his gifts come from him. Travis can heal, weave dreams, he instinctively knows what will make other satyrs happy, and he can tell another satyr when they walk in the room, among other things. That's how he knew about you."

"I was wondering about that."

"Travis is also the baccharist, which means he can conduct a bacchanal."

"Oh." Trent looked at Travis.

Travis got up from his chair as the door burst open and Arthur raced inside, stopping when he saw Mr. WaltersWalters. "Oh." Arthur smiled brightly. "You're here. I'm so glad. Uncle Travis said you might be coming today." Arthur stepped forward and shook Trent's hand before hugging both Travis and Cembran.

"Why don't you show him around the farm while Cembran and I finish cleaning up?"

"Yeah, okay." He seemed so excited. "Before I forget, Mom told me to tell you that they went down to the lake."

"Thanks. When you're finished, come down to the lake and we'll go swimming." Travis turned to Trent. "I should have told you to bring your suit. I'll bring an extra with us for you."

"Thank you." Trent followed Arthur outside and down the path toward the barns, chuckling to himself at Arthur's energy. "Hey, Arthur. Slow down, will you?"

Arthur stopped and waited for Trent to catch up, looking contrite. "Sorry, Mr. Walters."

Trent caught up and smiled. "Arthur, you've graduated—you can call me Trent."

His eyes lit up, , "Really?" Trent nodded. "Cool.... Thanks." Looking around, he asked, "Umm… do you want to see the sheep or the goats first?"

"Whichever you like." Trent motioned for Arthur to lead on and he followed Arthur to the sheep barn, where he saw the lambs with their mothers. Trent was surprised when the mothers let Arthur hold their lambs. After Arthur saw to all the lambs, he led Trent to the goat barn where he watched as Arthur played with the kids. "Should we get to the lake? I don't want to make you late for your own party."

Arthur checked his watch. "Yeah, you're right. We should head that way. Besides, I'll come back later this evening." Arthur put the kid he was carrying back with its mother and led the way down the path, through the forest, and into the clearing that housed the small, clear lake.

They were greeted by a chorus of "Congratulations!" from the dozen or more people gathered on the sandy beach. Trent watched, smiling, as Arthur was hugged, tousled, or beamed at by everyone there. They were obviously very proud of his former student, as well they should be.

"Hello!" Trent's attention was diverted from Arthur by a voice behind him. Turning around, he saw three young men smiling at him. "I'm Dovino, this is Jeremy and Phillip. We're friends of Arthur's." Their expressions were warm and genuine as hands extended in greeting.

"I'm Trent. I was one of Arthur's teachers this year. I met Travis at a school event and he invited me here today."

The three of them nodded knowingly, obviously seeing nothing out of the ordinary. "We're glad you could join us. We were just getting something to eat." Dovino motioned to the food tables located near the edge of the clearing. "Please join us."

Everyone seemed so friendly and open. Trent let a little more of his reluctance fall. "Thank you." As he walked to the table, other people stopped and introduced themselves.

"I'm Gathod, and this is Doug." Trent thought the couple stunning.

"Pleased to meet you."

Jeremy introduced him to his parents, Greg and Millie, as well as his sister Judy and her husband Rick. Trent saw Steven and Brock and said hello. There were so many people, Trent couldn't keep them straight, but that really didn't matter. Everyone was so friendly, so welcoming, that Trent really started to feel at ease.

Trent fixed a plate, got himself a beer, and found a place to sit. Food was eaten between snippets of conversation and well wishes to Arthur. At one point, Travis got up with Cembran standing next to him. "I notice that Arthur has finished eating." Everyone chuckled. "Or should I say inhaling his food." Smiles and good-natured chuckles resounded. "So I'm going to ask him to come forward." Arthur got up, all smiles, and stood in front of Travis. "This young man has made us all proud, so please raise your glasses to Arthur." Glasses were lifted high in the air. "To Arthur!"

A raucous "Hear, hear!" returned from the assemblage as glasses were clinked and toasted.

Cembran stepped forward and handed Arthur a small, wooden carving of a lamb. "Remember where you come from, what your strengths are, and that you're loved, above all." Arthur took the small carving and threw his arms around Cembran's shoulders, hugging him tightly. Words of thanks were whispered as they hugged.

Gathod and Doug stepped forward as Arthur released Cembran. "Arthur, this is from Doug and me." Gathod placed a silver sun-shaped amulet on a delicate chain around Arthur's neck. "To ensure your hopes and dreams are always your own."

Travis stepped forward, handing Arthur a framed picture of the farm. "To remind you that we'll always be here when you need peace from the world's noise." Arthur was starting to tear up as he hugged Travis.

Trent watched this, enraptured. These weren't the usual graduation gifts. Each one was so personal, a special remembrance from the giver.

Brock and Steven stepped forward. "Steven and I weren't sure what to get you. You've meant so much to all of us." Jim and Sue, his adopted parents joined them. "We talked things over with Mom and Dad as well as Cembran and Travis, and we came to an agreement." Steven handed Arthur a large, manila envelope. "This envelope contains the details of a trust, set up by all of us." Brock indicated everyone present and heads nodded. "This trust has been finalized and contains enough money to pay for four years of tuition, books, and housing at Michigan State University."

Arthur could take no more and he threw himself into Brock's arms, crying as Brock hugged him close. "You earned it, little brother, and we all know you'll make us proud." Arthur released Brock and hugged everyone in attendance, including Trent, saying thank you to each person.

Travis was the last person he approached. "I don't know what to say to you. You helped me find a home, a mom and dad, and a whole family. I can never thank you enough." Arthur hugged Travis so tight that his eyes bulged a little.

When he could talk again, Travis asked, "Have you decided on a major?"

"Yes, I'm going to be a veterinarian." Another round of congratulations and well wishes were expressed as Trent stepped back from the crowd to let others have their time with Arthur.

Trent used the opportunity to look around the clearing. Near the edge of the lake, away from the partiers, Trent saw a lone figure watching the festivities, a hand over his eyes to shield them from the sun. Slowly, Trent walked around the lake and approached the lone figure. Trent nearly gasped audibly as he got closer. This man was unlike anyone Trent had ever seen before. A tall, darkly handsome satyr—about that there was no doubt at all—with large horns and hair-covered legs like tree trunks, wearing only a pair of rough shorts and a shirt that barely covered his massive chest.

"I'm Trent." He extended his hand in greeting. The satyr looked at him without moving, a slightly confused look on his face. "Do you understand me?" Nothing; not even a shrug. Trent placed his hand in the center of his chest. "Trent."

He then placed his hand against the satyr's chest and waited. At the touch, the satyr stilled and his eyes widened before he uttered in a deep, rich voice, "Vauk."

Trent nodded and smiled, leaving his hand where it was. "Vauk." Then he picked up one of Vauk's hands and placed it against his chest... and waited.

"Trent." Vauk smiled for the first time and its brightness stunned Trent right down to his balls.

Chapter Seven

Trent looked into Vauk's eyes, mesmerized by something deep in those chocolate-brown orbs. He knew he should be afraid—Vauk looked so different from anyone he'd ever met—but he wasn't. Slowly, Trent mimed asking Vauk if he was hungry by rubbing his stomach with his hand and nodding toward the food tables. Vauk nodded his head slowly, almost tentatively. Trent reached to Vauk's side, taking that large, rough hand in his own, and gently led him back to the party, Vauk's head craning from side to side, watching everyone and everything.

Cembran met them as they approached and said a few words. Some of the tension in Vauk's body relaxed as Cembran smiled and stepped away. Without letting go of Vauk's hand, Trent led him to the food table. Vauk immediately started to eat directly from the buffet. Trent gently touched his shoulder and, when Vauk turned, Trent offered him a plate, the smile never leaving his face. Vauk looked confused, so Trent took a plate himself and added a few items from the table as Vauk watched him closely.

With a small nod, Vauk seemed to understand and, taking the plate Trent had offered him, he followed Trent's lead and neatly filled his own plate.

Trent got utensils for both of them and led them to a blanket on the warm sand. Vauk stood looking around until Trent took his plate and signaled for him to sit next to him. Vauk complied and Trent handed him back his plate.

Vauk started eating with his hands, scooping up the food with his fingers and then licking them clean. Rather than try to correct him, Trent began eating his meal with a knife and fork, letting Vauk enjoy his food. Trent noticed that Vauk kept looking at him and had stopped eating. Trent handed Vauk a set of utensils and slowly began to eat again, making sure each of his movements was exaggerated so Vauk could mimic them. It was a sweet moment and one Trent knew he'd remember for a long time. At first Vauk was clumsy using a knife and fork, but he persevered. At one point, Vauk cut a little too hard with his knife and the plate he was holding split in two. The look of surprise on Vauk's face was priceless. Trent tried not to laugh, but he couldn't help it, and he was relieved when Vauk joined him. Trent got another plate for Vauk, and while he was up, got beer for both of them as well.

As they ate together, other people looked their way smiling, calling out greetings, and waving. Vauk noticed them looking and a tensed few times, but the open smiles and warm tones of their voices seemed to allay his fears.

While they were eating, Arthur approached them and sat on the sand next to Vauk. "Aude, Vauk, abent re fausten?"

Vauk smiled at Arthur and nodded. "Aude, Arthur." Vauk's words sounded hesitant even to Trent's ears, but Arthur smiled brightly, like he'd just received a great gift.

Arthur watched Vauk for a minute before turning his attention to Trent. "Mr., umm, Trent," he began, his hesitation making them both smile, "are you enjoying yourself?"

Trent looked at Vauk and then at Arthur. "Yes, very much. Your family and friends are really special and they've made me feel very welcome."

"I'm glad you're having a good time." Arthur looked around. "Mom and Dad say that this is a special place, a place where we can be ourselves and be happy."

Laughter drifted from one of the other groups. "I think they're right, Arthur. This is a special place." With another smile, Arthur drifted away to talk with the other guests.

Vauk finished his food and picked up his beer, downing it in a robust gulp before wiping his mouth on the back of his hand, smiling fiercely at Trent.

Trent watched each move of Vauk's body, enjoying the way his muscles played under his tight, dark skin. As he was watching, he realized with surprise how well they could communicate with each other without the use of words. It was like they were somehow in tune with each other. The party continued around them, but Trent was engrossed with Vauk.

His reverie with Vauk was interrupted when Cembran approached, speaking a few words to Vauk and receiving a few nods and a smile in response. Cembran smiled to Trent, said a few words of greeting, and then slipped away, leaving the two of them alone again.

Trent heard splashing and turned to see that many people were swimming in the lake, splashing together and roughhousing. Trent watched as Cembran raced into the water, tackling Travis and sending them both under the water. The two of them surfaced a few seconds later, laughing as Cembran was pulled into Travis's arms.

Using a combination of hand and eye signals, Trent asked Vauk if he'd like to go swimming. Vauk shook his head slowly and got up from where he was sitting. Trent rose as well, watching his every move. Trent gazed into Vauk's eyes and the pain he saw reflected back at him surprised him. Damn. Vauk reached forward, his hand caressing Trent's cheek. The rough, hot skin slid across the skin of his face, and involuntarily Trent leaned into the touch, enjoying the closeness with this strong, powerful satyr.

Then it was gone. Vauk nodded slowly, his eyes darting around as he listened carefully. Then Vauk turned quickly and ran off into the woods in the direction of the farm. Trent could still almost feel Vauk's touch on his cheek as he watched him disappear. Confused, Trent plopped himself back on the blanket, his head sagging, wondering if he'd done something wrong. *But he touched me so tenderly.*

"It's okay, Trent." Lifting his eyes, he saw Cembran and Travis standing in front of him. Cembran sat next to Trent while Travis settled behind Cembran, his arms wrapping around the blond's waist.

"He left so quickly."

Cembran smiled indulgently. "He spent more time with you this afternoon than he's spent with anyone in the past year." Cembran went on to explain where they'd found Vauk and how they'd rescued him from the carnival. "We usually see him from a distance. Even my contact with him has been limited."

Trent wanted to know everything he could. "Then where does he live?"

Cembran looked over his shoulder at Travis, obviously his cue to take over. "We believe he has a shelter on the far side of the property that he uses for most of the year. During the coldest days of the year, he sleeps in the barn with the sheep."

"You *believe* he has a shelter? You don't know?"

"Yeah. None of us has ever seen it and we've also never looked for it either. He needs time." Travis smiled and Cembran twisted to look at Travis. "But I think he may be ready for more." Cembran's eyes widened and he whispered something softly and Travis nuzzled a response that satisfied Cembran's curiosity. "He certainly seemed to like you."

"He doesn't seem to talk much." It was more of a vocalized thought than a question.

Cembran nodded. "He seems to understand Old Satyr, but I'm not sure he's comfortable speaking at all. As near as we can tell, he didn't for almost fifty years and he seems to have little interest in speaking at all. The few words he said to Arthur were a surprise." Cembran smiled. "But Arthur seems to put everyone at ease, including Vauk. I believe he's probably spent more time with him than any of us."

Travis placed a hand on Trent's shoulder. "Take it one step at a time." Travis looked at his watch and stood up. "It's time to cut the cake." Travis motioned for Arthur to come out of the water.

A primal sound carried through the woods and echoed over the water, followed by a high-pitched yip and then a low, bellowing growl. The party turned silent as everyone looked at one another. Travis squeezed Cembran's arm and then took off at a run toward the farm. Cembran turned to Trent. "Come on! He may need our help!" He raced off toward the farm with Trent racing behind him.

The beach gave way to woods and then the farm fields as a shot rang out, followed quickly by another. Trent raced behind Cembran as they followed the sound of the shots to the far side of the sheep enclosures, where they saw Travis lowering a rifle and rushing to a prone figure on the ground. Cembran and Trent stopped running and hurried to where Travis was kneeling near the prone figure. As they got closer, Trent's breath hitched as he recognized Vauk lying on the ground, bleeding heavily from gashes on his legs and chest.

Trent's first thought at seeing Vauk's injuries was "I can't lose him." Why he felt this way he had no idea, and it surprised him.

Cembran knelt next to Travis. "You have to help him."

Trent sat next to Vauk's body, holding the large satyr's hand in his, while Travis and Cembran's talk spun around him.

"Travis, you have to!"

"I know. I'm just not sure how." The doubt was clear in his voice.

Trent watched as Cembran looked into Travis's eyes. "Listen to your heart. You know what to do. Just think, feel, and let your heart guide you. I'm here with you and I can feel you, Lemmle."

Trent held Vauk's hand to his heart as Travis took Vauk's other hand, closed his eyes, and concentrated. Cembran's hands rested on Travis's shoulders as he concentrated as well, sending his energy to Travis so he could concentrate on Vauk.

Trent's attention returned to Vauk, and he saw the wounds on his legs close and the skin knit back together, then the wounds on his chest closed and the skin started to repair itself.

With a deep sign, Travis let go of Vauk's hand and leaned back against Cembran, his face drawn in near exhaustion. "I've got you, Lemmle. Just relax and breathe." Travis rested against Cembran and his eyes slid closed as Vauk's eyes fluttered open.

Still holding the satyr's hand, Trent stroked the bearded cheek with his hand, smiling into those chocolaty eyes. Trent could see the same pain he'd seen before, but this time it seemed tempered, a little less close to the surface. Vauk tried to get up, but Trent gently settled him by stroking his cheek and placing a hand on his chest. Turning to Travis without breaking contact with Vauk, he asked, "What happened?" Trent tried to keep any agitation out of his voice.

Travis opened his eyes, still leaning against Cembran, taking comfort from his mate. "Near as I can tell, a bear," Travis glanced at the black form in the grass not twenty feet away, "wandered onto the farm. I think Vauk sensed his presence and tried to protect the animals."

Trent nodded. "That explains the sounds we heard at the lake."

"Yeah, I think Vauk was trying to protect the farm and got mauled by it." Cembran was stroking Travis's chest in a gentle, almost intimate manner.

Cembran joined the conversation. "I take it you shot the bear."

"Yeah...." Travis sighed softly and Trent looked at him, confused. "Vauk injured the bear, but I managed to shoot it before it killed him. I guess we were lucky." Travis hated to kill anything, even predators, but he knew it was a necessary evil.

Trent returned his attention to Vauk, looking once again into those eyes. "I know you can't understand me, but, damn... you're fearless." Trent smiled and held Vauk's hand to his cheek, and he realized the close proximity to Vauk combined with his strength and bravery was really turning him on. Thank god no one could see.

"Trent, I need to get Travis to bed." Cembran helped Travis to his feet. "Healing Vauk drained him of most of his energy. Will you be okay with Vauk?"

"Sure. I'll stay with him."

Cembran let Travis lean on him as they started toward the farmhouse. Arthur approached. "Uncle Travis, are you okay?" Concern colored his voice.

"He will be, Arthur. Would you get Gathod and ask him to meet us at the house? He'll be able to help."

"Okay... I'll be right back." Arthur took off at a run toward the lake.

"Cembran, is there a place I can take Vauk for him to rest?"

Cembran and Travis stopped walking. "He seems to be most comfortable in the barn with the sheep." Cembran noticed Trent's confused expression. "He refuses to sleep in the house. There are blankets and a pillow in a box in the last stall. It's where he stays on cold nights."

Trent nodded as Cembran and Travis continued toward the house. "Come on, big guy." Trent helped Vauk to his feet, and together they made their way to the barn. Trent could tell Vauk was tired and weak by his stumbling steps. Vauk seemed to know where he wanted to go and led Trent to the farthest stall in the sheep barn. Trent found the blankets and pillow where Cembran said they were and, after making a bed for him, he helped Vauk lie down. Once he was settled, Vauk's eyes closed and soon his breathing became regular and he drifted off to sleep.

Trent lost track of time as he settled in the stall, staying close to Vauk. It was getting dark outside when Cembran and Arthur poked their heads into the stall. "How's he doing?" Cembran's voice was barely a whisper.

Trent used the same soft whisper. "He fell right to sleep. How's Travis?"

"Sleeping as well. Do you need something to eat?"

Trent shook his head. "No."

"Do you want to come back to the house?"

"No. I'll stay with him in case he wakes up." Cembran nodded and then Trent heard their footsteps as they quietly left the barn.

The next thing Trent remembered was light shining through the barn windows as a hand caressed his cheek. Trent leaned into the touch and pressed his own hand to the hand on his cheek, making sure Vauk knew his touch was wanted, desired. Trent looked into Vauk's face and saw the same pain in his eyes, and to his surprise his lips were trembling slightly. Trent couldn't help wondering what had hurt him so badly. He figured it was more than the captivity, but the answers were locked inside a silent Vauk. Not knowing what to do, Trent held Vauk's hand to his cheek, not wanting to break the connection.

Then he felt the hand slowly pull away. Vauk stood unmoving, looking like he was trying to decide what to do, then he turned and, before Trent could get up, Vauk was gone, leaving only the sound of his feet exiting the barn.

Trent got up and walked to the barn door, but Vauk was nowhere in sight; only a few branches moving at the edge of the woods indicated where he'd gone. With a deep sigh, Trent headed toward the farmhouse.

Chapter Eight

T rent heard the phone ringing through the open windows. Getting up off his knees and taking off his gardening gloves, he stepped inside, picked up the phone, and walked back outside as he answered. "Hello."

"Trent, it's Travis." He could hear the man's energy coming right through the phone.

"Hey, Travis. How are you and Cembran?" Trent continued walking before sitting on the garden bench in the shade, content to relax awhile. He'd been gardening most of the morning and it felt good to sit.

"We've been good. June is a great month on the farm. Everything is green and the farm is full of kids and lambs. It's my favorite time of year." Trent could hear the delight in Travis's voice.

"Sounds wonderfully pastoral." He wasn't kidding; the scene touched something in him he'd never thought about before.

"Glad you think so, because we were wondering if you'd like to join us for the weekend? You could drive up on Friday. Saturday is the bacchanal, and Sundays are usually quiet and restful."

Trent smiled. "This will be my first."

He could hear Travis chuckling on the other end of the line. "One of many… I hope."

"Should I bring something for the bacchanal?"

"That's not necessary. Everything is already taken care of. I'll explain when you get here."

"Oh." That sounded a little mysterious and intriguing. "I'm looking forward to it." His first official satyr gathering.

"Excellent. Well, see you this weekend."

"Thanks. I'll see you then." Trent hung up and smiled to himself as he put the phone down and went back to his gardening, but his mind kept wandering to other things, like the possibility of seeing Vauk again.

So, Friday found Trent driving back out of the city, heading to Travis and Cembran's, whistling and singing along with the radio. He couldn't seem to wipe the smile from his face. Everything about the farm fascinated him, particularly since he'd been raised in the city. The most intriguing thing for Trent was the thought of seeing Vauk again. He just couldn't get the hulking, silent man out of his mind. Trent knew he was probably being unreasonable, but something about Vauk fascinated him. Trent had thought about it repeatedly, but no answers came; only more questions.

To keep himself occupied, Trent had spent the past few weeks working on house projects that had been neglected or put off during the busy school year, and he'd gotten a part-time job tutoring elementary school age kids at the local learning center. After working with high school students all year, these younger children were like a breath of fresh air, and Trent was really enjoying the work.

As he drove, Trent stifled a yawn and took a drink of his coffee. He had thought that with school out he'd be well rested, but that wasn't turning out to be the case for some reason.

Arriving at the farm, Trent pulled into the parking area. After unloading his bag, he made his way to the farm, knocking on Travis and Cembran's door. The farmhouse seemed quiet, and when no one answered, he set his bag on the stoop and looked around, trying to discern where they were working, but the farm seemed very quiet. After a few minutes, he heard some soft sounds emanating from the sheep barn. Shrugging his shoulders, he followed the path to the barn, stopping briefly to watch a few of the lambs playing in one of the pastures.

"Wonderful, aren't they?"

Trent recognized Travis's voice and turned. "Yes, they are." One of the lambs bounded to the edge of the pasture, coming right up to Travis, who extended his hand and received a soft nuzzle and a few licks on his fingers. "They all know you, don't they?"

"Most of them, yes. They trust us to take care of them."

"But, doesn't that make it difficult...?" Trent wasn't sure how to express his thought, but Travis seemed to understand.

"The goats are raised for milk; the sheep are raised for their wool. We don't slaughter or eat any of them and breeding is kept under control to keep flock numbers from growing too fast, because neither of us could bear to sell any of the babies."

"Oh." Trent's eyes got wide. "So that's part of the magic here. I couldn't understand it, but I think I can now." The air seemed to radiate peace and harmony, as though fear had no place here.

Travis smiled and nodded. "All the creatures here are as happy as possible. They're loved and they return that love." The lamb continued nuzzling Travis's hand as Trent scratched the soft wool between the lamb's ears. Travis grinned. "Being satyrs, we have a deeper connection to them than humans."

"I have a lot to learn." The lamb licked Trent's hand before turning and bounding back toward its playmates.

"Come on; let's go have dinner."

They met Cembran coming from the goat barn and the three of them went inside the house. Trent picked up his bag from the stoop and Travis showed him to the guest room. "Make yourself comfortable. Cembran and I will have dinner ready in a few minutes."

Trent set his bag near the bed and went to wash up before dinner. When he was done, he went into the living room and sat in one of the chairs at the table, watching the two of them work together. Travis and Cembran said little to each other as they worked, but the small touches and the loving look in their eyes whenever they saw each other made Trent long for that kind of easy, loving relationship.

"I was wondering... is Vauk all right?"

Travis and Cembran shared a quick, knowing smile. "He's fine and seems fully recovered, as far as we can tell. We see him by the lake most evenings."

"Oh...."

"Don't worry, Trent; you'll see him." Trent smiled and hoped Travis was right, as he and Cembran brought dinner to the table. Everyone sat down and the food was passed around. "It looks like a warm night. We could swim to cool off after dinner."

"Do you want to call and see if Dovino, Phillip, and Jeremy want to join us?"

Travis nodded as he swallowed. "I'll call when we're done eating." Trent was quiet through most of dinner, listening to Cembran and Travis talk about their day and the activities on the farm. After dinner, Trent helped clear the table, setting the dishes in the sink while Travis called the boys and arranged for them all to meet at the lake. "I'm going to head to the beach and build a fire."

Cembran took the dishes Trent was carrying. "Why don't you change and go down with Travis? I'll finish up here and join you."

Travis leaned in to Cembran, stealing a soft kiss, "Don't be too long, Lamb."

Cembran smiled into Travis's lips. "I'll just be a few minutes."

After changing into their bathing suits, Trent and Travis walked together down the path to the lake. The water sparkled with the last rays of the sun as they built a small fire. Cembran joined them just as the wood caught.

"Let's go in the water, Lemmle. I'm feeling lucky tonight."

"Oh, ho... you think you can beat me to the other side of the lake!" Travis's eyes were dancing as Cembran dropped his towel on the sand and raced into the water, followed quickly by Travis.

"That's cheating!" Cembran's laugh echoed until he settled in the water.

"What's happening?"

Trent turned and saw Dovino on the beach, closely followed by Phillip and Jeremy. "Cembran and Travis are racing."

All three boys smiled. "Cembran's been trying to beat Travis for as long as I've known them."

The three boys put down their towels, slipped off their shirts, and ran into the water, splashing one another and yelling. Trent took off his shirt and was about to join them when a tall, lone figure stepped into the clearing. "Vauk." Trent found himself grinning and he noticed a smile on the large satyr's face as well.

"Trent... I am glad to see you." The words were halting, but definitely understandable.

Trent couldn't keep the surprise off his face. "Vauk, I thought you didn't understand English." Damn, I must have looked like a fool the last time I saw him.

"I learn English in last two weeks." Vauk stopped and tilted his head to the side, apparently very confused. "You teached me."

Now it was Trent's turn to be confused. "How could I teach you? I haven't seen you since you were hurt." Either Vauk was truly mixed up or something really strange was going on.

"Every night, you come to me and show me how to make English words and when I wake up, I not forget. I hope you come here soon so I could show you for real how good you teach me."

Trent shook his head and sat on the sand. This made no sense. "How could I...?" Trent cut off his question, confused as to how to continue. Looking at Vauk, he could see similar confusion, tinged with disappointment and hurt. Trent patted the ground next to him and Vauk sat silently next to him. "Each night I came to you?"

Vauk smiled and nodded his head vigorously. "Whenever I sleep, you come to me."

Trent heard Travis and Cembran getting out of the water, laughing. Trent turned his head and saw Cembran with his legs curled around Travis's hips and his arms around his neck. "I beat you, I beat you." The satyr was chanting with glee.

"What do you want for your prize?" Cembran put his lips to Travis's ear and the laughing stopped, Travis's eyes filling with passion as he nodded slowly. "Okay, Lamb, you go to our shelter and get ready. I'll be in soon and then you'll get your prize."

Cembran unwrapped his legs and stood on the sand, smiling into Travis's eyes before stepping away. "Don't be too long." Cembran slapped Travis gently on the butt before heading to one of the small shelters just inside the trees.

Travis laughed softly to himself as his attention turned to the couple near the fire. The sound of the youngsters in the water drifted over the water. "Travis." Trent sounded different, like confusion touched with fear.

Travis sat down next to Trent, nodding at Vauk. "Is something wrong?"

"No… not wrong exactly, just confusing. I've been talking with Vauk." That got Travis's attention. "And apparently, I've been teaching him English."

Travis looked from Trent to Vauk. "Trent, he come to me when I sleep and teach me and when I wake up… I not forget."

Travis grinned from ear to ear. "Trent, have you been dreaming about Vauk?"

"I think I may have, but I don't really remember my dreams when I wake up. I never have—"

"I think you've been connecting to Vauk through your dreams and you've been teaching him English. You do have the ability and your dream-weaving capabilities are very strong. It's just surprising that you don't remember them."

"You mean to tell me I've been teaching in my sleep?"

"That's exactly what I think, yes. The last time you were here, you made a connection with Vauk and you tried to communicate with him on a basic level. Since then, I think you may have been teaching him by weaving his dreams into lessons so he could speak English. And from what I heard, it's working."

"I just wish I could remember."

"You might, now that you know you're doing it. You'll just have to see."

"Thank you."

"You're welcome. Now, I've got someone waiting for his prize and I don't want him disappointed." Travis got up and followed Cembran's route to the shelter, leaving Trent and Vauk alone on the sand.

The night was now nearly silent; the only sound was the crackle of the fire. While they'd been talking, the boys had gotten out of the water and gone home. The night air was starting to lose its daytime heat and Trent found himself scooting a little closer to the fire.

"Trent… thank you." Vauk's voice was soft and deep.

Trent's attention refocused from the fire to Vauk. "What for?"

"For teaching me." The fire reflected in Vauk's eyes and played in his hair, making his large horns look menacing, yet his voice seemed tentative and very soft. The disparity was almost jarring. "I know you did not know, but thank you."

"A teacher can only teach what someone is willing to learn, and while I don't remember the dreams, you must be a good student." Trent touched Vauk's hand, letting their heat mingle in the simple touch. "This is nice, being here with you." Trent wanted desperately to kiss Vauk, but he wasn't sure if the gesture would be welcomed, so he refrained. "How long have you been here?"

Vauk concentrated, searching for the right words. "I come to the farm almost a year. Travis and Cembran rescue me from bad men. I kept in cage." Trent could see Vauk shudder.

"I'm glad you're here." Trent scooted closer to Vauk, letting their arms entwine. "Really glad." Trent had been cold, but the warmth and closeness of Vauk's body made the slight chill vanish in a rush of heat.

"I like it here. I protect the… kind." Vauk shook his head. "Sweet… no… gentle," Vauk nodded, pleased with himself at finding the word he wanted, "animals. They like me and do not scare me like most people."

"Do I scare you?" Vauk thought a minute and then shook his head no. "Good, I'm glad."

"Can I ask question?" Trent nodded. "Why you not have horns like me?"

"I do." Trent concentrated and did something he rarely did and let his cloak go, displaying the short horns high on his forehead.

"You can do magic." Vauk's voice filled with amazement.

Trent smiled brightly. "You can do it too." Vauk's face turned skeptical. "I can show you how if you like."

"You can?" Disbelief was plain in his voice.

"Sure. I'll show you tomorrow… if you want." Vauk nodded and smiled.

Their conversation drifted slowly through the evening, their voices low. The more they talked together, the better Vauk's speech became. Occasionally, Trent would gently correct his speech, always with a smile and a light touch to his hand or shoulder. As the evening wore on, the night got cooler, but Trent was reluctant to leave. So, at one point, he scooted closed to Vauk, burrowing beneath the big satyr's arm. They continued to talk, their voices soft, and Trent started to drift off.

"You need sleep?" The deep voice penetrated Trent's half-asleep brain.

Trent mumbled something and burrowed closer to Vauk, the warmth and the deep, rich scent too good to part from. Trent nodded off and woke to strong arms under his body as he was lifted and carried. Too tired to object, he put his arms around Vauk's neck and let the big satyr take him where he wanted. He was set gently down on a soft mattress. Trent shivered as Vauk pulled away, tugging on his arm. Then the warmth returned, cradled to his back. "Mmmmmm." Trent burrowed close, holding on to the arm draped over his side.

Chapter Nine

rent woke when he heard soft footsteps and whispered voices. Vauk's chest still pressed to his back and he didn't want to move, the warmth and closeness felt so good. He could feel Vauk's chest expand, feel his breath in his hair, and damned if he wasn't as excited as he could ever remember.

Was that...? Trent could feel something pressuring his butt. Slowly, he leaned back. Yeah, it was. Vauk was excited too, really excited. He hoped it wasn't just a morning thing. Vauk squirmed against him, muttering something he couldn't understand, before hugging Trent tighter. Lying next to Vauk, Trent tried to remember his dreams from the night before. He could recall talking with Vauk around the fire, feeling sleepy, and Vauk carrying him. He hadn't dreamed that. Then he could remember being in his classroom at school, teaching youngsters how to read and write. Vauk was in the class, squeezed into the seat of one of the kiddy desks, and the class was soaking up all the information he could impart as fast as he could present it. It was like teaching the smartest kids possible. Wow, maybe I am teaching Vauk. Then he smiled that he'd remembered it this time.

Vauk shifted next to him and appeared to be waking. Trent stifled a giggle as Vauk yawned loudly into his ear. "Good morning." Trent shifted so he could see Vauk's face.

"Good morning, Trent." Vauk sat up, the blanket falling away from his body. "I have to see to the animals, make sure they are okay." Trent tried to keep the disappointment off his face. "Will you still show me how you make horns disappear?

"Sure."

"Good. I find you later after I check animals." Vauk stood up just outside the shelter entrance. He turned to leave.

"Vauk." Trent stood up and Vauk turned to look at him. Trent used the opportunity to raise himself to his toes and kiss the big satyr. The feel of Vauk's lips on his sent heat through his body and Trent had to restrain himself to keep the kiss from deepening too quickly. The last thing he wanted was to scare Vauk off. The big satyr's lips moved against Trent's as the kiss was returned and Trent heard a soft deep rumble of what he hoped was pleasure.

Trent slowly lowered himself, breaking the kiss. "I'll see you later." Vauk nodded, touching his lips with a finger as he turned and slowly walked down the path away from the shelter. Trent smiled at the large satyr's reaction and straightened out the bed they'd slept on before he too started down the path back to the farmhouse.

At the farmhouse door, Trent knocked lightly. Cembran opened the door and smiled as Trent entered the living room. Travis was seated on the sofa speaking to a man Trent remembered meeting at Arthur's party, but his name escaped him.

"Trent... you remember Doug?" Trent smiled—saved by Travis's good manners.

"Good to see you again." Trent extended his hand and the sheriff took it, the handshake firm. Travis motioned for both men to sit down. "I'll step outside if you need to talk privately." Trent turned back toward the door.

Doug looked over to Trent before speaking, deciding if he should continue in front of him. Doug reached his decision. "Maybe you should hear this." Trent sat down and waited for Doug to continue. "There've been rumors in town that I think you need to know about." Travis rolled his eyes; he didn't put much stock in rumor. "I know. I usually ignore it too, but this is different."

"How so?" Travis relaxed back into his chair. Cembran brought each of them coffee and then sat on the arm of Travis's chair, sipping from his cup. Travis turned his head and gave Cembran a gentle thank-you kiss before returning his attention fully to the conversation.

"The rumor spreading through town is that there's a large, horned animal prowling through the woods in this portion of the county. The descriptions range from a large wild goat to a wild jungle animal of some sort."

Travis shrugged. "There's nothing I can do about a silly rumor."

"No, but the carnival is coming back to town for the summer festival and it's the same one as last year. If they hear the rumor, they might figure out where their attraction escaped to and come looking for him."

Travis inhaled and exhaled slowly. "I'm not sure what we can do. We'll tell Vauk to be careful for the next few weeks." Travis sipped his coffee, concern written on his face.

Trent spoke up. "I promised Vauk that I'd work with him so he could learn to cloak his satyr characteristics." Everyone's attention shifted to Trent. "I don't know if he has the ability, but I'll try to teach him."

"Excellent." Travis brought the others up to date. "It seems that Trent has formed a connection with Vauk and he's been able to teach him English using their dreams."

Cembran whistled softly.

"What?" Trent wondered what that meant.

Cembran looked embarrassed. "Sorry. It's just that's really powerful dream-weaving. Probably the most powerful I've ever heard of. Most of us can weave dreams to some level, but to be able to teach someone, have them retain the knowledge, catalog it with what they already know, and be able to use it when they're awake is remarkable."

Doug finished his coffee and got up to leave. "I'll see you all this evening at the bacchanal."

Cembran smiled happily. "You'll be able to come?" Sometimes Doug's schedule prohibited him from being able to attend—much to Gathod's disappointment.

Doug grinned. "Gathod threatened me with bodily harm if I miss this month, particularly since I had to work last month." Everyone said their goodbyes, and Cembran finished preparing breakfast.

Trent spent most of the morning helping around the farm. He didn't know much about the animals, but he knew gardening, so he helped

Travis with the vegetables, weeding the new plants, and watering some of the tender seedlings. Trent immersed himself in the task.

"Trent, are you ready for lunch?" Trent looked up to see Cembran walking toward him between the rows of vegetables. He hadn't realized it was getting so late.

Trent's stomach rumbled. "Yeah, I guess I am." The time had really gotten away from him. Standing up, he followed Cembran back down the rows and into the house.

After lunch, Trent was again working in the garden when he felt, more than heard, someone approach. Tilting his head, he saw a pair of large, strong, hairy legs. His eyes swept upward, to where beefy thighs gave way to a flat stomach and powerful chest. He smiled as he looked into those chocolaty eyes. "Are you ready?"

Vauk nodded, returning Trent's smile. "Yes."

Trent stood up and reached for Vauk's hand. Trent really liked touching Vauk and he hoped it wouldn't make him uncomfortable. His fears were relieved when Vauk's fingers gripped Trent's. "Let's go down to the lake; the water will help." Vauk nodded in agreement, and the two of them walked together toward the lake, Trent grinning like an idiot. At the lake, Trent rolled up his pants legs and waded into the water, Vauk standing beside him. "Look down. See your reflection in the water?"

"Yes."

"What I want you to do is study your face and imagine what you'd look like without your horns. You need to get a clear picture in your mind." From the look on Vauk's face, Trent could tell he was having trouble, so he placed his hands in front of Vauk's horns, blocking them from his reflection. "Does this help?" Vauk nodded. "Keep that image in your mind... close your eyes." Vauk complied. Trent crooned softly into Vauk's ear, "Concentrate and tell yourself that's what you look like. Keep that picture in your mind." Trent hoped his voice was calm and reassuring. Being this close to Vauk, his senses bombarded with his scent, heat, and the sight of his powerful body, nearly had Trent shaking. "Keep that picture in your mind and open your eyes."

Trent watched as Vauk's eyes opened and for a few seconds, his horns were gone, but they quickly returned. Vauk looked disappointed. "It did not work."

"It did for a few seconds. We'll try again. Close your eyes." Trent worked with Vauk for the next hour, but the best he could manage was to mask his horns for just a few seconds. "It's okay. It'll just take some practice." Trent let his hands rub along Vauk's back, trying to soothe his frustration. "We can try again tomorrow if you like."

Vauk nodded slowly and turned to face Trent. "Thank you for trying. I should be able to do this. I just do not know why I cannot."

Trent touched him gently on the side of his face, Vauk's beard rough against his skin. "Maybe it's because you've never really had the need to hide, the same way the rest of us have." Trent slowly withdrew his hand.

Vauk thought for a minute. "Maybe. I grew up in a satyr village where everyone showed who they were. No one had to hide their looks. There were no... humans," Vauk looked at him questioningly and Trent nodded and smiled at his correct use of the word, "... around."

"Where was your village?"

Vauk's face lit up as he remembered. "In a forest in the mountains." His eyes became vacant, like he wasn't concentrating on what he was seeing. "As boys we'd play in the trees, happy and laughing. We were inseparable even as children. My family had a small farm on the edge of the village and every afternoon once my work was done, I'd meet Miki and we'd...." Pain and sadness filled Vauk's eyes and a tear rolled down his cheek. "I can't speak of this."

"Okay. It's okay. We don't have to talk about it now." Jesus.... What or who had hurt him so badly? Vauk wiped his eyes and composed himself. Trent stayed close, touching him gently on the arm. "You know that the bacchanal is tonight."

"Yes. Travis told me I was welcome."

"Are you... would you come with me?"

Vauk shrugged. "I do not know if I can." Trent tried to keep the disappointment off his face, but Vauk noticed it. "It is not you, Trent. I have not been to a bacchanal since...." Vauk let his voice trail off.

"I understand. But I hope you'll decide to come."

"I need to go. Thank you for trying to teach me."

Before Vauk could leave, Trent kissed him on the lips. This time, Trent added a touch of heat to the kiss, letting his lips play over Vauk's before slowly pulling back. "You're welcome." Trent watched Vauk's eyes dance just before he turned and walked toward the trees, turning back to glance at Trent before disappearing into the woods.

Trent slowly walked back to the farmhouse. "Damn it!" Trent yelped as he found himself flat on the ground. Looking around he realized he'd tripped over a small tree root. "Watch where you're going, Trent." Picking himself up, Trent pulled his head out of the clouds and walked the rest of the way back.

After spending some of the afternoon working around the farm, helping where he could, Trent took some advice from Travis and had a short afternoon nap. "The bacchanal tends to go late into the night, and the last thing you want to be is sleepy." Travis had spoken with a knowing look that made him wonder. So, after his nap, Trent showered and dressed for what he hoped would be a memorable night. Trent wasn't counting on Vauk showing up, but he kept hoping anyway.

As the sun was setting, Trent heard others arriving, so he wandered down to the lakeshore. A large fire had been built on the sand, and a group of satyrs sat around the fire, talking and laughing together. Each of them had allowed their cloaks to fall, so Trent followed suit. It was obvious to Trent that they all knew each other by their ease and camaraderie together. "Trent." He heard his name and saw Jim and Sue waving him to where they were sitting. "Join us." Trent sat next to Jim. "Things will start in a while." Jim then explained how the bacchanal usually worked. "Travis typically starts with stories. Everyone is encouraged, but not required, to tell stories about their lives. Then the music and dancing start, followed by…," Jim's eyes were sparkling as he looked at Sue and then back to Trent, "what satyrs do best." Sue giggled as Jim hugged her to him.

Trent quietly listened to the others talking around him, not quite at ease enough to really contribute to the conversation. Every now and then, someone would ask him a question and he'd get drawn into the conversation for a while, but then he'd drift back to the edges. More and more satyrs arrived and joined the expanding circle. As the last of the sun faded and darkness settled over the lake, Travis and Cembran stepped into the clearing.

"Welcome, friends, to our bacchanal. Tonight we have a new face with us. Trent Walters is joining us for his first ever bacchanal." The people around Trent whom he didn't know reached over to shake his hand and introduced themselves. "As is our custom, we'll start with the sharing of our stories. We each have unique and varied histories, some stretching back centuries," Travis hugged Cembran close, "and it's important to share who we are and where we come from."

Trent felt someone sit down next to him. "Hey, Trent."

"Arthur." Trent was pleasantly surprised to see him.

"Travis lets me stay for the stories." Arthur settled in to listen. "Then I go back to the farmhouse for the night."

Near silence descended on the group as the stories began. Listening to other satyrs tell their stories made Trent's own experiences seem less unusual, and he felt drawn to these people in a way he'd never expected. He felt included, like he'd found a place that he could truly be himself. Toward the end of the story time, Travis stepped to Trent and asked if he had a story to share.

"Yes, actually, I do." Trent stood up. "After listening to some of your stories, I'm learning that my story is not unique." Heads shook and a few others made soft "No" sounds, but Trent raised his hand. "For me, that's a wonderful thing. I grew up not knowing who my father was, or that I was a satyr at all. It wasn't until I matured that my characteristics and abilities manifested themselves. Luckily, I was able to figure out how to cloak myself."

"Who taught you how?"

"No one. I learned to do it largely by accident in front of the bathroom mirror. After that, I kept myself cloaked until I met some of you a few weeks ago. Since then, I've learned that I'm not alone, that there are others like me, and I've found a place where I can truly fit in." Everyone around the fire clapped as Trent sat back on the sand, grinning widely as he scanned the faces around the fire, hoping….

Travis stood. "Bacchus… we are here and you are welcome." The fire jumped and music started playing, seeming to come from all around. Trent said good night to Arthur as he stood up and stepped away from the gathering. The chairs and blankets around the fire were pushed back and everyone started to dance. Swirling music with rhythmic beats carried them as they moved around the fire. Couples held hands and moved together, their bodies getting closer and closer, their movements more and more like simulated sex. Trent stood back, watching the dance and looking out over the lake.

"Trent." Travis stopped dancing and stood next to him. "Join us." As Travis was speaking, Trent saw a figure emerge from the trees down the beach. Travis saw the movement as well. "Ahh." Travis nodded knowingly as he clapped Trent lightly on the back. "I understand who you've been waiting for." Travis then rejoined the dance, scooping Cembran into his arms.

Trent walked slowly away from the fire and the dancing, but the music seemed to travel with him and continued to surround him. Vauk stood still on the beach watching as Trent approached. "Vauk, I'm so glad you came."

"I was not sure I should come, but I wanted to see you and I felt a pull I have not felt in a long time." In the darkness, a lot of Vauk's features were obscured, but Trent could tell his body was still with tension.

Trent took Vauk's hand in his. "Come with me?"

Vauk made no movement. "Trent, the wildness is strong in me right now."

"Vauk, please dance with me." Trent pulled gently on Vauk's hand and he wasn't sure Vauk would follow. To Trent's delight, Vauk let himself be led toward the others dancing around the fire. As they got close, Trent whispered, "Will you show me how to dance like a satyr?"

Vauk nodded and stepped into the ring of dancers. Instantly, the music changed, becoming more primal and rhythmic. The lyrical lines of the music drifted away, replaced by strong tribal drums. Then Vauk started to dance. Trent's mouth hung open as Vauk moved around the fire like a sleek jungle cat, hunting its prey. Trent's arm was tugged and he felt himself being pulled into the ring of dancers as Vauk wrapped an arm around him and carried him along with his movements. Trent grinned when he realized that he was the prey in Vauk's feral mating dance. The other dancers took up Vauk's movements, leaping and prowling around the fire. Trent watched as Brock and Steven removed their shirts, and it looked to him like Steven was trying to remove Brock's pants before Brock pulled him toward the trees and the shelters beyond. A short time later, Dovino grabbed both Jeremy and Phillip, pulling them down the lakeshore before disappearing into the trees. Trent continued dancing as Vauk pulled him closer and he felt his own ardor rise deep inside him. Couples continued to leave and then rejoin the dance. Trent lost all track of time as Vauk held him closer and their movements joined and flowed together.

Trent was lost in a reverie—they could have been dancing minutes, hours, or days. Eventually, Vauk stepped away from the fire, walking directly to the drink table and drinking a huge glass of beer in what looked to Trent like a single gulp. Figuring that now was his chance, Trent picked up a blanket from the sand with one hand and, as Vauk set down his glass, he wrapped the other arm around Vauk's neck and tugged his head down into a hard, demanding kiss. When Vauk didn't pull away, Trent slipped his tongue between Vauk's lips, deepening the kiss. "Come with me." Vauk nodded in a slightly dazed manner and Trent took his hand, leading him back down the beach away from the fire.

Once they were away from the light, Trent spread the blanket on the sand. He then pulled his shirt over his head and opened his pants, shoving them to the ground, and stood before Vauk, naked, hard, and shaking with want, need, and passion. Vauk's eyes went wide as Trent jumped forward, flinging himself at Vauk before practically climbing the big satyr's body to latch their lips together in a bruising kiss.

Slowly, Vauk lowered Trent to the blanket while Trent watched those dark eyes. "Are you sure, Trent? I do not know if I can control the wildness." The concern in Vauk's voice touched something deep inside Trent. He could feel it in his heart.

"I'm sure. I want you, Vauk. The wildness included." God, he wanted him so bad, he was vibrating with excitement. Vauk's hands on his skin were driving him wild. Without another word, Vauk took off his rough-spun shirt and slipped out of his pants. Damn, the big guy was hairy everywhere. Vauk's chest was covered in dark hairy curls; his legs were matted with course black hair.

"Damn, Vauk, you're sex on wheels."

The comment was met with a bemused smile as Vauk lowered his body onto Trent's. "Sex… on… wheels? Is that good?"

"Yes." Trent tried to explain further, but his mouth was taken by Vauk in a hard kiss that stole his breath away. Trent's skin went wild as Vauk moved on top of him, the hair on Vauk's chest and legs rough against him. Trent wrapped his arms around Vauk's back as his legs were parted and fingers pressed against his opening. Vauk kissed him again as those fingers teased his skin.

"Suck!" Two large fingers replaced Vauk's mouth at his lips, and Trent lapped and sucked on the large digits. Trent arched against Vauk as he felt hot lips suck and nibble on one of his now hard nipples. Then the fingers withdrew, replaced again by Vauk's lips, before those two wet fingers pressed deep into Trent's body.

Trent threw his head back and cried out in ecstasy as those fingers breached him for the first time. "Oh god, Vauk. Do that again!" The fingers withdrew and plunged deep inside him again... and again, hitting the sweet spot each and every time.

"The wildness is coming!" Vauk's eyes were swirling as he tried to control the impulses coming from his baser instincts.

"Let it go, Vauk. I want all of you." The fingers slipped from his body and the air whooshed from Trent's lungs as Vauk plunged himself deep. Pain from Trent's suddenly stretched muscles surged along his spine, followed almost immediately by waves of pleasure as Vauk withdrew and plunged deep again. "Fuck, Vauk...." Trent could barely form words as his body was pounded, his own throbbing cock bouncing against his stomach as he met each of Vauk's thrusts. Trent enjoyed a good fucking, but Vauk's power and stamina were driving him to heights of pleasure he'd never known before. Vauk's wildness seemed to be releasing Trent's own wildness. Extending his hands, Trent raked his fingers across Vauk's chest before pulling Vauk down on top of him, sucking on Vauk's lips until he tasted blood.

Heat rose from deep inside, concentrating in Trent's groin. "Vauk... not... gonna... last." Trent's climax crashed on him like a rutting ram. Vauk threw his head back, the light reflecting off his horns. Trent felt Vauk's release surge into him as he climaxed, their howls of release blending together and echoing across the water.

Chapter Ten

Breath heaved into Trent's lungs as he collapsed back on the blanket, Vauk between his spread legs, still filling him. Palms stroked along his chest and stomach, soothing his hot, sensitive skin. Then Vauk's lips were on his, the kiss sweet, gentle, Vauk's tongue tracing their outline. "Aahhh." A small whimper escaped as Vauk withdrew, then strong arms wrapped around him, pulling him to rough skin, warmth, and back to hot, now soft lips.

"Did I hurt you?" Vauk's voice was soft and touched with worry.

Trent smiled into a kiss. "No. You were mind-blowing."

Now it was Vauk's turn to smile. "You and your sayings I do not understand. Is that good?"

Those arms clutched him a little tighter. "Yes, that's good. That's very good." Vauk's post-sex tenderness stood in stark contrast to their frantic coupling. He wasn't expecting Vauk to be so tender, and he leaned into the touch, his head resting against Vauk's shoulder.

The night air sent a shiver along Trent's sweat-damp skin. With a soft grunt, Vauk stood up, bringing Trent along with him. Strong hands supported Trent's butt as he wrapped his legs around Vauk's hips and his arms gripped his shoulders. "Need to get you warm." Vauk walked Trent toward the woods and to one of the currently unoccupied shelters. With a kiss, Trent was lowered onto a cushion and covered with a soft blanket.

"Don't...." Before Trent could finish his thought, Vauk was gone. He watched the opening, wondering what he'd done to make Vauk leave. Trent smiled with relief when Vauk returned a few minutes later, dropping their clothes and the blanket in the corner of the shelter before slipping under the covers. "I thought you'd gone." Trent molded his back to Vauk, smiling when an arm wrapped around him. "I'm glad you came back." Trent craned his head to meet Vauk's, kissing the big satyr tenderly. "Very glad." Trent scooted closer, wiggling a little against Vauk's hairy body. "You feel so good."

Vauk's hand petted small circles on Trent's stomach and chest, skimming lightly over his nipples. "So do you." The soothing touch of Vauk's hand, the warmth of his body, and soft sounds of the forest lulled Trent to sleep.

Movement next to him startled Trent awake. Vauk was sitting up, his horns nearly hitting the roof of the shelter. "I did not mean to wake you."

Trent sat up and leaned in for a kiss. "I'm glad you did." Trent pressed a soft kiss to Vauk's lips.

Vauk yawned and stretched as best he could in the small space before Trent gently pulled him back into another kiss, but this time, Vauk pulled away, reluctantly. "I would love to stay here with you, but I must see to the animals."

Trent looked confused. "Won't Cembran and Travis take care of them?"

"Not those animals. I need to care for my little ones."

Trent's face lit up like a kid on Christmas morning. "Do you mean babies?"

Vauk nodded, returning Trent's smile. "Would you like to see them?" Trent nodded, his grin getting wider. "Then we need to get dressed." Vauk stood just outside the shelter and started putting on his clothes while Trent watched every movement. Seeing the big satyr naked in all his glory was a sight for Trent to behold.

"What a sight, Vauk."

The big satyr turned his head and looked behind him. "What?"

Trent stood up, his eyes glued to Vauk. "You."

Vauk shook his head. "Me? No."

Trent stood up, letting the blanket slip from his body. "Oh, yes... you. Most definitely you." To emphasize his point, Trent let his eyes rake over Vauk and he felt those chocolate eyes returning the gaze. After looking his fill, Trent slowly picked up his own clothes and pulled them on.

With both of them dressed and the shelter straightened, Trent followed Vauk back toward the farm, past the barns and pastures, and into the woods on the far side of the farm. The warm summer day gave way to the cool shade beneath the dense foliage. Vauk obviously knew exactly where he was going and seemed to be following some sort of path, although Trent couldn't see it at all. After climbing over fallen logs, walking around mammoth tree trunks, and skirting damp bogs, Vauk led him into a small clearing. An enclosed shelter that couldn't have been any bigger than eight by ten feet was surrounded by a small pen and a few enclosed hutches.

"Is this where you live?" Vauk looked at Trent and nodded, unsure of Trent's reaction. "It's so beautiful here." The morning breeze rustled in the trees and they could hear the trickle of the nearby creek. "It even sounds beautiful." Silent but smiling, Vauk unlatched the lid of a wooden box next to the shelter and brought out a bucket of grain. Leading Trent around the corner of the shelter, Vauk called gently, standing at the edge of a small pen.

The head of a small fawn peeked around the corner. Vauk called again, held out a handful of the grain, and the fawn warily walked to him. "Hold still; she is a little afraid." Trent watched, not moving a muscle, as the fawn walked to Vauk and gingerly ate the offered grain. Vauk offered more grain and gently stroked between the long, alert ears, cooing and soothing the entire time. "Come forward, very slow." Trent stepped forward in slow motion. "Take a handful of grain and hold your hand out." Trent followed Vauk's instructions, making no sudden movements. Vauk pulled his hand back, waiting to see if the fawn would respond to Trent. The little button nose twitched and those long, alert ears shifted before the small head lowered and the fawn's lips nipped at the food. "Take a little more." Trent got another handful, and the emboldened fawn ate the food from Trent's hand and even let him pet her.

"You're a pretty little one, aren't you?" Trent used the same tone Vauk did, mimicking his soft cooing. "Where did you find her?"

"Near the creek." That big satyr head sagged just a little and his eyes saddened. "She was curled next to her dying mother. I brought her here and fed her with a bottle I got from Cembran."

Trent fed the fawn another handful of grain. "What's in the hutches?"

"I have a nest of baby rabbits and a young raccoon. The rabbits will be released in a few weeks; the raccoon as well."

Damn, the more Trent found out about Vauk, the more he liked him. Here was this huge, almost ominous-looking satyr who rescued and cared for orphaned animals. Trent stroked his hand down Vauk's bare arm. "You have a kind heart."

A dark expression briefly clouded Vauk's face. "I know what it's like to be alone... and unloved." Trent wanted to inquire further, but he didn't want to pry, and he wasn't sure the inquiry would be welcomed. "I need to feed the rest."

Trent followed as Vauk fed the bunnies and the inquisitive little raccoon. As they were finishing, Trent's stomach rumbled loudly. To Trent's relief, they both laughed. "Travis said yesterday that he and Cembran were having an after-bacchanal breakfast. Would you come with me?"

Vauk looked embarrassed. "I do not eat right."

"I don't think that matters." Vauk looked unconvinced. "I think everyone would be happy if you'd come."

"I will try, if you will help me."

"Of course."

Vauk put the feed away and made sure all the animals had water.

"Lead the way," said Trent.

Vauk smiled and led him back through the dense forest to the edge of the farm. "Thank you for showing me your home." Trent took Vauk's hand and they walked together toward the farmhouse, meeting Travis along the way.

"Are you both ready for breakfast?"

"Yeah, my stomach's been growling, and I think I heard Vauk's awhile ago too." Trent nudged the big guy playfully.

"I'm glad you're going to join us, Vauk." Travis seemed inordinately pleased for some reason, as he led them to the door and ushered them inside.

Cembran stood in the kitchen with Steven; the two of them appeared to be working together to make breakfast. As Vauk entered the house, the conversation stilled and all heads turned in their direction. Trent squeezed Vauk's hand gently before lacing Vauk's fingers with his, afraid he'd bolt at the attention. "Vauk, let me introduce you to everyone." Trent was relieved that Travis took the lead, because he couldn't remember everyone's name. "Cembran you know." Vauk nodded and smiled. "Steven and his truist, Brock." Travis indicated each person, making sure to use satyr terms for their relationships. He figured it would make Vauk more comfortable and help him understand. "You know Gathod and his truist, Doug." Again acknowledgments, hand shaking, and smiles. "Jim and Sue Kraus, Brock and Arthur's parents, and you know these three." Vauk nodded and smiled to Dovino, Phillip, and Jeremy. He'd seen them around the farm many times, but he'd usually kept his distance.

Vauk leaned close to Travis. "Some of them help rescue me?"

Travis nodded. "Many of them helped rescue you. Don't you remember?"

"I remember some, but mostly it is mixed up."

"Don't worry. All are friends here." Vauk was becoming agitated. He wasn't used to being around people.

"Mr. Walt... I mean, Trent, there's two chairs over here." Arthur was seated at the table with a book open in front of him. He marked his page and closed the book as Trent and Vauk made their way to the empty chairs.

"What are you reading?" Trent picked up the book: *The Care and Feeding of Goats*. "A little light reading?"

Arthur laughed. "I usually spend a couple weeks here during the summer. Last year I worked with the sheep, learning what I could. This year Cembran says I can work with the goats, so I wanted to read up on them first."

Trent filled in Vauk. "Arthur is going to be a veterinarian." Vauk's expression betrayed his puzzlement. "An animal doctor."

"I've always loved animals, and Mom says I've turned their garage into a zoo." Arthur's energy ratcheted up a little as he spoke. "Last week I found a snake in the backyard."

"Did you add it to your zoo?"

Shaking his head, Arthur said, "No, it was healthy, so I took it to a nearby field and let it go. I only keep the ones that are hurt and need my help."

"I have a deer, some baby rabbits, and a raccoon." For the first time, Vauk entered the conversation. Plates were set down in front of each of them.

Arthur's eyes widened, his expression sheer joy, ignoring the food. "Cool. I've got a couple turtles, a litter of kittens that I found, a bird with a broken wing, and a bunny that the neighbor's dog was playing with." Arthur scowled as he spoke of the dog. Trent started eating his breakfast, but Arthur kept talking. Obviously, animals were more important than food… at least right now. "I try to care for them so they can be released. I splinted the bird's wing and it seems to be healing, so I hope it'll be able to fly soon."

"All my little ones are…." He seemed to be searching for a word, so Trent whispered it to him. Vauk nodded and continued. "Orphans. I feed them and try to release them back into the forest." Vauk's expression clouded. "But I do not know what I will do with the fawn. I think she likes people too much."

Arthur took a bite of his breakfast, thinking as he chewed. As he swallowed, he smiled brightly. "How about Deer Woods?"

"What is this Deer Woods?" Vauk cautiously took a bite of eggs and then smiled. He'd been watching Trent eat, and he used his knife and fork. His technique wasn't elegant, but Trent smiled and patted his thigh as he continued using the utensils.

"It's a park area nearby where they have a herd of deer. They're cared for and kids can feed them." The excitement in Arthur's voice was contagious. "They take good care of them and protect them from predators. It's really cool."

Arthur started to eat and Vauk turned his attention to Trent. "Well, maybe…." Vauk looked a little lost. "How would I talk to these Deer Woods people?"

Trent patted the strong thigh nestled next to his. "Don't worry. If she can't be released and you need to find a home for her, then I'll help you."

"You will?" Vauk wasn't used to people helping him. He'd spent too many years in captivity.

"Of course." Trent leaned close, whispering into Vauk's ear. "Let's finish breakfast. I think we should talk." Vauk looked worried. "It's a good talk." Trent smiled. "I promise." Trent ran his hand along that strong thigh and he smiled when Vauk shuddered. They finished their breakfast and spent some time talking with the others. Vauk didn't speak much, but he did seem to get more comfortable as the morning continued.

"Are you enjoying yourself?" Cembran stood next to Vauk, speaking softly. Vauk nodded and smiled. "I'm glad you joined us. You're always welcome."

"Thank you."

Doug and Gathod, along with Steven and Brock, were gathering their things to leave. They took their leave, making a special point of saying goodbye to Vauk.

Sue stood up and signaled to Jim. "I think it's time we left as well. Arthur, are you ready to go?"

"Yes, Mom. I'm all set." Arthur gave Travis and Cembran each a hug goodbye. "Goodbye, Trent." Arthur shook hands with his former teacher. "Mr. Vauk... do you think I could see the deer next time I come?"

Vauk smiled and Trent felt it in his bones. God, he was gorgeous when he smiled. "Yes. I will take you to see the deer."

"You promise?!" Arthur's enthusiasm was barely contained.

"I promise."

Arthur threw his arms around Vauk, giving him a tight hug. "Thank you." Vauk wasn't quite sure what to do. Finally, he hugged the young satyr back and Trent released the breath he'd been holding. Trent should have known Arthur's enthusiasm would break through some of Vauk's defensive walls.

"Arthur, it's time to go."

Turning around, he said, "I know, Mom." He looked back at Vauk. "You won't forget, will you?" Arthur's eyes danced with excitement as he followed behind Jim and Sue.

Trent and Vauk said their own goodbyes and thank-yous to Travis and Cembran before stepping outside into the warm summer air. "Trent, you said we need to talk."

"Yes. Where would you feel most comfortable?"

Vauk looked toward the lake, and then shifted his gaze in the direction of his clearing in the woods. Trent waited for Vauk to answer, letting him make up his own mind. "Can we go to my home?"

"Sure. You'll need to lead the way." Vauk nodded and again led Trent to the small clearing, pointing out some of the landmarks as they walked. When they reached the shelter, Vauk checked on his little ones and then sat in the shade, motioning for Trent to sit next to him.

"What did you want to talk about?"

Trent leaned forward, his lips meeting Vauk's in a gentle kiss. "This, us… what happened last night. Last night was not just the bacchanal… for me, anyway. I really like you and I'd like to spend more time with you, but only if you want me to."

Vauk stared at the ground. "I do not know why you would. I cannot be very interesting to you."

Trent stroked his hand along Vauk's bearded cheek. "Vauk." The big satyr slowly looked up. "I like you because you're kind and caring. You help and protect those weaker than you." Trent tilted Vauk's head up, kissing those full lips. "You're strong, handsome, and whether you believe it or not, one of the most attractive men I've ever met." Trent kissed Vauk again, this time using his tongue to caress just inside his lips.

"I like you too. I am just…." Unsure of how to continue, his voice tapered off.

"I've seen the pain in your eyes sometimes. I know there's someone whom you loved very much." Vauk nodded. "That was a long time ago, right?" Vauk nodded again. "Maybe sometime you'll be ready to tell me about… Miki." Vauk's head shot up, his eyes filled with surprise. "I guessed. You mumbled his name in your sleep the last few nights. It's okay to miss him, and it's also okay to move on. The decision is yours and only you can decide what it is that you want and if you've waited long enough to take it when you've found it." Trent figured he'd said enough, so he got up and wandered to the fawn's pen. She was curled up, asleep in the shade, her legs snug beneath her. Trent watched quietly until he felt a hand on his. Trent turned around, leaning against the fence.

Vauk angled his head and lowered his lips to Trent's. This wasn't a kiss of passion, but a kiss of the promise of things to come. Pulling his lips away, Vauk took Trent's hand and led him to the door of his home.

Chapter Eleven

Trent said nothing as Vauk led him toward the door. He wanted to ask if he was sure. If this was what he really wanted. But why tempt fate? Previously, Trent had initiated almost all contact. Now, finally… Vauk was telling him in his own way what he wanted, and he wasn't going to argue. Vauk opened the handmade door and led Trent into his home. The single room was small, but well built, with a pallet in one corner covered with furs, and a small table with a single chair. A small window that looked recycled from another building faced the woods. The most surprising thing was that there didn't seem to be a source of heat, not even a fireplace.

Vauk led Trent to his sleeping pallet. Placing his hands on Trent's cheeks, he slowly and gently pressed their lips together. The kiss lingered as lips and eventually tongues explored and tasted. Trent loved the taste of Vauk and he whimpered as they kissed. Trent put his arms around Vauk's neck, reveling in the feel of hot lips and probing tongue. A soft, whimpering moan escaped Trent. Vauk echoed it back as their bodies pushed closer together, their heat mixing together through their clothes.

"You kiss good… real good," Vauk whispered, as they took a quick breath before their lips met again. This time Trent sucked on Vauk's lower lip, his own rubbing against the roughness of Vauk's beard.

"So do you." Trent continued the kiss as he felt Vauk's hands travel across his shoulders, down his back, and over the swell of his butt. Trent pulled Vauk closer, increasing the intensity of their kiss as tingles of pleasure rushed along his spine. Soft whimpers and moans filled the small space and echoed back to them, increasing their passion.

Vauk's hands slid to the back of Trent's legs, lifting him up, and then circling them around his waist. "I want…." Small snippets of expression were spoken, usually cut off by another kiss, like neither of them could bear to have their lips parted.

Carefully, Vauk lowered Trent onto his bed, covering the long, lean body with his own. Trent vibrated beneath him, loving the feel of the strong, hot, muscular satyr on top of him.

"Trent… would you let me?" Vauk's eyes, deep and probing, locked onto his partner's. With a nod and a kiss, Trent gave his permission, knowing he'd give whatever Vauk asked, placing himself in Vauk's hands.

Vauk shifted, kneeling next to Trent's prone body. His hands glided over Trent's exposed skin. The shirt Trent wore was pulled up and over his head, and the hands wandered, caressing and petting the newly visible skin. "You are beautiful." Vauk leaned forward, kissing Trent's now-swelled lips before lowering his powerful head farther to capture and tease a now-hard nipple. His tongue circled and swirled before Vauk blew on the hot skin. Trent whimpered and squirmed as a thumb circled over the other nipple. "So very beautiful."

Trent hissed as Vauk's teeth scraped over his skin, burning, thrilling, hot, and wet, all at the same time. He reared up, hands to the fabric covering Vauk's chest, but his fingers were gently stilled, placed on the furs by his side. Lips danced and moved over his chest. Vauk's lips— god, he loved Vauk's lips. Trent sucked in his breath, anticipation peaking as fingers brushed above his pants. Breath held… please… please… please. Vauk smiled, almost hearing Trent's silent plea, reading it on his face as the fingers snapped open the button of his jeans, parting the fabric gates.

Sensation ceased, and Vauk moved away, Trent's disappointment palpable. Then the hands were back, pulling his pants past his hips and down his legs, while fingers brushed against his skin.

Trent's eyes remained on Vauk, wondering what he was going to do next, never doubting somehow that the result would be thrilling pleasure as he lay naked and exposed beneath Vauk's heated gaze. Usually Trent talked during sex; hell, he usually rambled. But Vauk's intensity and his ability to thrill with just a touch left Trent's words unnecessary.

Slowly… hot, nimble fingers caressed and stroked the skin of his feet, no area left untouched, no cell unstroked. Ankles were felt and flexed, every contour being learned, every bump memorized. Calves caressed with fingers, laved with a hot tongue, each touch driving Trent wild. Thighs and legs kneaded, hot lips kissing a path to Trent's manhood, but never quite reaching their destination—much to Trent's utter frustration, as his whimpering attested. Hips kissed, tongue leaving long, wet paths, Trent writhing as Vauk worked sensitive spots, each reaction burned into Vauk's memory. Stomach kissed, teeth gently scraping, tongue tasting hot, salty skin. Chest sampled, hard nipples nibbled and teased, aching for more, as Trent's entire body shivered in expectation and desire.

Finally, after detours and exploration, the lips found their way home, latching onto Trent's in a kiss of passion and desire.

Trent pawed at the front of Vauk's shirt, desperately trying to get through the fabric. "I want you too…."

Vauk stood and opened his shirt, removing the garment and dropping it to the floor. Trent's eyes locked on Vauk—each bit of skin revealed was scrutinized, from the powerful chest to the indented navel; from the large, dark nipples to the trail of hair that disappeared into Vauk's pants. Vauk watched Trent's gaze and let his hands travel down his stomach before opening his pants, slipping them down his powerful, tree-trunk legs, letting them puddle on the floor.

Trent raised his arms in invitation and Vauk accepted. Their bodies pressed together, erections sliding past each other, moans elicited with each move, each slide of their bodies. Vauk's lips pressed to Trent's, fueling his already raging desire for this huge man who the night before had taken him with such force and today was as tender and caring as anyone he could remember. The difference, the variation, thrilled him beyond measure. Trent knew what he wanted, lifting his legs to lock them around Vauk's waist, opening himself to this incredible being.

Fingers slipped down his thighs, across exposed buttocks, to tease the skin of his opening. "Yes… don't stop… yes!" Trent arched against Vauk, needing as much skin-to-skin contact as possible. Trent felt the weight on his body shift slightly, and then slick fingers pressed against him, seeking entrance. With a kiss and a whimper, permission was granted and those large digits sank into his body. "Yessss!"

Lips nibbled Trent's ear. "That is good?"

Trent turned his head, capturing Vauk's lips as the fingers went deep, hitting that special spot. "That's really good!" Trent's head flew back as the spot fired again and again, triggered by the magic fingers that filled him. Trent's eyes went wide, locking onto those chocolate orbs as the fingers slipped from his body, replaced by Vauk's hard, full cock.

Steadily, inch by inch, Trent was filled again as he was kissed and caressed, "Oh, god!" Trent groaned a long, slow groan as Vauk sank into him, stretching, filling.

In slow motion, Vauk withdrew almost completely, eliciting a whimper, before pushing back inside, earning him a deep, throaty groan. His pace was agonizingly slow, designed to build desire and passion... and it was working. Trent was vibrating with excitement, his need to come almost overpowering. Yet Vauk kept him just below the peak, never giving him quite enough. Each movement inside him brought more heat, more need, slowly building to a peak that he just couldn't quite reach.

Trent's ear was nibbled, his throat sucked. "Will you come for me?"

That was it. With a shout, Trent keened, shooting between their bodies, clenching hard around Vauk, who quickly followed, crying out his own climax.

Vauk did his best to not completely collapse on top of Trent, but he gave in when Trent pulled him down, wrapping his arms around him, stroking the big satyr's back as they kissed, enjoying the afterglow. It took awhile before either of them could move. After cleaning each other, they lay together, curled in each other's arms.

Trent dozed, cradled in Vauk's powerful arms. When he woke, he turned to find Vauk looking at him. "Were you watching me the entire time?"

"You are beautiful, even when you sleep."

Trent smiled and kissed Vauk for the compliment. They held each other close, whispering soft words, caressing skin, and sharing warmth for close to an hour. "Vauk, I want to ask you a question, but I'm not sure I really should." Vauk met his eyes and he wasn't sure if he should go on. Finally Vauk nodded softly. "Would you tell me what happened? Tell me about Miki?"

The pain and sorrow he'd seen before welled in Vauk's eyes and he turned away. "You don't have to." Trent stroked the powerful shoulder.

Breath heaved in and out. Vauk turned back to Trent and he watched as he battled with his decision. "Maybe it is time." Trent could see the anxiety on Vauk's face, and he scooted closer, increasing their physical contact and gently kissing those lips. Looking into Vauk's eyes, he saw that the pain had shifted to determination.

"I am not sure where to start."

"Start wherever you want."

"Sometimes I have trouble remembering right. Everything is mixed up sometimes." Trent petted and squeezed a thigh. "Miki, Sasha, and I grew up together in the village. As kids, we three could not be separated, spending all our time together. As we grew up, Miki and I got closer, and once we reached maturity we fell in love."

"Did Sasha feel left out?"

"Sasha liked girls, but we stay friends. My father was disappointed that I would not have children, but he understand and even give us his blessing when Miki and I became truists." A huge smile lit Vauk's face as he spoke. "I remember the warm night when he and I gave each other our Triuwes." Vauk stopped talking and Trent didn't move, not wanting to break the spell or interfere with what was obviously a very happy memory. "We were happy together for many years."

The smile faded from Vauk's face. "Miki and I went to a small lake to swim. We spend the afternoon making love, swimming, and lying in the sun. On the way home, we were jumped by men I did not see as we walked through the woods." His voice became rough and heavy. "Miki managed to get away, but I was captured by some rough men who tied me up."

Anger welled in Trent as he saw the pain in Vauk's face. "I was carried through the woods and thrown in the back of a truck." Tears ran down Vauk's cheek. "After they drove for a long time, the truck stopped and I was pushed into a cage at what turned out to be a circus."

Trent brushed away a tear. "How long ago was this?"

"Just after the last war in Europe."

Trent was shocked. "You mean World War II?"

Vauk nodded. "I did what they wanted, hoping for rescue, but no one came. For the first six months or so, I could still feel Miki and had hope. But one morning I wake up and I could not feel him." The tears started flowing in earnest. "After that I did not care anymore and I became the animal my captors thought I was. Instinct took over and I let it." Vauk wiped his eyes, brushing away the tears. "I really do not remember much after that until Cembran and Travis found me at the carnival and rescued me almost a year ago."

"So you were…." Trent couldn't finish the sentence around the lump in his throat.

"For almost sixty years. Occasionally, I'd be moved from one cage to another, and at some point I was shipped to this country, but I do not really remember it."

"What would stop you from feeling Miki?"

Vauk's eyes filled with sadness and the tears started again. "The only thing that can break the Triuwe bond is dying. I could feel him until he died."

Trent pulled Vauk to him as the huge satyr grieved for the love he'd lost so many years before. The pain and sorrow were so deep, so powerful, that Trent felt tears run down his own cheeks as Vauk sobbed like a child against his shoulder. Vauk shifted and tried to pull away, but Trent held him tight. Finally, Vauk returned Trent's hold and let himself be comforted. "It's okay… let it out."

Rubbing his eyes and sniffling slightly, Vauk lifted his head off Trent's shoulder. "I am sorry," he said, his eyes looking toward the floor.

"You're sorry? Vauk, I'm sorry. I shouldn't have…."

God… how could I be so insensitive? He was obviously hurting and I had to push.

"You did not know. I am… ashamed that you see me like this." Vauk's eyes remained glued to the floor.

Placing his fingers below Vauk's chin, Trent gently lifted the big satyr's head. "You have nothing to be ashamed of. Grieving for Miki and for your own lost freedom is okay. Letting go of the pain is good. Now you can deal with it instead of hiding it inside you." Vauk didn't look convinced. "Let me ask you this. Would Miki want you to feel this way?"

Vauk didn't move for the longest time. Then he shook his head slowly. "He was always so full of life. The first to laugh, the first to joke and play... and the first to love." A small smile replaced the look of despair. "He would want me to be happy."

Trent leaned back, stretching out on top of the soft fur bedding. Taking his new lover's hand, he guided him onto the furs as well, curled around that large body, and held him tight. "Rest awhile." The kiss was gentle, soft, and Trent loved every second of it, their lips slowly exploring, taking their time, reassuring and comforting.

Trent thought they might drift off to sleep, but instead they held each other close, Vauk allowing Trent to silently comfort him. Sitting up, Vauk said, "I need to check on the little ones."

"Okay." Trent got up and gathered his clothes from the floor.

"You don't need to leave. I will just be a minute." Vauk pulled on his pants and slipped into his shoes before leaving. Trent could hear him outside moving around the house, talking softly to the animals. The door opened again a few minutes later and Trent watched as shoes were toed off and pants hit the floor just before he had hot, sexy company on the bedding again.

"Why don't we play a game?" suggested Trent. Vauk lifted his eyebrows, obviously intrigued. "Let's practice cloaking again. When you improve you get a kiss."

"What do I get if I get it right?" A wicked smile spread across Trent's face. Leaning forward, he whispered into Vauk's ear for a full minute. Vauk's expression changed from smiling to intent, and as Trent continued whispering, a low, deep moan escaped with no way for Vauk to stop it.

"Is that reward enough for you?" Vauk swallowed deeply and nodded. "Then let's get started."

Vauk practiced cloaking for the next hour or so. The best he was able to do was cloak his horns for a minute or so. It was an improvement over the last attempts, but still proved difficult for Vauk to master. Finally Vauk huffed in frustration. "I just cannot do this!"

"Yes, actually, you can. You've been able to cloak your horns a few times. It's not the ability you lack. I'm just not sure what it is."

"Oh." Vauk looked frustrated.

Trent settled behind Vauk, pressing his chest to the big satyr's back, hands stroking the skin of Vauk's chest and stomach. "It's time for your reward."

Vauk leaned back and turned his head. "But I…."

Trent silenced him with his finger. "The first rule in my class is 'never argue with the teacher.'" Trent tweaked Vauk's nipples as he kissed him hard.

Vauk enjoyed his reward immensely.

Chapter Twelve

Stretching and yawning, Trent decided it was time for bed. He'd watched enough television. God, how inane can you get. Pulling himself out of his comfy chair, he couldn't help thinking of Vauk and how he'd be seeing him again tomorrow. This weekend was the July bacchanal and Trent was excited, really excited. A few weeks ago, Trent had gotten a job working at a learning center, tutoring young kids who needed summer help. He loved working with the elementary and middle school age kids for a change. But, each weekend, as soon as he finished his last Friday tutoring session, he was on the road heading north toward Vauk and his satyr friends. He felt included; for the first time in his life, he truly belonged.

He and Vauk still had their nocturnal teaching sessions, although they'd become less frequent. But even when they didn't, Trent could feel Vauk's presence whenever he slept, like comforting background music—not in the front of his mind, but always there. Vauk's language skills had progressed very quickly, so they'd moved on to other things. The lesson on table manners had been fun. The dream started in a classroom setting, morphed to the table at Travis and Cembran's, and then changed again to a picnic by the lake. That progressed to after-dinner dream sex. Trent woke up sticky, smiling, and still horny. The next weekend, they'd packed a picnic lunch and reenacted their dream sex by the shore of the lake. The reality beat the dream hands down.

One of the happiest developments over the past month was when Vauk released the young raccoon and the rabbits he'd been caring for. Trent had accompanied him when he carried the hutch into the woods and released the rabbits. They scurried around, exploring their new environment, looked back at Vauk, and then raced into the woods. To Vauk's delight, a few days later, they were back digging a burrow at the edge of Vauk's clearing. Vauk released the young raccoon later the same afternoon. When Vauk opened the cage, he'd sniffed around, gave Vauk a final thank-you rub on the leg, and disappeared into the forest. Vauk had been thrilled to see the babies he'd cared for off on their own, even though Trent knew he'd miss taking care of them.

Padding into the bathroom the night before he was to leave, Trent cleaned up, stripped down, and climbed into bed. He was almost too excited to sleep, but forced himself to relax, and he finally drifted off.

Trent woke with a start, the morning light just peeking through the windows. Automatically, he reached for the pad he kept on his nightstand. He'd gotten used to writing down his dreams before the memories started to fade. As he tried to recall his dream, he shivered, unsettled and confused. His mind filled with unsettling images and weird, disjointed, confusing feelings. That was so strange. His dreams had been really choppy and bizarre, not flowing and coherent like they'd been for the past month or so. Trent tried to recall details, but all he remembered was a swirl of confusion and broken images.

Throwing back his covers, he dropped the pad back on the nightstand and headed to the bathroom, confused and unsettled, but unsure why. After taking a drink, he opened another window to catch the early morning breeze, and got back into bed.

The unsettled feeling stayed with him and wouldn't let him sleep. After lying in bed for an hour, he got up again, giving up on sleep. Once he was up and dressed, Trent called the farm.

"Hello."

"Cembran, it's Trent."

"Morning," Cembran yawned. Trent knew Cembran had probably been up for hours, but he still wondered if he'd gotten him out of bed. "Excuse me."

"Sorry if I woke you." Trent hoped he didn't.

"No… we had a bad night. Travis tossed and turned all night, keeping me awake as well."

"Can I talk to him?"

"He's still in bed. I'm letting him sleep."

"Seems to be going around. I didn't sleep well either." Must be the heat. "I was wondering if it would be okay if I showed up early. I'm not working today and…."

Trent could almost see Cembran's smile through the phone. "Sure, come on up. You can join us for breakfast. We're always glad to have you and I know someone else will be happy to see you too."

Trent chuckled. "I'll see you soon then."

"Okay. Drive safe."

Packing quickly, including some special treats that Trent had found Vauk really liked—chocolate, Champagne—as well as some new surprises, Trent loaded the car, locked the house, and watered the garden before getting in the car and starting the trip to the farm. Now accustomed to the drive, it went by quickly, with Trent smiling the entire trip. He was in love. He'd finally allowed himself to express the thought to himself, and as soon as he had, he'd felt so light and happy. He wasn't sure how it would go over at school in the fall, but he'd already determined that while he wasn't going to announce his lifestyle, he wasn't going to hide or deny it.

Pulling into the usual parking place at the farm, he gathered his things and headed down the now-familiar path to the farm.

The door opened as he approached, and Travis stepped outside, yawning. "Still tired?"

Travis put his hand over his mouth and tried to stifle a yawn. "Yeah; didn't sleep well." Travis stepped outside and waved Trent inside. "Breakfast is almost ready." Travis yawned again. "I'll be right back, Lamb." Travis called inside once his yawn passed.

"Don't be long."

"I won't, Lamb."

Trent went in, setting his things by the door. He'd take them to Vauk's after breakfast. Trent then joined Cembran in the kitchen. "Can I help?"

"Would you set the table? I'm almost done here."

"Sure." Trent got the silverware, dishes, and glasses from the drawers and cupboards, setting the table.

Travis came back inside, and Cembran brought the food to the table and they all started eating. Trent remarked, "Everything always tastes so good here. There's just something about this place."

Travis slipped his arm around Cembran's waist. "I think it's the cook." Cembran leaned close and received a gentle kiss.

Trent smiled. "Well, there is that."

Throughout breakfast, the three of them talked while Trent kept one eye on the door. Travis and Cembran noticed but said nothing, just exchanging knowing looks. After breakfast, Trent offered to help clean up, but Cembran shooed him out of the kitchen. "I'll do this; you go find Vauk." His smile was bright. "You've had one eye on the door since you got here." Cembran swiped the dish cloth at Trent, laughing. "Go find him."

"Thanks." Trent hugged Cembran. "For everything."

Cembran laughed and fussed. "Go on."

Trent smiled as he gathered his things, stepped outside, and headed down the path to the far pasture and the beginning of the faint trail to Vauk's. He was careful as he walked through the woods, watching for the landmarks Vauk had pointed out. This was only the third time he'd done this alone, so he paid extra attention, not wanting to get lost.

The clearing was quiet when Trent stepped from the trees. "Vauk." Trent expected the door to open, but there was no movement. Trent knocked and then opened the door. "Vauk?" No answer. The interior of Vauk's cabin looked the same as always, but no Vauk. The bed was made, the table clean, just like always.

Setting his things neatly by the door, Trent went back outside. "Vauk!" No response. Wandering around, he came to the pen housing the fawn. She ambled up to Trent. "Where's Vauk, little one?" Then Trent noticed that the fawn's water bucket and food container were empty. "That's strange. Did he forget you?" As soon as he said that, he realized how weird things were. Vauk would never forget to feed or water her.

Trent filled the fawn's water dish from the rain barrel and got some food from the box. The poor thing ate and ate before drinking half the water. This was very strange. Trent refilled the food and water containers before looking closely around the clearing. Seeing nothing else unusual, he decided to walk back to the farmhouse to check with Travis and Cembran.

As he walked back, he couldn't shake the feeling that something was most definitely wrong. The more he thought about it, the stronger the feeling became.

Trent emerged from the woods, walking toward the farmhouse. He met Travis as he walked by the sheep barn. "Didn't expect to see you for a while."

"Vauk wasn't there and the fawn hadn't been fed or watered. Have you seen him lately? I think there's something wrong."

Travis stopped. "I saw him yesterday morning. He talked about you, as a matter of fact. He was excited you were coming." Travis shook his head, thinking. "This is really strange." They picked up their pace and resumed their walk toward the house. As they approached, they saw Doug hurrying down the path from the road. "Morning, Doug."

The three of them met in front of the house. "Trav, let's go inside. We've got a problem." His expression was serious, and Trent felt his guts twist with worry.

Travis opened the door and the three men filed inside. "What's going on?" Travis motioned toward the chairs in the living room.

"My deputies were patrolling the summer festival grounds when they overheard the carnival workers laughing and celebrating the recapture of one of their attractions."

Trent's hand flew to his mouth as he gasped. Doug's attention shifted from Travis. "I don't know where they found him, but I believe they've captured Vauk."

"Oh, God!" Trent leapt from his chair. "We have to get him back!" He marched toward the door.

Travis intercepted him, putting a hand on his shoulder to calm him. "Let's not go off half-cocked. If they do have him, we need to plan how we can get him back." Travis guided Trent back his chair. "We can't break him out again; he'll be too heavily guarded." Travis turned to Doug. "Do you have any ideas?"

"I think we need to get a look at him first. Make sure he's unharmed and that it's truly Vauk. If nothing else, we can let him know we're there and trying to help him. Officially, there's only so much I can do without endangering him and all of you in the process." Doug was quiet for a while, thinking. "I could say that since he's been living wild, that a vet should look him over. That might allow us to get close."

"We could give it a try. At least it's a start."

Trent was wound tightly and very impatient. "But what are we going to do to get him out?" Regardless of what anyone said, Trent just knew that Vauk was in trouble and that he'd been captured. It helped explain the weird dreams he'd had.

"We'll think of something, but we need to know it's truly him and we need him to know that we're trying to help." As much as Trent didn't like it, he knew Travis was right. No one had come for Vauk before and he'd be damned if Vauk was going to feel completely abandoned again.

Cembran came in from feeding the goats and Travis filled him in. "We'll be back as soon as we can."

Sadness clouded Cembran's face. "Try not to worry, Trent. We'll figure out something. I just know it."

The three men left, practically racing down the path to where Doug had parked his cruiser. After they'd climbed into the car, Doug turned on his lights and siren and flew down the road. It would have been cool if Trent hadn't been so worried. At the edge of town, Doug pulled into Rex Payne's driveway. "Wait here. I'll see if Rex can go with us." Doug left the car and returned a few minutes later with the good veterinarian. Rex was the vet Travis and Cembran used at the farm for their animals. Once everyone was seated, Doug headed the final distance into town.

"Doug, you want to tell me what this is about?" asked Rex.

Doug turned to Travis to explain.

"Rex, what I'm going to tell you is going to seem strange and hard to believe…." Travis was trying to determine how much he should tell Rex when Trent interrupted.

"Look, Doc, some men from the carnival have captured what they believe is an animal."

"What they believe?"

"Yes, but he's not an animal and we need to see him. And you're our ticket to do so." They pulled into town.

Doug cut in. "Rex, we'll explain later. I promise. Right now we need you to play along." He looked at the three men and nodded slowly. "Think of it this way, Rex: you're helping someone in desperate need."

Doug parked close to the carnival at one of the roadblocks. The four of them got out of the car and Doug led the group to the carnival trailer that acted as an office and headquarters. Doug pounded on the door and it was opened by an enormously fat man with a cigar between his teeth.

"Yeah!" His eyes widened when he saw the sheriff's uniform.

"Sorry to bother you, but we understand you captured a wild animal that you believe escaped from the carnival last year."

"Yeah, we did." Trent wanted to hurt him. That smug look on his face just made him mad. Travis touched his shoulder to calm him down.

Doug continued, aware of the tension. "Since it's been running wild, we'd like to have a vet check it over. Public safety and all."

The fat man's eyes twitched as he looked over the group. "Don't see why not." The trailer rocked as the huge man waddled down the steps and onto the ground. "Let me get the boys and you can take a look."

"Where is he being kept?"

The carnival boss pointed to a small trailer near the edge of the carnival grounds. "It's locked tight. I'll meet you there in a minute."

Travis touched Doug's shoulder. "I'll stay back in case—"

Doug cut him off, not wanting to hear more.

Rex and Trent followed Doug to the trailer. A small vent in one side seemed to be the only source of fresh air. Trent said, "Doug, give me a minute."

Trent stood by the vent. "Vauk, are you in there?" No response. "Vauk, can you hear me? Please be okay."

"Trent," the voice was soft, tentative, and sounded scared.

"Yes, it's me." Thank god, at least he was okay… sort of. "I'm here with Doug and Travis."

"Help me!" It sounded like he'd been crying.

"We will, but you need to help us too."

"How?" Fear welled in his voice.

"Clear your mind and push the fear and wildness away. Breathe deeply. Try to cloak yourself. Remember what we practiced."

"I'll try." He sounded calmer, but really unsure.

"Get a picture in your mind of yourself without the horns and tail. See it. Visualize it." Trent had an idea. "Think of the last time we made love. How happy we were. Think of making love to me without your horns and tail. Tap into that energy."

The carnival boss approached and Trent had to step away. "I'll be back." Trent walked slowly to Doug and Trent.

The fat carnival boss was still chewing on his cigar. "My boys will open the trailer, but for your own safety, stand back so they can restrain him before you approach. His eyes trailed to Trent and then back to Doug. "Who's he?"

Rex spoke up. "He's my assistant." The boss huffed. Rex continued. "Go check that there's adequate ventilation."

Trent nodded and moved back to the vent, appearing to check it over. "Try hard, Vauk, please." Trent nodded to Rex. The conversation around him ceased and the boss motioned for the boys to open the door.

Chapter Thirteen

T he lock was removed and the door swung open, letting in a little light. In the far corner of the trailer, huddled against the sides, was a naked man. Rex inhaled deeply. Doug looked on in surprise. No horns, no tail, and legs that looked human.

Trent wanted to scream, "You did it!" He managed to keep his tongue, particularly since he saw Vauk's eyes were plastered closed in a look of sheer concentration.

Doug stepped in front of the opening, taking charge. "Who authorized this?"

The fat man blustered as he stepped forward. "It's my property. He escaped last year. I have every right—"

"Since when do you have the right to kidnap and imprison people?" Doug glared at the carnival boss as he called for backup. "No one is going anywhere." The boss's mouth flew open and the cigar tumbled to the ground. The fat man looked inside, turned white, and grabbed his two men. "That's a man, not an animal! You fools! What did you think you were doing??"

"But boss... we...." Their voices sounded contrite, but their eyes were blazing with anger.

Doug stepped forward. "You two, get down on the ground. Now!" Doug called in what he had into his radio, getting additional reinforcements while he handcuffed the two men. "This is kidnapping, boys." After he'd cuffed the two men, he turned to the carnival boss. "Don't go anywhere! I want to talk to you as well. Either you cooperate, or I'll arrest you too!" The carnival boss nodded slowly. The authority in Doug's voice overrode everything else.

A few minutes later, Doug's reinforcements arrived, reading the men their rights and loading them into cars. "Rex, would you get the blanket out of my trunk?" Doug asked. He threw him the key and he hurried off, returning a few minutes later.

Trent took the blanket and stepped into the trailer, wrapping the blanket around Vauk's naked body, whispering, "You did good, Love."

Vauk's eyes opened and his concentration faltered. Doug noticed and closed the door to give them some privacy. "You did really good." Trent kissed Vauk, holding him close.

"You came for me." The words were very soft.

"Of course I came for you. I love you."

Vauk's head snapped up, his eyes meeting Trent's. "You do?"

"Oh yes. I love you very much. I'll always come for you." Trent pulled Vauk to him, rocking and comforting.

The door opened and Doug poked his head in. "Is he okay?"

Trent released a deep breath, still holding Vauk to him. "I think he will be."

"We need to get him out of here without being seen."

Trent nodded. "Can you do it again, Love?"

Closing his eyes, Vauk concentrated and he was able to cloak himself again. Trent made sure Vauk was covered and then held him as he stepped out of what had been his cage and onto the pavement. Doug was speaking to the carnival boss, arranging for him to come to the station to give him a statement. Rex led Trent and Vauk to Doug's car. They both climbed into the backseat.

Vauk rested his head against Trent's shoulder. "Do you really love me?"

Trent kissed the skin closest to his lips, loving having Vauk close and not wanting him to move. "Yes, I do. I love you." Why was it so hard for Vauk to believe?

"Good, my Tapfer, because I love you too." Trent felt his heart swell at Vauk's declaration.

"Tapfer? What's that mean?"

"It means… knight, rescuer, one who's brave. It's what you are, because you came for me, because you saved me."

Travis opened the door and got in the backseat with them. "Doug will be here in a minute to take us home."

"Thank you for getting me."

"It was Trent. He knew something was wrong. We just helped."

Vauk looked up into Trent's eyes. "You did?"

Trent nodded, petting the skin on his arm. "I knew you'd never leave the fawn unwatered and unfed." Vauk became agitated, but Trent calmed him with a touch. "It's all right; I fed and watered her this morning. She's fine." Vauk relaxed and again let Trent hold him.

The driver's door opened and Doug got in the car. "Let's get you home." Doug started the car, put on the siren and lights, and sped toward Rex's office.

Rex turned around in his seat. "Travis, do I want to know what's going on?"

Travis smiled. "Maybe not, but know that you helped someone today."

When they arrived at Rex's office, he opened the door. "Maybe the next time I'm at the farm you can explain things to me, but for now, I'll just go back to work." After saying good-bye, Rex got out of the car, and they continued their speedy journey to the farm. Throughout the trip, Trent held Vauk close.

"Are you going to be okay?"

"Yes, I will now." His voice trailed to a whisper. "You came for me." The surprise in Vauk's voice nearly made Trent cry. How could anyone not come for him? Trent wondered what had happened all those years ago. But he pushed those thoughts aside as they arrived at the farm.

Vauk kept the blanket around him as he and Trent got out of the car. "Thank you." Vauk told Doug. Trent got out of the car right behind Vauk, keeping the big guy close.

"You're welcome. I'll stop by later, after I speak with the men from the carnival."

Travis stayed behind for a few minutes as Vauk and Trent followed the path to the house. As they approached, Cembran opened the door and ushered them inside.

Cembran got them seated and immediately went into the kitchen and started fussing, making food. Travis came in as well, going into their bedroom and returning with some clothes, handing them to Vauk with a soft smile. "You can use the guest room to dress and lie down if you need to."

Vauk nodded, got up and walked silently to the room, closing the door behind him. Trent waited a few minutes before knocking on the door and poking his head in. Vauk was sitting on the edge of the bed. Trent went into the room, closing the door behind him. "Come on, Love. Let's get you dressed." Trent helped Vauk into his clothes. "Lie down for a while; you must be exhausted." Trent slipped off his shoes while Vauk lay back on the bed, and then joined him, holding the big satyr close.

Vauk started to squirm. "I need to tell you what happened."

"Okay, but why don't you rest now and you can tell us what happened after lunch. I'm not going anywhere. Sleep now. I'll still be here, I promise." Trent stroked the hair from Vauk's forehead, kissing him gently on the lips. "Rest, Love."

Vauk settled down and drifted off to sleep. A few minutes later Cembran poked his head in. "Is he asleep?"

Trent nodded. Conversation from the other room drifted in through the open door.

"Lunch will be ready soon."

"Okay. We'll let him sleep 'til you're ready." Cembran smiled and closed the door, cutting off the voices from the other room. Trent closed his eyes as well and soon slipped into sleep, his arms wrapped around Vauk. Later, Trent woke to the sound of the bedroom door opening, Cembran's bright face peeking through the opening. Trent smiled and the door quietly closed.

"Love," Trent rubbed Vauk's broad back. "Are you hungry?"

"Yes." Vauk started to move. "I should get up." Vauk swung his legs over the edge of the bed and slowly raised himself to his full height.

"Feel better?" Concern was written on Trent's face and colored his voice.

"I do." Trent took Vauk's hand and kissed the knuckles before opening the door.

Doug, Gathod, Cembran, and Travis were all sitting in the living room, and they looked expectantly at Vauk when he entered. Doug spoke first. "I've spoken to the men who took you and to the carnival boss, and I have some questions for you."

Vauk opened his mouth to speak, but Cembran cut everyone off. "Lunch is ready, and this can wait until we've eaten." Doug looked like he was going to say something, but then closed his mouth. Cembran went into the kitchen. "Doug, I love you like a brother, but sometimes you're too sheriff for words."

Doug smiled, "Yeah, I know. And you're right; this can wait until after lunch."

Everyone sat around the table and Cembran served massive amounts of food. "Lamb, were you expecting an army?" joked Travis.

Cembran huffed softly as he took his chair. "They probably didn't feed him very well and I figured he'd be hungry."

Travis grinned as he kissed behind Cembran's ear. "So you made enough food for…." Travis's thought was interrupted when the door opened. Jeremy came in followed by Phillip and Dovino. Cembran looked smug, and Travis rolled his eyes. "Grab a plate and join us."

Lunch was a cacophony of conversation, everyone discussing, rehashing, or bringing everyone else up to date on the day's events. Once everyone had eaten their fill, Cembran and Travis cleared the table. Travis had to kiss the smug look off his truist's face as the empty dishes were carried to the kitchen.

Once everything was settled, everyone moved into the living room. Doug started the discussion. "Vauk, are you up to telling us what happened?"

"I'll try." Trent took Vauk's hand, squeezing it gently. "I was following an injured squirrel on the north side of the property. I'd just caught the poor little thing when I felt a sting on my neck. Two men raced from the woods. I tried to run, but my legs wouldn't work. After taking a step, I dropped the squirrel and fell to my knees."

"The next thing I remember, I was in the back of a car, my hands and feet were tied, and there was something over my head so I couldn't see."

"Did you hear anything?" Doug asked the questions while everyone else listened.

"At first everything was really mixed up, but I remember them saying 'the boss wants him back in a cage.' The other man then asked, 'You think the carnival's good enough?' The first man replied, 'Where else you gonna put a freak?'" Everyone listening remained quiet, but puzzled looks were exchanged. While Doug made notes, Trent squeezed Vauk's hand and leaned close. "You are not a freak, Love."

Vauk squeezed Trent's hand in response and continued. "The car stopped and I was pulled out and carried into a trailer. All my clothes were cut off and then the hood was taken off my head."

"Did you see anything?"

Vauk shook his head. "It was too dark in there."

"Did they untie your hands and feet?"

"No. I used my horns to wear the rope on my hands and then untied my feet. Occasionally I'd hear voices outside, but no one came until after dark, and they only put some food and water inside. It was so hot in there with no water. I didn't try to move much." Vauk's voice was starting to strain. "The next thing I remember was hearing Trent's voice."

Doug patted Vauk on the shoulder. "Thank you. I know that wasn't easy." Doug consulted his notes. "That seems to fit with the information from Maynard Harmon, the carnival manager. He told me that he hired those men to work in the carnival about two weeks ago. Provided paperwork to prove it and other workers corroborated his story. Yesterday, they asked for a few hours in the afternoon and according to him, returned telling everyone that they'd recaptured the attraction that escaped last year and that they'd put him in an empty trailer."

Trent spoke up. "Didn't he check?"

Doug consulted his notes. "He said that he hadn't had time, they'd been too busy. He was going to check later today, but we got there first."

Travis leaned forward. "The carnival manager didn't send the men to look for Vauk?"

"According to him, no. When I asked him that question, he said that they'd redeployed the tent and trailer space they'd used for Vauk months ago and that they were making more money than the Manimal show ever did. He even added that he was trying to figure out what they were going to do with Vauk when they packed up. Space was going to be tight."

"Doug, do you believe this guy?" Travis sounded skeptical. Trent looked at Vauk, trying to figure out how he was taking all this. He was worried, but Vauk seemed to be okay.

"As crazy as it sounds, I do. The details he gave me seem to check out, including the old Manimal tent. It's now used for virtual reality machines that are raking in the money."

"All of this just doesn't make sense. Why would these men act on their own? What was their motive? I take it they weren't rewarded by the carnival."

"That appears to be correct."

"What did the men have to say?"

"They aren't talking, except to say it was an accident. They're a couple of tough characters, but they don't appear to have criminal records. Weird accents though. We're checking their immigration status to see if they're in the country illegally."

Vauk jumped from his chair and started pacing around the room, shaking visibly. His breath came in short gasps as he walked and shook. Trent got up and tried to calm him.

"It's okay, Vauk. Please calm down. No one is going to hurt you."

"I don't know."

Trent could understand Vauk's anxiety, particularly with all he'd been through in the past day or so, but he felt there was something else. "Do you remember something?" Vauk nodded, still shaking. Trent led him back to his chair. Vauk sat back down and started to curl into the chair, and Trent could see him withdraw.

Gathod, who had been quiet through the discussion, stepped forward. "Vauk!" Big chocolate eyes looked at Gathod. "We know you've been through a lot, but something has you really scared, and it's something you just remembered." Vauk said nothing, his eyes locked on Gathod. Trent took the big satyr's hand, trying to soothe him. Gathod continued. "You need to tell us. We can help, but only if you share what you think you know." Vauk turned away. Gathod's voice became sharper and Trent was about to put a stop to it when he felt Cembran's hand on his shoulder. "Do I have to have your baccharist order you to tell us?"

That seemed to get through, and Vauk shook his head slowly, tears running down his cheeks. "The men who took me," his voice was very soft, almost childlike. "They sounded like people from where I grew up... people from a nearby village."

Trent patted Vauk's hand gently. "That could be a coincidence, Love."

Vauk shook his head violently. "No! When I was in the car, before I fully woke up, I could have sworn... that one of them said my name."

Chapter Fourteen

T he room erupted in expletives, followed by questions. Doug wanted more information and started firing off inquiries. Travis tried to get things calm, but the men all talked over one another, getting nowhere and doing nothing, except upsetting the one person who needed their help.

"Stop!" Trent's teacher voice carried over the din. The noise immediately stopped. Travis held up his hand, signaling everyone to wait. "Are you sure, Love?" Trent's voice instantly became comforting and intimate, his question only for his love.

"I think so. Things are mixed up, but I think it was one of them saying my name that helped me sort of… wake up." Vauk was still curled in the chair.

"I still have a few questions…," Doug started.

Trent shook his head, keeping his temper, which was starting to flare, in check. "He's had enough." The others nodded in agreement. Taking Vauk's hand, he tugged him gently to his feet, "Come; you need to rest."

"I need to see my little one to make sure she's all right."

"Will you please rest first?" Vauk nodded and allowed himself to be led to the bedroom. Trent looked at the young satyrs. "Have any of you been to Vauk's?"

Dovino stepped forward. "I have once. I found it by accident when I was exploring."

"Can you find it again?"

"Sure."

"Would you go there now? There's a fawn in a pen. Make sure she has food and water, but move slowly and don't spook her. Then inside by the door are my bags. Would you bring them back here?"

"Absolutely. We'll be happy to do that for you." The three of them left together, closing the door behind them softly.

"He needs to rest and have some time alone."

Cembran stepped to Vauk, hugging him tightly. "You are part of our family. I know this is hard for you, but I wanted you to know that all of us care for you and want you safe. Rest. We'll be here if you need or want anything." Cembran stepped back and Trent guided Vauk into the bedroom and closed the door.

The room was quiet, and the sound of the farm and the forest drifted in through the open windows. "Let's get you undressed." Trent helped Vauk slip off his clothes and then guided the big satyr onto the bed. Trent then took off his own clothes and lay down next to Vauk, their bodies curling together.

A large arm pulled him close. "Thank you, Tapfer."

Trent grinned against Vauk's lips. "You're welcome, Love." Trent's fingers combed through Vauk's thick hair. "Rest now. After your nap, I have some special surprises I brought for you." Their lips met softly, gently. "Roll over on your tummy." The big body next to him turned over, showing Trent that broad back. Slowly, lovingly, Trent's hands moved over the taut skin, soothing and comforting.

A soft knock didn't interrupt what Trent was doing. The door opened and his bag was set inside by unseen hands. Then the door closed and they were alone again.

Trent slipped off the bed, rummaged in his suitcase, and returned with a small bottle of massage oil. "This is one of your surprises." Oiling his hands, Trent stroked Vauk's shoulders and neck muscles until they relaxed and loosened. The broad back was soothed and the firm buttocks kneaded. Trent smiled as steady breathing and a soft, muffled snore reached his ears. Shifting carefully, he rested next to Vauk, pulling a light blanket over both of them.

Hours later, the sun was waning as Trent woke, his body curled with Vauk's, each holding the other closely. Trent moved slowly, trying not to wake his lover. He wasn't successful. "Where are you going?"

"I'll be right back, Love." Trent climbed off the bed and pulled on his pants before quietly leaving the room. He returned a few minutes later. "Cembran is making dinner if you're hungry."

"Is everyone still here?" A look of dread briefly clouded his face and Trent could imagine that Vauk wasn't ready to rehash what had happened... again. He just needed to rest.

"No. It's just Travis and Cembran."

Vauk visibly relaxed and swung his legs over the side of the bed. Trent stepped between Vauk's long legs. Leaning forward, they kissed. Hard. Trent's lips pulled on Vauk's, tangling his fingers in his hair. Vauk responded tentatively at first, but then with increasing ardor.

"Let's have dinner and then I can be alone with you, because I want you so bad. Want to show you how much I love you... how much you mean to me." Trent kissed his Vauk again and then forced himself to step back, smiling. "If I stay too close to you, we'll never get dinner."

Vauk groaned low and deep, pulling Trent back into his arms. "Let's have a quick dinner." Vauk's kiss was demanding; he wanted Trent to know he wanted him as much as Trent wanted him. After a breath-stealing kiss, Trent backed away again, his body tingling, telling him to stay where he was, dinner be damned. Slowly, reluctantly, they pulled on their clothes and opened the door.

"Hey, there you are." Cembran was smiling from the kitchen, Travis behind him, nibbling on his neck. "Dinner will be ready soon." Cembran turned around and swatted Travis playfully with the dish towel. "I'll never get dinner ready if you keep distracting me." Travis's arms circled around Cembran as he pressed close. Cembran gave up and leaned back against Travis. They shared a tender kiss and then Travis backed away, smiling, his eyes saying, "We'll pick this up later."

"How much time before dinner?"

"About half an hour. Just make yourselves comfortable," Cembran called from the kitchen as he worked.

Vauk turned to Trent. "I need to see to the little one." Trent could see the concern on Vauk's face, but he was afraid to leave him alone.

"I'll go with you." Vauk looked at him and shook his head. "You can argue with me or we can get going."

"Okay. Cembran, we'll be back shortly."

Cembran smiled and continued his work. "Don't be too long."

Vauk was already at the door by the time Trent had assured Cembran that they'd be back in time for dinner. Once they were outside, they moved rapidly down the path and then through the woods. In the clearing, the fawn heard them approach, and when she saw Vauk, she raced to him, nuzzling his hand. Trent got feed and filled her water while Vauk played and talked to her, letting her know that everything was all right. After reassuring herself, she ambled to her feed and starting eating.

The last vestiges of twilight were fading as they approached the farmhouse. Opening the door, they were assailed by the wonderful smell of Cembran's dinner. "You're just in time. Dinner's ready."

The four of them sat together around the table. Trent hoped they could keep the conversation light, but it wasn't to be.

"Vauk, Cembran and I were talking and we'd be very pleased if you'd move into the spare room." Vauk said nothing, surprising Trent, who expected Vauk to decline immediately. "You're a part of our family, our community, and we want you to be safe."

Vauk stopped eating. "I don't need someone to babysit me." Trent patted Vauk's hand, putting down his fork.

"Of course you don't, but I want to ask you something. Do you really want to continue living in the woods alone?" Vauk's eyes fluttered. "When you first got here, you needed to be on your own, to heal and to feel like you were free again." Travis picked up his fork. "We just want you safe and happy above all else."

Vauk was quiet, looking from Trent to Travis to Cembran. "What do you think, Tapfer?" Cembran looked up from his food, smiling knowingly at the use of the unusual endearment.

"I'd feel better if you stayed here, but it's up to you. I want you happy and safe as well."

"What about the fawn? I can't leave her alone…."

Travis swallowed his food. "We'll build a pen here for her, right near the woods so it'll be shaded and still safe for her. Travis took another bite. "I take it she can't be released."

Vauk had a mouthful of food, so Trent answered. "I wouldn't think so; she's bonded with Vauk."

"Then she can stay here."

Vauk swallowed. "Like a pet?" The word carried disdain.

Travis didn't hold it against him. "As another of the creatures we care for."

The answer seemed to please him. "Okay."

Trent smiled. "You'll move in here then?"

"Yes, Travis is right. It's time I lived with others again."

The dishes clinked as they continued eating. "I hate to bring this up, but we need to talk some more."

"I know; I just can't right now."

Trent finished his food, sitting back in his chair. "What does Doug think?"

Travis looked at Cembran, who nodded, and then back at Trent and Vauk. "Doug is looking for answers in the human world, not in the satyr world."

"Oh."

Cembran cut in. "Doug loves Gathod very much, but he's human and sometimes doesn't understand. It's not his fault, and he does his very best for us, but I agree with Travis—we need to explore a non-human possibility."

Travis could tell Vauk was becoming agitated. "I think we've talked about this enough for today." Travis pushed back his chair and helped Cembran clear the dishes. "Go… sit. Cembran made dessert and we'll talk about more pleasant things."

They spent the rest of the evening devouring Cembran's cherry pie and drinking some of Cembran's incredible homemade beer. "You know, Cembran served me this beer that first night we met."

Cembran looked happy as he sat on the arm of Travis's chair, his arm around his shoulders. "Do you remember the freak storm?"

Trent smiled and watched them slowly get lost in each other and their memories. Setting his empty glass aside, he took Vauk's hand and quietly led him to the bedroom.

The door closed behind them with a soft click, cutting off Travis and Cembran's happy, and now private, trip down memory lane. Trent smiled. "Those two are really wonderful, aren't they?"

"Uh-huh." Big hands latched onto Trent's hips. "I don't want to talk about them." Trent's mouth was captured in a hot kiss. "Enough talking for today." Trent nodded as Vauk continued ravishing his mouth, a small whimper of agreement escaping.

Trent then felt Vauk's hands on the buttons of his shirt and he backed away. "Not yet." Trent's eyes were dancing and his lips were already swollen from Vauk's kisses. "Get naked, Love, and lie on your back." Trent turned around and rifled through one of his bags. When Trent looked over his shoulder, Vauk hadn't moved. "I'll be there in just a minute." Trent found what he was looking for and smiled to himself when he heard Vauk stripping behind him.

Keeping his surprise hidden, Trent stripped as well and then climbed on the bed. Vauk was all spread out, arms out, chest rising and falling with each excited breath. Trent straddled the big satyr, knees on the bed, his butt across his lover's hips. "I brought you one of your favorites."

From behind him, Trent produced a box of European chocolates. Vauk reached for the package, but Trent moved it out of his reach. "Lie back, big guy." Trent opened the package and took out a dark chocolate truffle, putting it between his teeth but not biting it. He then leaned forward and brought his lips to Vauk's. The chocolate melted gently, spreading across their lips and tongues.

"Mmmm, that's the best chocolate ever."

"It is, Love. Chocolate and you... the perfect combination." Trent got another truffle and put it to Vauk's lips. His lover opened wide and his lips sucked in both the chocolate and Trent's fingers, nibbling softly on both at the same time. Trent chuckled at the blissful look on his lover's face.

Vauk's big hands slid along Trent's legs, caressing his thighs as he fed Vauk another chocolate. "Tapfer, what about you?"

"Oh, I'll get mine." Trent took the final chocolate from the box and swirled it around Vauk's nipples, leaving chocolate trails across the broad chest. "Mmmm, chocolate-covered Vauk, my favorite." Trent squirmed with excitement, and as he did, the hair on Vauk's stomach and groin tickled the inside of Trent's thighs, butt, and balls. The roughness was exquisite.

Leaning forward, Trent started licking the chocolate from Vauk's body, nibbling at each hard bud as he removed the chocolate. The sweetness of the chocolate combined with the saltiness of Vauk's skin was heady in the extreme. Vauk was moaning deeply as Trent's tongue roamed freely over his skin. Trent could feel the pent-up energy beneath him. The more he teased and the more he revved Vauk up, the closer the wildness inside his lover got to the surface.

"I love you, Vauk." Trent leaned forward and reached to the nightstand as a pair of lips latched onto a nipple with a deep, low, feral growl. "Take what you need, Love. Let it out." The growl continued as Trent grabbed the lube, squirted some on his fingers, and plunged them into his body. His lover rewarded him with a deep, growly moan as he pulled out his fingers and wrapped them around Vauk's pulsing cock. More lube was added and then Trent lifted and lowered himself onto Vauk, taking him inside with a long, continuous movement. Trent watched as Vauk's eyes got wide and his pupils huge. Lifting himself again, Trent plunged down onto Vauk with a yelp of desire.

"Is that what you want?" Vauk nodded as he bleated softly, trying to keep himself under control. Trent was having none of it; he wanted Vauk to release everything. Repositioning his legs, Trent bounced on Vauk's body, lifting himself and then plunging down again and again. "Let it out, Love. Take what you need." Vauk started thrusting his hips up to meet Trent. "More, Love. Give me everything…you… the wildness…all you have!"

Vauk sat up, wrapped his arms around Trent, and rolled them on the bed, driving himself deep as he did just what Trent said.

Each stroke hit the pleasure center inside him as Vauk pounded into him. Using one hand to steady himself, Trent used the other to twist one of Vauk's fleshy nipples, making him cry out and increase his pace.

"Yes, Love… give it to me!" Balling up his hand, Trent pounded the pad of his hand against Vauk's chest. "I want it all… everything you have!" Vauk threw back his head, a predatory roar accompanying his explosive release, pulling Trent into his own mind-numbing climax.

Vauk withdrew and collapsed onto Trent, his body covered in sweat. "Did I hurt you?"

Trent heaved a deep breath. "No, Love, you were perfect."

Vauk hugged Trent tightly, resting his head next to Trent's on the pillow… and Trent waited.

It started slow, a hitched breath, a tightening of his hug around Trent. "Let it out, Love." Then a shudder of the big body on top of him. "It's all right; let it go." Then a gasped and held breath, followed by a soft cry and a rush of tears. With another breath, Vauk broke down sobbing.

"Why me?" More sobs. "What did I ever do?" All the pain and confusion, held for so many years, was finally free.

Trent stroked Vauk's back, soothing and comforting, letting him know he cared. Slowly, Vauk's breathing returned to normal and the tears trailed off. Trent continued to pet, caress, and love.

"Are you feeling better?" Trent kissed Vauk's cheek, the only skin he could reach at the moment. Vauk shifted off Trent and lay spent on the bed.

"Yes, thank you."

Trent answered with a soft kiss before getting a cloth. After cleaning them both, Trent settled Vauk on the bed, pulled up a light blanket, and turned off the small bedside light. Vauk was asleep almost immediately.

Trent carefully got out of bed, slipping on his robe and heading to the bathroom. Opening the bedroom door, he was surprised to see the light still on in the living room. After taking care of business, he padded toward the light. Travis and Cembran sat together on the sofa in their robes, two glasses of wine on the table in front of them.

"Would you like a glass?"

"No, thank you." Oh god. Trent turned red with embarrassment and turned away. "Did we…?"

Neither Travis nor Cembran cracked a smile, even though Trent knew they'd been heard. Hell, thinking back, he figured they might have been heard in the next county. "We heard nothing."

They both finished their wine and stood up. Travis gave Trent a hug good night and then disappeared into the master bedroom.

Cembran hugged him good night as well. "I'm glad he has you." He turned to put out the light.

"I knew what Vauk needed, but I don't know how I knew."

Cembran smiled as he clicked off the lamp. "Don't question it. It's just part of the love."

"But…."

Cembran sat back down on the sofa, barely visible in the moonlight, and patted the cushion next to him. "When a satyr finds his soul mate, they start to grow together, feel when the other is in need or trouble, and almost instinctively know what they need."

"Do you have that with Travis?"

"Yes, and so do some of the other couples you know. When I first met Travis, I thought we were unique, but Steven and Brock have described something similar."

"Does everyone feel this way when they're in love?"

Cembran chuckled softly. "Yes and no. You can be in love with someone who isn't your soul mate. Some of us never find them, just like humans. So when it does happen, it's very special."

Doubt spread through Trent. What if Miki was Vauk's true soul mate? "Is it possible," Trent hesitated, fearing the answer to the question, "to have more than one soul mate?"

"Of course. Our soul is a wondrous thing and I think it has the ability to reach out to bond with many people. Look at Jeremy, Phillip, and Dovino. I believe they're soul mates, all three of them. Any of them would be incomplete without the other two." Cembran patted Trent's knee. "Go back to bed and stop worrying." Cembran stood up and quietly entered the bedroom he shared with Travis, while Trent headed back to bed as well.

Vauk was sound asleep when Trent slipped back into bed. A big arm curled around his waist, pulling him close. Trent sighed, contented and happy, as the cool night breeze blew over his skin. Snuggling close, Trent drifted off to sleep in the arms of his lover.

Part Three
Rebuilding

Chapter Fifteen

T rent was still asleep when Vauk woke for the first time. The sun was peeking through the window and voices from outside drifted in. "Travis...." Giggles and squeals of delight. "Stop that. I have chores... and so do you." Cembran was obviously trying to stop his giggling, but it wasn't working. "Shhh... you'll wake them."

Deep laughing. "Race you to the hayloft."

"You are so naughty." Quick footsteps followed. "Last one there...." The rest trailed off.

"You are gonna get it when I catch...." Travis's voice trailed off as well.

Vauk smiled to himself, listening as the voices outside drifted away. He owed a lot to those two and it made him happy that they loved each other so much. Heck, it gave hope he'd never thought he'd have again. Settling his head back on the pillow, he pulled the smooth, sexy, warm body of his new lover close and drifted back to sleep.

Vauk was dreaming. He had to be dreaming; this was too good. Things like this didn't happen to him in real life. Fingers curled around him, stroking him to hardness. Vauk moaned in his dream. In real life, he wasn't sure and it didn't matter, sort of in an "if this is a dream, I don't want to wake up" sort of way. Vauk pumped his hips and the fingers tightened. Perfect... too perfect... yes, I'm dreaming. Then the fingers were gone and he settled back down.

He was enveloped in a cocoon of hot wetness, stroking and pulling. This wasn't a dream. Cracking his eyes open, he moaned softly. Trent had his mouth on him, sucking him in. He couldn't form words, so he ran his hand across Trent's hip and thrust gently into the thrilling wet heat. This movement was met and encouraged as Trent altered his rhythm to Vauk's thrusting.

"Tapfer...." Vauk was almost whining softly. A hand cupped Vauk's butt, pushing him forward, encouraging him. "So good to me." Vauk could feel an impending explosion, moaning softly as the pleasure built until he couldn't control it any longer. With a soft groan, Vauk spilled himself down his incredible lover's throat, and as he did, he felt warm, wet heat spray against his side as Trent climaxed next to him.

Trent shifted on the bed and Vauk pulled his hot, sexy lover on top of his big, hairy body, kissing him hard.

God, he loved this man—something he never thought he'd be able to do again after the loss of Miki. But it had happened, and he thanked Bacchus for his kindness for giving him this young satyr with his smooth skin, lithe body, and a carnal appetite to match his own. "What did I ever do to deserve you?"

Trent looked into his eyes. "You were just you."

Vauk felt Trent's hands wind through his hair, fingers teasing the base of his horns. His lips took Trent's, conveying the love that matched the words they'd used before.

For the first time in a very long time, Vauk felt truly awake and alive. Since shortly after his capture and for the length of his decades-long captivity, Vauk could remember nothing clearly. It was as though he had been unconscious the entire time, like an animal with no memory or thought, only instinct. The mists surrounding him hadn't started to part until he'd heard the words Cembran had first spoken to him.

Those words, simple and direct, triggered something in Vauk, something he'd almost long forgotten. Then his rescue and the slow return to consciousness and life. He remembered some of the last year, though much of it was still a blur. But he particularly remembered Travis and Cembran's kindness and patience.

About six weeks ago, he'd met Trent, the man now happily resting on top of him. Trent had helped him, given him a means of communication, helped him start to assimilate, and let him into his dreams so he could learn faster. And when he'd been recaptured, it had been Trent who'd come for him. A tear of happiness rolled down Vauk's bearded cheek. It was Trent—Vauk wrapped his arms around him—who had told him he loved him. Trent wiggled a little and then settled again, his eyes now closed and his breathing steady. Vauk whispered to his dozing lover, "Love you... my Tapfer... my hero." Vauk slowly let his own eyes drift closed again.

They were awakened awhile later by a soft knock. The door opened a crack. "Breakfast in fifteen minutes." Then the door closed again and Vauk felt Trent stirring. "Morning, handsome." Trent's eyes met Vauk's.

"Good morning yourself." Trent felt so good. "I don't want to get up."

"I don't either." A tummy rumble reduced both of them to giggles. "I guess my stomach's decided for us."

"I guess so." Trent rolled off Vauk reluctantly, and slowly got to his feet, pulled on his robe, and waited for Vauk so they could head to the bathroom together.

Trent started the shower and stepped under the water. Vauk poked his head around the curtain. "Do you want company?"

Trent twisted around, wiggling his tight butt. "I've been waiting for you." Vauk smiled and stepped into the shower, pulling Trent's tight, lithe body to his. "We don't have time, Love." Trent sounded mischievous as he pressed his butt against Vauk.

"We always have time for this." Vauk tilted Trent's chin and kissed his lover gently, their lips sliding together in a gentle, loving kiss. The water cascaded over them as Trent twisted slowly and they held each other. Their hands washed each other, stroking skin, touching, connecting with each other in a very intimate and personal way. After washing, rinsing, and drying each other, they dressed and joined Travis and Cembran for breakfast.

Cembran served a breakfast of healthy proportions, with the four satyrs eating heartily. "What's on the agenda for today?" Trent asked between bites.

Travis swallowed. "I got the materials to build the pen for the fawn. The boys will handle the chores, so I thought we could work together to get it started." Vauk was moved, and he smiled, happy that they were going to build a permanent home for his little one. He really wasn't looking forward to giving her up. "We probably won't be able to finish it today, but we can make a good start."

Trent continued eating, remarking between bites, "Count me in." The happy look on Vauk's face was worth the hard work ahead.

"As long as you don't expect me to run that post hole digger thing you bought, I can help." Travis knew Cembran didn't like the machines he used on the farm—they made him nervous.

"Trent and I can dig the holes; you and Vauk can set the posts."

"Sounds like a plan."

Cembran got up and started clearing the table, while the others finished their coffee. "It'll take a few minutes for me to clean up, and then I'll be out."

Trent and Travis stood up, but Vauk remained seated. "Is something wrong?" Travis was concerned that Vauk might have changed his mind about staying with them and moving the fawn to the farm.

Vauk shook his head. "Thank you both for everything. You have done so much for me already. I've been trying to figure out why you've been so good to me and how I can ever repay you."

"You're family, Vauk. Maybe not by blood, but by choice—our choice—and hopefully your choice as well." Vauk nodded and then smiled. "Good. Now let's build a home for your little one."

The four of them worked together for the rest of the morning, digging holes and setting fence posts, which had to be set extra deep because of their height. They broke for a quick lunch and then spent the early afternoon setting the last of the posts.

Travis wiped his brow as he looked over their work. "That's all we can do for today. Tomorrow we can string the fence once the concrete sets. "Is she going to be happy here?"

Vauk smiled brightly. "Yes, she's going to love it." His earlier confusion was gone, his face beaming with pleasure.

Everyone was hot and sweaty, wiping their brows, shirts wet with sweat. "How about a quick swim?"

The suggestion was met with eager nods, so after cleaning their tools, they headed back to the farmhouse, changing into bathing suits—shorts in Vauk's case—and headed to the lake.

The cool water felt wonderful on their hot, sweaty bodies, and after swimming and cooling off, Vauk found himself reclining on the beach in the shade of a large tree, his head resting on Trent's lap. Gentle fingers stroked his hair. "Rest if you want, Love. I'll be here."

Vauk closed his eyes and nodded off, the summer breeze drying his skin.

Trent jumped as Vauk inhaled sharply and jerked his head up, looking around. "Are you okay, Love?" There was concern in his voice at the confused look on Vauk's face.

"I felt him." Vauk smiled fondly, and then his happiness faded and turned to guilt when he looked into Trent's loving eyes.

"Felt who, Love?"

"Miki. I've dreamed of him often, but this time I could feel him, like…." The ramifications of his revelation sank in. If he could feel Miki, then he might be alive and… what about Trent?

Vauk started getting agitated and excited. Part of him wanted Miki to be alive, but what if he was and now Vauk loved Trent?

"It's just a dream, Love."

Was it a dream? "It felt so real. I could actually feel him, like I used to—in my soul, deep down."

The terrified, hurt look on Trent's face as the ramification of Vauk's announcement sank in tore at Vauk's heart. "Oh." Trent tried to remove his shock, disappointment, and a surprising sense of loss and jealousy from his expression. He'd just found Vauk and he was going to lose him so quickly… and to someone who was supposed to be dead.

"Jesus!" Travis had been resting with Cembran a few feet away. He suddenly jerked up, crying out and holding his head. "What the hell?" Everyone's attention focused on Travis as he shivered and shook.

Cembran held and comforted his mate. "What happened, Lemmle?" The worry was plain in his voice.

"I felt something… something weird… dark…." Travis shuddered. "Almost malevolent." Travis looked around, his gaze turning to Vauk. "Are you okay?"

"Yes. Why?" Vauk was confused by Travis's concern.

"I don't know, but what I felt seemed to be directed at you."

"Me?"

"Yeah. Did you dream or feel anything?"

Vauk beamed uncontrollably. "Yeah, I felt Miki, the way I used to a long time ago."

Travis shuddered again and then tried to stand, slowly getting to his feet. "I'm sorry, Vauk, but I don't think so, because I felt it too, just before…." An uncontrolled shiver shot through Travis. He hated disappointing Vauk, but he didn't want him to have any false hopes. "If it was your Triuwe bond with Miki, I wouldn't have been able to feel it."

Vauk looked crushed. "If it wasn't Miki, then what was it?" Vauk looked incredibly downcast.

Damn, he hated to do this to him. "I don't know. I wish I did, but whatever I felt was, for lack of a better word… evil." Trent walked to Vauk and hugged him close. "I'm so sorry."

"How do you know?" Vauk didn't want to believe Travis; he wanted Miki to be alive.

Cembran answered. "Travis is very sensitive to dream manipulations. He can even feel when the dreams of others are being entered and used."

Travis released Vauk, stepping back. "Usually what I feel is happy, but this… this was frightening in its anger and strength."

"What do we do? I don't want him hurt." Trent was scared for Vauk, the fear pushing away the earlier hurt.

Travis drew and released a deep breath. "I don't know, but we'll try to find out." Standing up, he said, "I'm going to call the troops, see if they can stay in the morning so we can put our heads together." Cembran accompanied Travis as he walked back to the house.

"I'm sorry, Trent." The dejected look on Vauk's face was almost too much for him.

"What do you have to be sorry for?"

Vauk tugged Trent around so he could see his face. "I guess I feel guilty."

"For being happy that Miki might be alive?" Vauk nodded slowly, eyes downcast. "Don't be. I love you, Vauk. I love you enough to want you to be happy. I hope that I can be the one to make you happy, but if Miki could do it better, I'd let you go." Trent's eyes teared up. "It'd break my heart, but I'd let you go." A tear ran down Trent's cheek and he wiped it away.

Vauk tugged him into a breath-huffing hug. "I love you, Tapfer. I don't know what you see in me, but I love you so much." They clung to each other, each feeling miserable for the other.

Trent lifted his head to look into Vauk's eyes. "What I see in you?" Trent rolled his eyes. "I know you don't see it, but I love you for your strength, your kindness, the fact that you're so physically strong, but aren't afraid to show your emotions, and," Trent's eyes twinkled through the tears, "you are the sexiest person I've ever met in my life."

Vauk's head shook vehemently. "Me? No... you."

Trent cut him off with a hard kiss, his tongue exploring the big satyr's sexy lips. He smiled against hot lips. "See, that's another thing I love about you—you think I'm sexy and I think you're sexy. That's really hot!"

Trent was getting him worked up again, those lips, that body, and he wanted him, bad... very bad. And controlling those urges was difficult. Vauk's hands roamed over Trent's clothed body, their eyes meeting and locking. "I know...." This was another of those moments when he could almost read Vauk's mind. "I want you too." Slowly, Trent pulled away, Vauk's low growl making him chuckle softly. The growl built as Trent nibbled on his ear. "Think how good it'll be at the bacchanal later." Gods, this man was wicked... sinful... incredible. "Besides, Travis will be back soon, to prepare for tonight." The kiss held promise and simmering passion.

Vauk stood up and tugged Trent to his feet, breathing hard. "We should check on the little one, make sure she's okay." Taking Trent's hand, they walked down the path to the house together.

Emerging from the woods, just cresting the rise at the edge of the farm, they stopped. "I love this view—the house, the barns, the sheep and goats dotting the fields. It's the best place I've ever seen. It's so peaceful here." Vauk noticed a longing in his voice.

"Do you wish you could stay?" Vauk hoped he'd say yes.

"I'd love to stay, but I love my job too, and it's too far to commute. Maybe someday...."

Walking again, they crested the rise, following the path to the house.

"Mr. Vauk! Mr. Vauk!" Only one person called him that.

"Arthur!" The young satyr ran to him and threw himself into a hug.

"Mr. Vauk, I was looking for you. Will you show me the fawn?" Vauk nodded. Letting go of Vauk, Arthur hugged Trent as well, although with a little more reserve for his former teacher.

"We were just heading that way."

Arthur could barely contain his joy. "Wonderful." Something about the guileless enthusiasm of the young satyr really appealed to Vauk, and the three of them walked across the fields and down the barely marked path to the clearing, with Trent pointing out the fence posts of the fawn's new enclosure as they passed.

In the clearing, Arthur raced to the fawn's pen, waiting for her to make an appearance. The still-spotted fawn peeked around the corner of Vauk's shelter, saw Arthur, and bounded to him. "Wow, she really likes you." Vauk was in awe of the love Arthur seemed to have with all the gentle creatures on the farm. He knew he had the gift, but the young satyr's affinity with animals surprised even him.

Arthur giggled as the fawn licked his fingers. "She's hungry. Can I feed her?" The excitement in his eyes was precious.

"Sure, the feed is in the box."

As Arthur raced to get the feed, Vauk bent to stroke the fawn's neck. "We're going to move you soon, little one."

Trent knelt next to him. "I think she's excited about the move." Arthur returned and the fawn's attention shifted to the food bowl.

"Can you find your way back, Arthur?" He nodded, his attention engrossed with the fawn.

Getting up together, they walked back through the woods toward the farm. Still in the woods, Vauk pulled Trent off the path, pushing him against a tree. "Sometime I'm going to make love to you in the woods. Out here beneath the trees with the breeze, and your soft, smooth skin shining in the sun. Making love like the satyrs of old." Vauk's arms circled around Trent, his head tilted and their lips met. "I love you, Tapfer."

"I love you too. I want to ask you, will you come to the bacchanal with me? I'll understand if you don't want to." Vauk had plenty to think about and Trent thought he may need some time alone.

Vauk still wasn't sure how he felt about being around so many people. With a deep breath, he said, "If you'll be with me, I'll go anywhere." Trent's kiss was hard, his tongue plundering Vauk's mouth, his body plastered to Vauk's, vibrating with excitement.

"I don't want to move, this feels so good."

Vauk kissed Trent's soft, kiss-swelled lips. "If you think this feels good, just wait until tonight, Tapfer." Trent's moan couldn't be stopped as his lips were taken again. If this was a preview of tonight, Trent couldn't wait.

Chapter Sixteen

The bacchanal was in full swing. Trent had spent much of the afternoon with Vauk. After visiting the fawn, they'd spent a lot of time in the woods, walking and kissing. They'd also talked. A lot. As scared as Trent was of the possibility that Miki could still be alive, they'd still talked it through. It was obvious to Trent that Vauk was very conflicted, but he was also convinced that Vauk really did love him. Vauk didn't know what he'd do if Miki were actually alive, but he at least acknowledged to Trent that Travis might be right. They were off by themselves, sitting in Vauk's shelter after playing with the fawn. "Travis reacted right after I felt Miki; that can't be a coincidence."

"I agree, Love." Trent had determined to put his own fear aside and try to be supportive.

"But, who would do that? And how could they?"

"Travis will get to the bottom of it, if anyone can."

"It's funny. In a way, I wanted to feel Miki, and in a way, I was afraid of it." Trent waited for Vauk to continue, saying nothing. "Miki's been out of my life for a long time. I still love him, but I've grieved for him and I've been able to move on... and I found you."

"We'll figure it out and we'll deal with it—together. Whatever it is." Trent had kissed Vauk softly. "Do you still want to go to the bacchanal, or is it just too unsettling?"

Vauk broke into a sheepish grin. "I'm looking forward to having your body vibrating beneath me tonight." Trent trembled with anticipation.

The story portion of the bacchanal had been interesting and the dancing had been under way for a while. Everyone had been welcoming and seemed happy that Vauk was joining in the festivities. Steven and Brock had been particularly welcoming, being sure to introduce Vauk to everyone. Trent and Vauk had been dancing together, their bodies moving as one.

Partway through the dancing, Steven pulled them aside. "Vauk, will you show me how you dance like that?" Vauk's eyes went wide in surprise. He looked at Trent and then nodded slowly. Trent stepped back, standing next to Brock as they both watched Vauk show Steven how he danced.

"God, I love to watch him," Brock commented breathlessly, his eyes never leaving Steven.

Trent nodded his agreement. "I know what you mean," he said, his own attention riveted on the dancing Vauk.

"Being in love is wonderful, isn't it?" Brock spoke without ever moving his eyes from Steven.

"Yeah. How long have you and Steven been together?"

"Over three years, and each day feels better than the last."

Forcing his gaze away from Vauk, Trent said, "Can I ask you something?" Trent let his gaze drift back to Vauk, as he started twirling and gyrating wildly, carrying Steven along in his wake. Trent's eyes met Vauk's and they shared a smile.

"Sure."

"How did you know he was the one?"

Brock pulled his attention away from Steven. "Do you want the secrets of the universe too?" Brock's mischievous eyes twinkled in the firelight. "The best answer I can give you is that you'll just know when it's right." Brock's gaze shifted back to Steven.

A few minutes later, Steven broke away and grabbed Brock, tugging him into the dance. Vauk was right behind him, pulling Trent along with him, their bodies moving together, with Vauk jumping and twirling both of them in a dance that increased in tempo and frenzy. At one point, Vauk let Trent get ahead and they found themselves on opposite sides of the fire. Vauk whirled and leapt over the flames, landing right in front of

Trent, picking up the smaller man and whirling them together. "Geez, Vauk… showoff!" Trent was laughing as they continued dancing.

Vauk pulled them together and Trent felt the heat, smelled his scent, his sweat, the scents going right to his groin. "This is great!" Trent pushed his butt back against Vauk, grinding into him as they danced. He was still being whirled and guided around the fire as he let Vauk lead, let his feet have free reign. Desire built with each step, with each of Vauk's touches.

Suddenly, the music changed, the primal beat replaced with long flowing strings. The dancers shifted, and many standing around the edges joined in the slower dance. The dancers held their lovers close. Trent felt Vauk pull him back against his lover's chest, hands slipping beneath Trent's shirt, sliding over his chest and stomach. Slowly they kept moving, Vauk guiding them, Trent's head resting back against Vauk's shoulder. The music got softer, the firelight fading as Vauk led them away from the fire.

Their shelter just inside the trees formed on the periphery of his vision, his attention focused on Vauk's roaming hands and the tender touch of his lips, as they continued moving to the now-soft music. Vauk's roving hands lifted the edge of his shirt, pulling it over his head and off his body, a soft rumple as it fluttered to the ground. His pants were opened, pushed past his hips, and then pooled at his feet. The hands kept roaming, his hips and buttocks now getting in on the action.

"Vauk…." The name came out as a soft whine as Trent toed off his shoes and stepped out of his pants, Vauk still standing behind his nude body, lips sucking the skin on his neck, hands skimming his skin with hot caresses. Trent desperately wanted to feel Vauk's skin against his, but then he'd have to stop what he was doing, and Trent was completely under the spell of those hands.

Suddenly, his view of the lake and trees changed to treetops and star-studded sky as he was lifted in Vauk's strong arms and carried to the shelter. Their movement stopped, but Vauk made no motion to put him down. Instead, Vauk's hands moved under his back and butt, laying him out across Vauk's arms. "Oh, god!" Trent shivered and throbbed as warm, wet heat surrounded him, sucking hard, tongue swirling. "Vauk… so good… so hot." The heat dissipated and Trent opened his eyes as he was placed on the soft padding in the shelter, Vauk's lips taking his in a hard kiss. "God... Vauk... do that again... please."

"I will. Oh, I will." Vauk stood next to him, skin shining in the light of the candle lanterns, strong legs, narrow hips, and wide chest towering over him. Their eyes locked as Vauk opened the buttons of his shirt, removing the garment and dropping it on the ground. The shoes and pants were next, slipping down the strong, hairy legs before joining the clothing pile.

"Damn, Love, you steal my breath away." And he did too. Trent could barely breathe, looking up at the powerful satyr towering over him, all muscles, rich skin, jutting manhood, and heaving chest. Yeah, maybe he took Vauk's breath away too. Vauk's eyes clouded with lust and Trent smiled to himself as Vauk continued breathing deeply. Yup, it seemed he had breathing issues too.

Powerful legs straddled his body as Vauk knelt over Trent, their lips meeting, bodies pressing together, sharing hot, searing skin. Up to now, Trent had always let Vauk take the lead during sex, figuring the big satyr would be more comfortable in control. But tonight that was going to end. Trent pulled Vauk to him, and with a quick movement that caught the big guy by surprise, Trent rolled them so that now he was straddling Vauk's hips, his eyes shining as he looked down on the strong chest, dusky nipples, chocolate eyes, and huge satyr horns. "Tonight, you're mine, Love." Trent bent forward, kissing Vauk hard while his fingers circled around Vauk's hard shaft.

Trent could tell Vauk was a little apprehensive. "Trust me, Love." Trent stroked along the thick length, fingers playing around the base of the dripping head. Vauk nodded feebly as Trent kept up his erotic ministrations, watching Vauk's eyes shine with pleasure. "Never hurt you, Love." Trent kept stroking as Vauk squirmed beneath him.

Reaching for the lube, Trent squeezed some on his fingers, inserting two into himself. Vauk whimpered softly. "You wanna watch?" Mischief dripping from his voice, Trent murmured, "Okay, but no touching; only watching." Vauk nodded in agreement and Trent shifted his body. Still straddling Vauk, but now turned toward his toes, he leaned forward, thrusting his fingers into himself.

A deep, throaty growl sounded behind him and Trent took that as his cue to add another finger. "Tapfer... don't tease me so." Vauk was vibrating beneath him and Trent loved it—after all, Vauk usually drove him wild, and he was pleased he could return the favor. Shifting again, Trent turned around, looking again into those deep chocolate eyes.

Pulling his fingers from his body, he added more lube and stroked Vauk to hard, throbbing, slippery perfection. Lifting his body, he positioned himself above Vauk and sank down onto him. His eyes rolled back as the thickness stretched him, the burn familiar and very short-lived. Sinking further, the length filled him as his breath sighed from his lungs.

Vauk's hips rose to meet him and Trent continued taking all of Vauk's considerable length into him. Once he sank to the base, he squeezed, clamping tight onto Vauk, holding him possessively within his body. The big satyr whimpered softly with ecstatic pleasure. "Love being inside you." Vauk pulled Trent forward, their lips meeting hard, Vauk sucking and nibbling on Trent's mouth.

"So good." Trent sat back up and slowly raised his body. "Damn good." Then he plunged down onto Vauk.

"Tapfer...."

Every time Trent lifted his body, Vauk's breath hitched; every time he plunged down again, his lover huffed and moaned something unintelligible.

"Love... you... Vauk." Trent continued riding the big satyr for all he was worth, his fingers plucking the now-hard nipples as he continued plundering Vauk's body. "I'll," plunge, "fight," plunge, "for you." Plunge.

Trent started stroking himself as he continued riding his hot lover. Vauk's moans were becoming more urgent and increasingly primal. "Yeah, Vauk, come for me." Trent could feel his own climax building and he bore down, giving Vauk everything he had.

Vauk's back arched and his hips thrust, pushing Trent toward the roof. With a deep, low cry, Trent felt Vauk climax deep inside him.

Trent wasn't far behind. With a final stroke, Trent erupted, covering Vauk's chest with his release as he screamed, "Mine!" at the top of his lungs.

The blackness receded slowly as he came back to himself. He'd collapsed on top of Vauk and his lover's hands were stroking his back. It felt good, really good. Soft lips met his, and fingers ran through his hair, warm skin beneath him. "I guess I've been claimed." Trent listened closely to Vauk's words, but didn't hear any argument, only contentment and happiness.

"You bet your horns. You're mine and I'm yours." All that talk this afternoon about Miki had gotten to Trent more than he'd realized.

"But... what if...?"

"No ifs, Vauk. I'll fight for you if I have to, because I don't think I can let you go." Trent rested his head on Vauk's shoulder, making no move to shift off of Vauk, blinking back the fear that threatened to overwhelm him. "I love you, damn it." His voice was almost cracking. "I can't just let you go."

Arms tightened around him. "I can't either." The candle lanterns swung in the breeze, the soft, warm glow lighting their expressions of love.

The music from the ongoing Bacchanal drifted into their shelter, a soft reminder of the party going on a short distance away. "Do you want to go back?"

"No."

"Do you need something to eat?"

"No."

"Do you want anything?"

"Only you, my love. Only you." Trent got up, cleaned them both, and blew out the lanterns before curling up in Vauk's arms again. He still wasn't fully convinced that Vauk wasn't holding out some hope that Miki was still alive. In fact, he was sure Vauk was, and Trent was afraid of what would happen if Miki were, but he hadn't been lying; he'd fight for Vauk. He just hoped he wouldn't have to.

As if he were reading his thoughts, Vauk said, "Tapfer... stop worrying, okay?"

Trent nodded, resting in the crook of Vauk's body. Strong arms wrapped around him, Vauk's unusual endearment for him releasing some of the worry. "Go to sleep." Trent tried, but Vauk's breathing had evened out long before he finally fell asleep.

A soft noise outside the shelter woke him from a sound sleep. "Breakfast in half an hour." Trent opened his eyes, the morning sun lighting the trees outside. Vauk's arms still held him tight, the big guy still snoring lightly, his chest hair rubbing gently against his back. Slowly, Trent rolled over, kissing Vauk gently; hands traveled south, cupping his butt. Trent kept kissing softly: lips, neck, shoulders, sucking gently on a nipple.

A soft murmur and stroking hands confirmed that Vauk was awake.

"Breakfast will be ready soon."

A soft moan followed by a grunt signaled that Vauk wasn't quite ready to get up. Playfully, Trent ran his tongue along Vauk's side, which he knew was one of his ticklish spots. Vauk tried to scoot away, but Trent kept up the attention. Soon Vauk was rolling away, chuckling softly. Suddenly, the big body pounced, pinning Trent under him. "Hmmmm... let's see...." Vauk lifted Trent's arms over his head and started licking softly along his side. Each touch sent peals of laughter through Trent and he tried to fidget away.

"Vauk, that's not fair...."

"Why not?" Another lick followed by peals of laughter.

"You're bigger than me." Vauk stopped his tongue tickling, letting Trent catch his breath. "I like this."

"What? The tickling?" Vauk lowered Trent's hands, figuring he'd had enough.

"No." Trent raised his head, kissing Vauk's lips softly. "This...." He hissed again. "And this...." Trent's hands reached down, grabbing Vauk's hard butt as he lifted his legs, locking them around Vauk's hips.

"Oh." Vauk captured Trent's lips, pulling them together as he slowly joined them together. Their bodies moved slowly, languidly, wanting the slow loving to last, chests filled with heaving breaths. Hips rocked and moved slowly, staying in tune with each other.

"Vauk." Trent uttered a long, drawn-out sound, pulled from him by the passion.

"Tapfer." Their eyes locked together, hands caressing and stroking as the world collapsed to just the two of them. Their passion built slowly, neither in a hurry, both wanting it to never end. Their climaxes sneaked up on them, creeping up to them and almost taking them by surprise. This was love, this was mutual reassurance; all else could wait.

Their breathing returned to normal as they curled into each other's arms. Slowly, after kisses and touches, they started to move, pulling on their clothes and walking from the now-quiet lakeshore down the path through the woods, toward the farm.

As they approached the farmhouse, they could hear many voices through the open windows. Opening the door, they were greeted by smiles. Cembran and Sue were just dishing up breakfast. Arthur was getting out the utensils and napkins, setting them on the table. Travis, Brock, Steven, and the three young satyrs were carrying chairs, making sure there was seating for everyone.

Trent excused himself and headed to the bathroom. Once inside, he glanced in the mirror. His lips were swollen, his hair mussed, eyes glowing, and his neck carried a small mark. In short, he looked completely debauched. Washing his hands, Trent ran his fingers through his hair and joined the rest of the after-bacchanal breakfast crowd.

As he left the bathroom and walked to the table, Steven leaned close. "Didn't help." Trent looked at Steven questioning. "You still have that just-fucked look. Lucky you." Trent bumped his shoulder against Steven, unable to keep the happy grin off his face.

"Breakfast is ready!" Sue called from the kitchen in her warm, sing-song voice. Everyone helped bring the food to the table. Plates were piled high and they filled every available chair as everyone sat down to eat.

The door opened as Travis was filling his plate. "Gathod, there's plenty."

"Thanks. I'm starved. Doug had to go to work this morning." Gathod got another plate and helped himself. Conversation swirled around the room. Steven and Brock sat next to Trent and Vauk, the four of them talking and eating.

Arthur inhaled his breakfast, put his plate in the sink, and then poked his head over Vauk's shoulder. "Mr. Vauk, can I go feed the fawn?"

"Sure."

"Cool. Mom, I'll be back in a while."

Sue looked up from her conversation. "Okay, but don't be gone too long."

"I won't." Arthur raced for the door.

After breakfast, Cembran stacked the dishes in the sink and rejoined everyone in the living area. "I asked you to stay this morning because we need your help." The room got quiet as Travis spoke.

"Has something else happened?" Sue asked for the group.

"I think so. We all know that we rescued Vauk from the carnival about a year ago. Last Thursday, he was recaptured. Luckily, Trent realized something was wrong and we were able to free him again."

Brock leaned forward. "Did Doug get anything from the men who took him?"

"Not much yet. But he still tried. They're being held without bail." Both Steven and Brock nodded. "The thing is that yesterday afternoon Vauk felt his truist, Miki."

"When was the last time you felt him?" Jim asked in a soft voice.

Trent knew this was hard for Vauk about and he squeezed his leg gently. "About six months after I was captured."

"And nothing since then?"

"Not until yesterday."

"Hmmm." Jim sat back in his chair, shaking his head slowly.

Travis continued. "I also felt something. It was definitely directed at Vauk, but I also felt something malevolent… almost evil."

Gathod furrowed his brow. "If Vauk was truly feeling his truist, you shouldn't feel anything; only him."

"I know." Travis released a long sigh and the room got quiet except for some low murmurs between Jeremy, Phillip, and Dovino. "What is it, guys?"

Dovino spoke for them. "If Travis hadn't been around and you felt Miki, what would you do?"

"What do you mean?"

"Well, let's say that you didn't feel Miki after all and that Travis is right and he felt someone else." Everyone's attention focused on Dovino. "Let's say that you were alone when you felt Miki. What would you do?"

"I'd go...." Comprehension dawned. "Home."

"Exactly.... So if someone wanted to get you back to your village, the fastest way would be to—"

"Let me think Miki was alive." The sadness in Vauk's voice was heart-wrenching.

Dovino nodded. "Yeah," he said, his voice soft.

Vauk looked truly heartbroken and on the verge of tears. "But why? What did I ever do to deserve this, any of this?" Confusion and pain filled Vauk's voice.

"It's okay, Love. We'll figure it out." Trent hugged Vauk tight, looking around the room for help.

Travis took control again. "Vauk, who would want to hurt you or want you out of the way?"

"I don't know." A tear ran down Vauk's cheek.

"Who stood to gain from your disappearance?"

"No one I can think of. I mean, my father was the baccharist of our village, but we'd already decided that I wouldn't take over for him. I wasn't interested. If I were in line for the position, I could see the issue, but we'd already informed the village of our plans."

Everyone started talking at once, speaking over one another. "One at a time, please." Trent's teacher voice worked again. "Vauk, your father was the baccharist?"

"Yes."

Travis spoke up. "Do you have a brother?"

"No, I was an only child."

"So by tradition you'd eventually become the baccharist after your father."

"Yes, but the village knew that wouldn't happen, so there wasn't anyone to benefit."

The room got quiet with everyone lost in thought while Trent did his best to comfort a clearly agitated lover.

"Vauk." Travis tried to make this as easy as possible. "You said yourself that the men who captured you sounded like people from near your village." Vauk nodded. "And Doug said the men kept referring to 'the boss.'"

Trent kept comforting Vauk. "What are you getting at, Travis?"

"Here's what I think: Someone arranged for your capture all those years ago. Somehow they got wind that you'd gotten free, probably because you started to come alive. They sent the men, who interestingly enough are not satyrs, to capture you again. But when that didn't work, whoever's behind this now feels they need to get you back to the village and they've decided to play with your emotions to do so." Travis looked around the room for confirmation. Most of the heads in the room were nodding slowly.

"Let's say you're right, Travis. What do we do? Take him back and see what happens?" Trent shivered.

"No. Whoever is behind this is strong and powerful—powerful enough to have Vauk captured twice, and strong enough to be able to make him feel Miki."

"Then what?" Trent was becoming agitated.

"We watch and wait. Whoever is doing this will probably try again to lure you home, and when that fails, I suspect they might come here, and that's where we want them. Where we have the advantage and can help you."

Vauk found his voice. "What should I do in the meantime?"

"Let us know if you feel anything more; be careful, and go on with your life."

"How can I?" The frustration in Vauk's voice was obvious.

"Vauk," Gathod placed his hands on Vauk's shoulders, standing behind him. "If you let whoever this is run your life, then they win. You need to be strong and know that we're all here for you."

Trent looked up at Gathod and mouthed a thank-you.

Steven and Brock got up to leave. "We're here for you. Just let us know if you need or want anything." Each of them hugged Vauk tightly, said their goodbyes, and left. Gathod followed them out after saying his own farewells.

Arthur returned as Gathod was leaving and bounded up to Vauk. "She's doing well and seemed happy to see me. We played chase."

"Chase?"

"Yeah… she'd chase me around her pen and them I'd chase her. We had fun."

"You mean she let you in her pen without running away?" Vauk was amazed.

"Sure. We're buds."

Vauk could only shake his head in amazement, and then he got quiet and sulky.

Trent snuggled close to Vauk, his nose nuzzling an ear. "You want to be alone for a while?"

"No, I need to keep busy."

Travis jumped to his feet. "Well then, let's finish your fawn's new home."

Cembran got up and walked to the kitchen, but Sue stopped him. "I'll do these." Sue shooed Cembran out of his own kitchen with a smile. "You boys go build a pen."

Cembran shrugged. He knew better than to argue with Sue, and besides, it was a gorgeous summer day and he'd much rather be outside. So, without argument, he handed the kitchen over to her and followed the rest of the boys outside.

The fencing was put up in record time, and before lunch, Vauk's little one had her new home. To everyone's surprise, she let Arthur lead her to her new home using a collar and leash, following docilely as Arthur led her through the woods. Once she was in her new pen, she raced from edge to edge, exploring her new, larger home.

Vauk couldn't have been more pleased, and Trent relaxed a little seeing the smile on the big satyr's face.

That chore complete, everyone went inside for lunch. After eating, Trent and Vauk spent quiet time together in Vauk's shelter until it was time for a reluctant Trent to head back to the city.

Chapter Seventeen

Vauk paced back and forth across the room. With each new sound he'd spin around, looking at the door. "Vauk, you've been pacing for the last hour." Travis entered the room from the master bedroom with Cembran right behind him. "I know you're anxious, but the pacing isn't going to get him here any faster."

Vauk stopped moving and stood, biting a fingernail, as he looked at the door, willing it to open. "I know," his breath huffed out, "but when I called he said he'd be here right away."

Cembran chuckled, scooting around Travis and swatting Vauk on the shoulder. "Don't be so literal. What Trent meant was that he'd get here as fast as he could."

"Oh." Vauk had to remind himself that his language skills were still developing and that sometimes he misunderstood things.

"Don't feel bad; it still happens to me sometimes. Just be patient and he'll be here." Cembran walked into the kitchen. "I'm making some iced tea. Would you like a glass?" Travis had made iced tea the previous weekend and Vauk found he really liked it.

"Yes, thank you." Vauk smiled at Cembran and then started pacing again.

Travis sat on the sofa. "Sit down and tell me what's got you so upset." Vauk flopped in the chair across from Travis. "Has something changed?"

"No, I'm just tired of feeling these things. I feel Miki sometimes and it feels so real."

"I know. Sometimes I feel it too. But what happened to make you so jittery?"

"Last night…." The door opened and Trent rushed inside. "Trent!"

Trent rushed forward, throwing his arms around Vauk. "Sorry it took so long. I had to cancel my tutoring sessions for the day and I couldn't get some of them on the phone."

"I was so worried."

"I know you had a rough night." Trent squeezed Vauk tightly, not wanting to let him go.

"I just don't understand what's happening."

Trent nodded. "Let's talk about it."

Vauk sat back down in the chair, pulling Trent onto his lap, holding him close. "I was having one of those learning dreams with you."

"Yeah, I know." He and Vauk still had the teaching dreams—not as often as they used to, since Vauk's language skills had progressed, but they still occurred about once or twice a week, particularly when Vauk encountered something he didn't understand. "But something woke you up."

Vauk shook his head. "I didn't wake up. Something or someone interrupted it and I started dreaming about Miki. He was calling to me. 'Vauk… come home. I love you and miss you.' He was standing in the house we shared together, looking just like he did the last time I saw him. When I woke up, I felt so happy. Then I remembered that Miki's dead and that someone else is making this happen."

"Is that when you called me?"

"Yeah. I needed to speak to you, to see you."

Trent looked at Travis, hoping for some insight or help. "I didn't feel anything at all, but that really doesn't mean much, other than whoever's doing this is getting better at covering their tracks."

"How do we know it truly isn't Miki?" The not knowing was really starting to get to Vauk.

Travis released the breath he was holding. "I'd hoped it wouldn't come to this, but I figured that you'd need to know one way or another."

Cembran brought glasses of iced tea for each of them and sat next to Travis on the sofa.

"What are you getting at?" Trent turned to look at Travis.

"I was hoping that when you didn't go rushing home, whoever was doing this would realize it wasn't working. When the feelings continued, I figured that Vauk would need to know if Miki was alive. So I contacted Darifo, Dovino's father, in Switzerland. He has contacts in other satyr communities. Through what he described as a friend of a friend of a friend, he was able to find out that Mikhail Junak…" Vauk nodded, "died in 1949, which would be about six months after you were captured."

Vauk was stunned. He knew this shouldn't be a surprise to him, but the news hit him like a tidal wave.

Trent could see the moment the news registered for Vauk; his eyes lowered and his shoulders sagged. It was as if finally giving up hope had deflated him. Trent didn't know what else to do, so he just held him.

Tears ran down Vauk's cheeks, and the big satyr lowered his head onto Trent's shoulder and sobbed like a small child. Travis and Cembran got up, set down their glasses, and quietly left the house, leaving Vauk alone with Trent to finally grieve for Miki's loss.

"It's all right. You can let it out." Damn it, this was the second time he'd held Vauk while he grieved, and it probably wouldn't be the last. At least Vauk's emotional roller-coaster that had started a few weeks earlier was finally over. Trent got off Vauk's lap, standing next to his chair. Taking the big satyr by the hand, he gently tugged him to his feet. His brain told him that Vauk should lie down and be allowed to grieve, but something deep down was pulling him in another direction.

Wrapping an arm around Vauk's waist, he coaxed, "Come with me." Vauk let himself be led and Trent slowly walked him outside and into the late July sun. Trent guided Vauk down one of the paths through the fields. "Where are we going?" Vauk's words were choked, his throat constricted, nose running. Trent handed him a tissue.

"We're going to see your little one." Vauk looked at Trent confused and unsure. "I don't know why, but you need to see her." Slowly they walked, Trent's arm around Vauk's waist, guiding him forward.

As they approached the pen, the young doe, which was starting to lose her spots and fill out, bounded toward them, gazing at Vauk through the fence, pawing at the ground trying to get to him. "Go inside. I'll be right here."

Vauk looked dubious, but walked to the door into the pen and slowly pulled the gate open. Hearing the gate, the young doe sniffed and looked around. Seeing Vauk, she waited until he was inside before bounding to him, bumping him in her haste.

"Oh, little one." Tears streaked down his cheeks as the young doe nuzzled against his hand and ran the side of her head against his leg. Trent watched as Vauk continued weeping softly while his little one comforted him.

"Trent, what's wrong with Mr. Vauk?" Arthur's voice knocked him out of his own thoughts.

"He's hurting right now."

"Why?"

Trent debated telling him, but Arthur was old enough to understand. "We found out today that Miki's dead. I think up to now, some part of him was holding out hope he was still alive."

"Oh." Arthur was quiet for a while as the two of them watched Vauk play with his doe. "It's good you brought him here." Trent turned to Arthur, confused. "Animals love no matter what. Whenever I'm sad I always search them out—they forgive fast and love simply and unconditionally."

The doe heard Arthur's voice and raced to the middle of the pen, turning back and looking at Vauk, then at Arthur, and back at Vauk again. "Mr. Vauk, she wants to play chase."

"Huh?"

Arthur cupped his hands to his mouth. "Let her chase you around the pen." Vauk ran away from the doe, and sure enough she took off after him, bounding behind him and bumping him in the leg. Arthur called again, "Now chase her."

Vauk couldn't believe what he was hearing, but he turned around and started running. The doe leapt in front of him as he chased after her. After a while, the doe turned again and started chasing Vauk.

"Come on, Trent. Let's play too." Trent followed Arthur into the pen. Vauk was breathing heavily, and Arthur started racing around the pen. Back and forth, again and again, they took turns chasing after one another.

At first, Vauk's sad look returned, but watching Arthur and the doe play was like a soothing balm. Vauk's face relaxed, then his mouth turned up, and a smile followed. The doe head-butted Arthur on the backside, sending him head over heels. Arthur got up, laughing. Vauk let loose a hearty laugh that resounded across the fields.

"Trent," Arthur approached breathless, "it's your turn."

Trent put up his hands, shaking his head. "I don't think so." Not after the spill Arthur just took.

"Come on, Tapfer… she really wants to play."

A little unsure, Trent decided to play along. He raced around the pen, the doe right behind him. Once she caught him, he chased her. It was great fun.

When the doe had worn all three of them out, they sat in the shade, watching her munch on the grass. "Mr. Vauk, did you ever name her?"

"No, I always just called her little one."

Arthur chuckled. "She isn't so little anymore."

"No, she's growing up."

Trent interjected. "She deserves a proper name."

"I guess, but what?"

Trent knew what he wanted to suggest, but kept quiet. Arthur on the other hand had no such compunction. "Why not call her Mika?"

Vauk stopped, his body becoming rigid and still. Waiting for Vauk's reaction, Trent felt himself tense; Arthur continued as if Vauk hadn't reacted. "I know you loved your Miki, just like Uncle Travis loves Uncle Cembran. Let her remind you of that love."

Trent figured Vauk had been starting to build walls again, but Arthur walked right through them. "You're right." Vauk stood up and turned to the doe. "Mika." Slowly the doe walked to him and began nuzzling his hand.

Arthur started petting her as well. "You like your new name, don't you?" Making all sorts of cooing noises, he continued. "Yes you do." Arthur sat next to her and Vauk did the same. Trent watched as Mika settled between them, content and happy.

Trent scooted closer, wanting physical contact with Vauk. "Tell us about Miki." Vauk looked at Trent like he was crazy. "We didn't know him, Love. So tell us about him." The confused look remained. "When someone dies, we often share stories about them; it helps us remember the good things."

"What should I tell you?" Vauk gestured with his hands. "What do you want to know?"

"Tell us something happy, some memory that you want to share."

Arthur settled in. "I love stories," he said, beaming with anticipation.

"Vauk." Trent touched his shoulder. "Tell us how you fell in love."

"Please...." Arthur beg-whined, and Trent had to stifle a laugh.

"Why would you want to hear about that?"

All kinds of reasons sprang to Trent's mind: *because you need to talk about it, because I'm curious, because I need to know and don't want to compete with a ghost.*

Arthur beat him to the punch. "Because we love you, Mr. Vauk." Once again, Trent marveled at Arthur's way of cutting through difficult situations with simple, honest, heartfelt answers. Trent sincerely hoped he maintained his innocent, loving nature as he grew older.

Vauk thought for a while, trying to decide where to begin. "Miki, Sasha, and I grew up together, along with Alex and Vasha. We were all the same age, but Miki, Sasha, and I were inseparable friends. We met in school when we were about eight years old. God, we were hellions. Miki would conceive our deviltries, Sasha would plan them, and we'd work together to carry them out."

Arthur's eyes glistened with mischief. "What did you do?"

Vauk smiled, remembering happily. "The school was old and rumored to be haunted. We rigged the shutters, bell, and even a few of the desks to move." Vauk was grinning now. "We set it up so when strings were pulled, the shutters would bang, the bell would ring on its own, and one of the desks would slide across the floor. The best part was that when they were tugged, the string would come loose and we'd palm them and slip them in our pants. We scared the class and the teacher half to death."

"Did he find out?"

"Eventually, but only after weeks of teaching in a 'haunted school.' He spanked us good, but it was worth it." Tears of laughter rolled down Vauk's cheek.

"After school, we always met at my house. Miki's father was a friend of my father's and sometimes we'd meet at his house. Sasha's family was really poor. Miki's dad died when he was young, fell off their roof when he was trying to fix it, so he never had much growing up, but that really didn't matter to us. We were best friends, we looked out for each other." Vauk wiped his eyes. "They were the brothers I never had."

"When did you and Miki fall in love?" Trent stroked Vauk's leg, letting him know he was there if he needed him.

"At some point during the war, a bomb fell on the village, damaging a few buildings. Miki's righteous indignation went through the roof and he decided to join the resistance. I remember sitting in our kitchen with him, Sasha, Alex, and Vasha, drinking and laughing the night before he left."

"Why didn't you go with him?"

Vauk took a deep breath and released it slowly. "The entire village looked on the war as something between the humans. We didn't get involved. The village is in a valley and covered by trees, and humans can't see it anyway. So everyone, except Miki, stayed in the village and out of the war. Anyway, two years later, Miki returned to the village. I heard a knock on the door. When I opened it, Miki stood on the step, a shell of what he used to be, skinny, drawn, and gaunt. He hadn't eaten in days. But his eyes were the same bright blue. He held out his arms for a hug, but I kissed him instead. I knew right then—he was back... he was mine... and I wasn't letting him go again. What really surprised me was when Miki returned my kiss, and loved me back." Vauk stopped, his voice getting rough, not sure if he wanted to go on.

"It's okay; you don't have to go on if you don't want to."

"In some ways, Miki never got over the war. Loud noises always made him scream and jump. The first clap of thunder sent him running for cover. But we were happy. My father took Miki into our family, accepting him as a second son. He even presided over our Triuwe ceremony." Trent patted Vauk's thigh. He already knew how the story ended and he wanted Vauk to remember the good things, not dwell on the pain and separation.

"Ar-thur!" The call from Cembran floated over the fields and the boy waved at Cembran before getting up.

Arms clung around Vauk's neck, he beamed, "Thank you for the story." Then he disentangled his arms from Vauk and started to walk to the gate, only to race back, startling the doe. "I love you." Arthur hugged the big satyr again before taking off at a run, answering Cembran's call.

The doe settled back on the grass next to his leg as he lazily stroked her. "You know I gave Miki my Triuwe." Trent nodded. "You understand that I can't do that again."

"I'd understand if you never wanted to do it again."

"No, Trent… it isn't that. Each satyr can only give his Triuwe once and only once."

"Oh." Trent wasn't sure what Vauk was getting at.

Vauk's arms pulled Trent to him. "I love you, Trent. That hasn't changed. I just wanted to make sure you understood what you'd be giving up to be with me."

"I don't understand why you're telling me this."

Vauk nodded slowly. "You've seen the special bond between Travis and Cembran, Brock and Steven, and Jim and Sue."

"Yeah, it's almost like they know what the other is feeling. Sometimes I swear they can almost read each other's minds."

"They can't read each other's minds, but that bond, that connection comes from being Truists. That's something you deserve, but can never have with me."

"I could give you my Triuwe."

"Yes, you could, but then I'd be able to feel you, but you couldn't feel me. The connection would be one way." Trent was about to say it didn't matter, but Vauk put a finger to his lips. "I wouldn't let you do it anyway; it wouldn't be fair."

"Vauk, it doesn't matter."

"How can it not matter?" Vauk's voice rose, almost yelling.

"Vauk, it doesn't matter because I can't miss something I never had in the first place." Trent leaned forward, kissing Vauk, tongue tracing his lips. "I have to go back late this afternoon and I was wondering if you'd like to come with me for a few days. I have to work tomorrow, but we'd have the weekend together and I could show you around." Vauk looked interested, but reticent. "I have a big soft bed and a hot tub in the private backyard."

"What's a hot tub?"

"Seven hundred gallons of hot, bubbling water dancing and playing around our naked bodies."

"Oh, can we…?" Vauk's eyebrows rose suggestively.

Trent leered right back. "I'm counting on it." Both of them took turns leering at each other. Trent wanted to push Vauk to the grass, strip off their clothes, straddle his big satyr, and ride him for hours, but damn it, he wasn't sure this was the time.

"All kidding aside, I'd love to show you around Grand Rapids, but if you'd feel more comfortable staying here, I'll understand."

"I've spent a long time grieving for Miki. I think it's time I start living." Vauk grabbed Trent, pushing him back on the grass. "Really living again." A short time later, they were both naked, Vauk buried deep inside Trent, making him scream. "Is that what you want, Tapfer?"

"God yes! Live, Vauk. Don't stop. Live… really live!"

Chapter Eighteen

A sigh escaped Trent's lips as he lowered his body into the hot, bubbling water. "Come on in, Love. You'll like it. I promise."

Vauk was standing just inside the door, a towel low around his waist. He looked different. At the farm, Vauk rarely cloaked himself, but here it was a necessity. And it took some getting used to on Trent's part. He was becoming very partial to the look and feel of his big, strong satyr lover. "It looks too hot. I'll cook."

Trent threw his head back, laughing heartily. "I promise you won't cook; they're just air bubbles." He held out his hand and slowly Vauk stepped forward, touched the water with his hand, and smiled. Trent reached up and pulled away the towel. Timidly, the big satyr stepped into the bubbling hot tub as Trent trailed his fingers over Vauk's most tender and fascinating places. Slowly, the big guy lowered his body into the water.

"That tickles the bits."

"What?" Trent chuckled softly and smiled widely at the unfamiliar expression.

"My bits… you know." Vauk gestured below the water.

Trent continued chuckling. "I like the bits, tickled or otherwise." Trent stood up, the water coming just below his hips, giving Vauk a show of just how tickled he was.

The darkness surrounded them as Trent shifted, sitting on Vauk's outstretched legs, bringing their lips close. "Love you like this, all hot and wet and tasty." Trent licked a nipple before he cupped Vauk's head in his hands and brought their lips together. Lips slid together as tongues played and explored. Vauk's hand supported Trent's back while the other slid down his chest before slipping beneath the water. "Vauk... that's...."

"Like that, Tapfer?" His voice was barely a whisper.

"Yeah." Vauk's hand slid along his length. "Just like that." Trent let the back of his head dip into the water.

Vauk felt Trent melt against him, giving himself over to what he was doing, trusting him. Making those soft pleasure sounds just for him. "Love you, Tapfer." For Vauk, one of the biggest changes was his vulnerability. With Miki, he'd been the protector, the strong one, both physically and emotionally, but with Trent, it was different. His feelings seemed to be in turmoil and hard to control. And while he was still physically strong, Trent was fast becoming his emotional anchor. He gave of himself during sex and otherwise, whenever Vauk needed him. It was almost too good to be true.

Vauk placed a hand under Trent's butt, lifting him up, splaying him on top of the water. One hand was all it took, the other stroking hot, wet, smooth skin from neck to knees.

"God, that's so good." Vauk could feel Trent's body vibrating through his hands, his own desire stoked and throbbing. He wanted Trent—needed him—badly, but he was taking his time. The wildness that sometimes consumed him was quiet. "Don't tease me, Love."

"Not teasing... just loving." His hand kept stroking, running between long legs, slipping between firm cheeks to tease sensitive, puckered skin. Hips caressed, hands splayed across a hard stomach.

Vauk lowered Trent just a little, his throbbing manhood pressing between firm, tight globes. "Want you, Love. Take me please."

"Not yet, Tapfer. This is just the warm-up."

The big head shifted forward, hands steady, as teeth nibbled on a firm nipple. Trent hissed as the sensation built almost to the point of pain, then a hot tongue, soothing and sucking. "Gods...." Trent was breathless. "That's so hot."

"You like it when I use my teeth?" Vauk's voice wrapped around him like a silky, sexy blanket in the darkness.

Trent raised his head. "Hell yes, your teeth, lips, fingers, cock... as long as it's yours, I love it."

Vauk lowered Trent again, pushing at his entrance, but going no further. "Love this, love how you trust me." Trent pressed his butt a little lower, the pressure on him exquisite, but not quite enough for entry. A low moan of frustration built and escaped from Trent. "Need... more...."

Vauk's hands shifted beneath Trent, standing up, lifting them both out of the water. "Where are you taking us?" Trent's mind was so clouded with desire he could barely think.

"You told me you had a hot tub and a big, soft bed." Vauk stepped out of the tub, the water sheeting down his skin. "That was the hot tub; now it's time for the bed." Vauk carried Trent into the house and down the hall to the bedroom.

Placing Trent on the huge bed, Vauk stood at the edge, looking over the long, lean body beneath him. "Want you so bad, Love."

Climbing on the bed, Vauk lifted Trent's legs, exposing him to his gaze. "You'll have me, but first...." Vauk's tongue slid over and around Trent's entrance.

"Gods, Vauk!" Trent bucked gently back against the pleasure and heat.

Vauk smiled at Trent's reaction, repeating the action with his tongue, swirling around the muscle, pushing in, opening him.

"Stroke yourself; I want you to come while I tongue you."

"Fuuuuck." Trent drew out in a long sort of moan as he complied, fingers wrapping around himself, stroking long and hard. "Not gonna last!" Vauk put a hand on his lower belly while his tongue thrust deep. "Yeah.... Just... like... that...! Oh, Gods!" White, ropy semen shot onto his stomach.

Scooping up Trent's release, Vauk lubed himself with it and thrust into Trent, going deep and hard.

"Yeah, love how you fill me!" Vauk's thrusts were hard, pounding, crushing, as he rode Trent deeply, the bed shaking. Each thrust was full, long, and incredibly fulfilling. Trent cried out his passion. "More... want all of you!" Vauk was too gone to respond with words, his body doing his talking for him. "Love you, Vauk." Passion filled both of them, bodies connected, spirits melding, sharing passion and love.

Vauk's moans became more intense, more urgent, and Trent cried out, echoing back the moans. Release built for both, becoming unstoppable. "Tapfer!" Vauk called his release as he shot into his lover. Trent followed right behind, crying out his own passion, eyes glistening with ecstasy.

Breath heaving, Vauk slipped from Trent, collapsing on the bed next to him, pulling his lover up onto his larger body, kissing him softly, affectionately. Loving, chocolate eyes stared into large blue orbs. "Love you."

Trent's arms wound around his neck, and soft lips skimmed over his. "Love you too." He did, so much it hurt, and it scared him sometimes. It really didn't matter if they couldn't be truists; Vauk had stolen his heart and nothing else mattered. Trent knew he was probably setting himself up for heartache, but he had to take the chance.

Trent slipped off Vauk and out of the bed. Vauk heard the soft hum of a motor click off. Trent returned with a warm cloth and towel. After a quick cleanup, he climbed back on the bed, again lying on top of Vauk's big body, knowing that he loved the feel of Vauk against his skin as much as Vauk loved the feel of Trent against his own.

"I could go to sleep right here."

Vauk's strong arms curled around Trent, holding him tight, the smaller body rising and falling with the big satyr's breathing. Slowly, reluctantly, Trent shifted off Vauk, pulling back the covers on the bed. Vauk yawned and climbed under the covers, resting on his side, waiting for Trent to join him. "Come on, Tapfer." Trent smiled as he joined Vauk, the big satyr pulling him close, spooning into his back.

"What if I feel something tonight?" The soft whisper barely reached Trent's ears.

Trent yawned, his mind already drifting toward sleep. "I'll probably dream of you. I usually do after we make love." Trent rolled over. "Just know that I love you, that it's only a dream and that I'm right here." Vauk's answer was to pull Trent closer, holding him against his skin as they drifted to sleep.

The room was dark, and the sounds of the city outside had quieted. Vauk started awake, breathing hard, Trent still asleep next to him. "Tapfer." Vauk gently shook Trent's shoulder.

"You okay, Love?" Trent's voice was colored with sleep.

"I was dreaming." Vauk sounded confused and out of sorts.

Trent sat up, covers pooling in his lap. "Yeah, I was with you. It was one of our teaching dreams, except this time you wanted to learn what it would be like to take me on my desk." Trent knocked Vauk's shoulder playfully as he tried to remember everything. "You started toward me, but then began disappearing, reappearing again, and finally you were gone."

"Yeah, I remember. I left and then Miki was there and I could feel him." Trent comforted his still-confused lover. "This time, though, before Miki appeared, I heard voices. I couldn't understand them, but they were there." Vauk's face became rigid. "They felt scary, menacing, and then Miki appeared."

"It's okay, Love." Trent settled back on the bed, pulling Vauk down with him, curling them together, holding his lover tight.

"Do you think I felt whoever's doing this? Like Travis did at the lake?"

"That's possible. I suppose it's very possible." Vauk settled down, preparing to go back to sleep. "Did they seem familiar?"

"I don't know." Vauk paused. "Maybe." It took awhile, holding each other, but sleep took them again.

Trent woke, the sun shining in the windows, and slowly got out of bed, careful not to wake Vauk. Checking the clock, he knew he'd have to get moving if he were going to be on time for his first tutoring session. He quietly padded to the bathroom, cleaned up, and went back into the bedroom to get dressed.

Vauk stirred in the bed. "You're up."

"Shhh. Go back to sleep. There's food for breakfast." Trent leaned over the bed, giving Vauk a soft kiss. "I'll be back early this afternoon, and we can explore and see stuff." Vauk shifted and started getting out of bed and dressed. "Love, go back to sleep." Trent settled him back in bed.

Vauk yawned as Trent kissed him and then finished dressing. He was asleep again by the time Trent left the house.

Arriving at the learning center a few minutes before his first appointment, Trent waited in the lobby, checking in with the receptionist before heading to his designated room. Jimmy, his first appointment, arrived and Trent got to work, helping the third grader with his math.

By the time his last tutoring session was done, Trent was ready to go home. He knew Vauk would be waiting for him and he was anxious to show him around.

Opening the front door, Trent called "Vauk," as he stepped into the house.

"In here." Trent followed the voice to the family room. Vauk had the TV on, scowling and shaking his head. "Is this for real? These people are nuts."

Trent looked at the TV and laughed. "No. That's a soap opera. It's definitely not real. And yes, they are nuts."

"I don't understand."

"It's just entertainment; none of it is real." Vauk turned off the TV, relieved. "Are you ready to get some lunch and have some fun?"

In an instant, Vauk was on his feet, standing in front of Trent. "Hi, I'm glad you're home." The kiss was soft, really sweet. It surprised Trent that Vauk, being so big, so strong, was also so tender and affectionate. "It's strange here without you." Vauk looked around the room. "It's so noisy all the time. The people next door, cars on the street." Vauk looked up. "Even noises from the air." Vauk shuddered. "How can you stand it?"

Trent's arriving-home smile fell a little. "I guess I'm just used to it."

"There used to be all kinds of noises at the carnival, but I never heard them. I guess it's like that. But the farm is so peaceful." Vauk's arms pulled him close. "I like visiting because you're here, but I don't think I could live here."

"Oh." Trent's face fell. Damn. He hadn't even realized he'd been hoping Vauk would like it here and want to stay, maybe live here with him someday. Quickly, he tried to cover his unexpected disappointment.

Too late. "You're disappointed, aren't you?"

"Maybe a little. I think I was hoping you'd like it here."

Vauk rested his forehead against Trent's. "I would probably get used to it in time, but what would I do? I know animals, and trees, and…."

Trent kissed him softly. "I know. It wasn't realistic on my part. You belong on the farm. It's just that I don't really fit there. Not to work. I'm a teacher, not a farmer." Trent rested his head on Vauk's shoulder, rationalizing his disappointment away as best he could. "I love you and want to be with you. Today, I could barely concentrate, just thinking about you."

Vauk stepped back a little. "I don't know the answer either." The confusion and frustration on Vauk's face was somehow very touching.

Trent knew things could continue as they were, with him traveling to the farm on weekends, but he wanted to be with Vauk all the time. "We'll figure it out, somehow." God, he sounded like Scarlett O'Hara. At least he wasn't the only one confused and a little frustrated. "Shall we go eat before I pull you back in the bedroom?" Trent took Vauk's hand and together they left the house and got in the car.

Trent drove cautiously, avoiding the freeways. On the trip down, Vauk had gripped the armrests with white-knuckle intensity, the speed really getting to him. "There are so many people, everywhere." As they drove through downtown, Vauk looked up at the tall buildings. "People live up there?"

"Yeah. In fact, people pay a lot of money to live up there."

"Why? What do they do for trees and grass?" For the first time, something deep inside Trent clicked. All those times he'd worked in his garden, in the fog and rain, heat and humidity, sun and clouds, he needed to be in contact with nature, just like Vauk did. He thought about living in a high-rise and he could almost feel the satyr inside him rebelling. "They aren't satyrs, Vauk. They don't need trees and grass… like we do." He got it, and he knew why he could never ask Vauk to live in the city. He'd never be truly happy and maybe….

Trent pulled the car off the road and stopped. "I was going to take you to the museum, but I have a better idea." Trent checked traffic and turned the car around. "Bear with me a few minutes. I know what you'll like." Trent headed east out of downtown toward the edge of town. "I

know you hate the highway, but it'll take forever using surface streets."
Vauk nodded tentatively and Trent turned onto the freeway on-ramp.
Trent zoomed through traffic, getting off the freeway and pulling into
Meijer Gardens a few minutes later.

"What is this place?" Vauk seemed fascinated as Trent pulled into
the parking lot.

"It's a large botanical and sculpture garden."

Vauk pointed at the tall glass building ahead of them. "What is that?
It looks like a big glass house."

"Yup. It's a large greenhouse for tropical plants." Ignoring the looks
from other patrons, Trent took Vauk's hand and led him down the path,
past sculptures of children playing, toward the entrance. "We can go
inside and look around before walking along the paths outside, okay?"
Vauk tilted his head slowly, his eyes boggling at what he was seeing.
They ate together in the cafeteria before heading into the main
greenhouse.

Once inside, Vauk practically vibrated with excitement. The gardens
were running a butterfly exhibit and the main tropical greenhouse was
filled with colorful, fluttering wings. Vauk's head swirled and turned,
unsure where to settle his gaze, one strange tropical plant after another
drawing his attention. Gently, Trent guided Vauk along the paths,
towering palms reaching for the glass ceiling, orchids and bougainvillea,
bird of paradise, and lush vines growing everywhere.

In a soft breathy, excited voice, Vauk said, "Trent, look." A butterfly
had settled on Vauk's sleeve. "It's so beautiful." One of the docents
approached slowly, watching. Suddenly the air filled with colorful
wings, fluttering near Vauk, landing on his outstretched arms and
shoulders, even his back and chest. The docent inhaled slowly. "I've
never seen anything like this before." The docent turned to Trent, his
face a picture of surprise and disbelief.

Vauk's face and eyes suddenly looked like those of a child
discovering something wonderful and new. Trent approached slowly
along with the docent. "Looks like you found some friends." The docent
was becoming visibly concerned and stepped toward Vauk, but Trent
stopped him with a touch. "He won't hurt them." Vauk grinned from ear
to ear and slowly started to turn around, the movement causing a stir in

the living color that covered him. Then the colorful wings flapped and took to the air, spreading through the garden again.

"That was incredible," the docent sputtered in soft disbelief. Vauk shrugged slowly and they continued their stroll through the greenhouse, leaving the docent looking on in bewilderment.

Outside, hand in hand, they wandered through the nearly deserted paths, past the re-creation of da Vinci's monumental horse sculpture, through the wetlands and meadow. In the wooded section of the gardens, they strolled leisurely along the path, quietly being together, no words needed, just quiet togetherness.

A yelp of pain and fear broke their companionable silence. Vauk's hand slipped from Trent's and he ran toward the source of the cry, Trent right behind him.

"Don't let it get away!" The voice was hard and mean, followed by shouts and yelling.

Cresting a small rise, they saw three teenage boys chasing a small blond streak. Vauk raced toward the small creature, bellowing in his deep voice as he ran, his cloak slipping, satyr features fully visible. The boys froze, seeing this huge creature with large horns barreling toward them. The blond streak raced away from the boys and jumped into Vauk's arms.

"What the fuck kind of freak are you?" the leader spat as he pulled a knife. Trent tried to call a warning, but the kid was too fast, lunging toward Vauk, thrusting the knife. Trent closed his eyes, not able to watch Vauk get hurt.

Thoughts bombarded him, thoughts that weren't his own: aggression, fear, adrenaline coursing through him. What the hell? Opening his eyes, the scene looked surreal. Vauk, horns visible, holding a small dog. What the fuck? He was looking at himself, standing behind Vauk. Looking down, there was a knife in his hand. How did I get here? The strange, jumbled thoughts were almost too much. God, I'm inside the kid's head. He could feel all the kid's emotions and feelings, jumbled thoughts and aggression. The knife clanged against a log and then he was falling....

His face was being licked and he was lying on the ground. Grinding his eyes open, Trent looked up at Vauk. "Are you okay, Tapfer?" A hand stroked his cheek. "You scared me." Trent looked around; the teenagers were gone and they were alone.

"What happened?" Confusion reigned supreme, matched by Vauk's expression.

"Don't know. He had a knife, suddenly he dropped it, ran away, and then you fell on the ground." Vauk took Trent's hand, "Can you stand up?" Trent nodded and Vauk helped him to his feet, still holding the dog.

"My head." Trent rubbed his forehead, slowly regaining his balance. "I was inside the kid's head and saw you and me. I got him to drop the knife."

Vauk scrunched his face. "Were you seeing through him? Could you hear his thoughts?"

"Yeah, I think so. But how…?"

"Don't know."

"You need to cloak yourself, Love." Vauk's satyr features disappeared.

"I'm sorry."

Trent smiled, and then cringed as his head throbbed. "Don't be. Those boys were probably ready to wet themselves when you raced toward them." Trent started laughing, holding his head with one hand and his stomach with the other. "Besides, no one will believe them anyway." Trent kept laughing and Vauk joined in. "I bet they need to go home and change their pants about now."

As their laughter died down, Vauk set down the dog. "What do we do with him?" The blond terrier jumped and bounded around their feet. "He's obviously been here awhile." The dog streaked around them, his tail wagging his backside.

"No collar, and he's really dirty."

"He needs a home."

Trent grinned. "Is that your way of asking if we can keep him?"

Sheepishly, Vauk said, "Yeah."

"Let's go home. I've had enough excitement. We'll check and see if anyone knows about him. If he's truly homeless, we'll stop on the way home and get some dog things."

"Thank you, Tapfer." Vauk leaned forward, kissing Trent gently on the lips, while a tongue licked his chin. "He doesn't want to be left out." Still laughing, they walked together, Vauk still carrying the dog.

As they approached the greenhouse, a retiree volunteer docent approached. "Did you just come from the woods?"

"Yes." They looked at each other.

"Did you see anything unusual?" The kind-looking older man inquired.

"Just some kids chasing the dog." Trent motioned to the terrier in Vauk's arms.

"Nothing else?"

"No, should we have?" Trent knew he had to play dumb.

The old man shook his head and then turned his attention to the dog. "I'm glad you caught him. We've been trying for a month." He reached toward the dog. "I'll call animal control to come and get him."

Vauk growled in response. Trent intervened. "We're going to take him."

The docent smiled and let them pass so they could walk to the car.

They spent the rest of the afternoon shopping for dog supplies, and having the terrier looked at by a vet who pronounced him surprisingly healthy. Then they went back to the house for a late dinner and snuggling together on the sofa.

"What should we name him?"

Vauk thought for a few minutes. "How about—Luka?"

Trent smiled, kissing Vauk softly as Vauk pulled him on top of him. "Luka it is." Their kisses grew more intense and needy, signaling it was definitely time for bed.

Luka remained curled on the end of the sofa as they got up and headed to the bedroom, where the lovemaking continued until they were both exhausted, sated, and very happy. Settling down to sleep, they curled together, dozing off as Luka jumped onto the bed, settling at the bottom near their feet.

Trent woke a few hours later, shifting and turning in bed. A soft grunt from the large satyr next to him was followed by a groan and then the large body was on top of him, pinning him to the bed. It was the start of a robust lovemaking session that resulted in the covers on the floor, Luka bounding from the room, the bed bouncing, shouted releases, and two happy and slightly sore satyrs falling back asleep curled together.

Trent woke to an incessant ringing and all he could think was he needed it to stop, badly. Squirming away from Vauk, he reached for the phone, yanking it from the cradle. A few minutes later, he carefully hung up the phone. "Vauk. Vauk." Trent shook his bed partner awake.

"What? Tapfer, go back to sleep." Arms wrapped around him, pulling him back against the big warm body.

"Vauk, that was Travis. There's a man at the farm. He says he's your brother."

Chapter Nineteen

"What?" Vauk shook his head, unsure he'd heard Trent right. "Travis said what?"

"He said that a man knocked on their door this morning, looking for you. He said that he's your brother." Trent was starting to wonder what was going on himself. "You never told me you had a brother." He wasn't sure if he should be hurt or not.

"I don't have a brother. Or at least I didn't…." Vauk's voice trailed off.

Trent got out of bed and started dressing. "Travis asked us to get up there right away."

"Oh." Vauk just sat on the edge of the bed, stunned into immobility. "I don't know anything about my family anymore. Everything's changed."

Trent sat down next to him. "Well, if you now have a brother, maybe he can fill you in."

"Yeah… maybe…." Vauk looked up at Trent. "But, what if he's the one messing with my dreams, trying to make me think Miki's alive?"

"Good thought." Trent took Vauk's hand in his. "We'll need to be careful."

Vauk nodded his agreement. "Just in case, don't leave me alone with him."

Trent smiled, leaning close, kissing softly. "Wouldn't dream of it, Love." With another kiss, Trent got up. "We need to get dressed." Trent let his eyes wander over his naked satyr. Getting dressed was the last thing he wanted to do. "Although, a naked Vauk is always a good thing."

A smile peeked at the corners of Vauk's mouth. "I might scare the neighbors as I walked to the car."

Trent hooted. "Scare the neighbors? Half of them would chase after the car screaming for another look at the naked hunk."

Vauk's own laughter lasted a few minutes before his glum face returned. Trent pulled him to his feet. "Let's get dressed so we can figure this out." Just when he thought the roller-coaster ride was over, it started again.

Vauk nodded and started dressing. "Did Travis say anything else?"

"No. I don't think he knows anything else. He just asked us to come right away."

In near silence, they finished dressing, packed their bags, and loaded the car.

Less than an hour after Travis's phone call, they were on the road, heading toward the farm, with Luka's head out a window, ears blowing in the breeze. The closer they got to the farm, the more nervous and agitated Vauk became.

"How do you want to handle this?" Trent asked. Vauk furrowed his brow. "Do you want to see him right away, or do you want time to get your thoughts together, maybe see Mika first."

"I want to get this over with, and then we can see Mika." Vauk seemed lost. "I don't know…. How do you greet a possible brother you never knew you had?" Vauk seemed completely lost. "I'd probably be thrilled to have a brother if these feelings I keep having were real."

"I think I understand." Trent parked the car next to Travis's truck. "I'll be with you."

"Thank you, Tapfer." Vauk was a bundle of nerves as he got out of the car. Trent came around to his side of the car, took his hand, and together, they walked along the path to the farmhouse, Luka following along on his leash.

The farm was quiet, unusually quiet for noontime, as they approached the front door. Trent knocked and waited. The door was opened by a stern-faced, almost scowling Cembran. Trent actually stepped back. He'd never seen such a dour look on the usually happy, radiant face. "Cembran, are you okay?"

The dark look melted away, "Sure. Sorry. I was thinking about...." His words drifted off. "Come in." His voice now carried its usual brightness. "Who's this?" Cembran bent down and scratched the small terrier's ears.

"Luka." Trent picked up the dog, holding him in his arms. "We found him yesterday. Vauk rescued him from some tormenting kids."

"He seems wonderful." Cembran continued scratching his ears and the darting tongue tried to lick Cembran's face.

Trent and Vauk stepped inside and Cembran closed the door behind them. "Is this Vauk?" A large, tall figure stood from one of the living room chairs. "I'm Christoff, your brother, or, more precisely, your half-brother. Dad remarried and had me thirty years ago." He grabbed Vauk's hand, shaking it robustly as Vauk looked stunned. "I've been looking for you for a long time."

The energy in the young satyr was incredible. "Christoff," Trent broke in as he stopped for a breath.

"Sorry. I tend to run on when I get excited." The smile on his face was radiant. "I'm just so happy to have found my brother after all this time." He was practically bouncing he was so wound up.

"Why don't we sit down?" Travis ushered everyone into chairs. Trent sat next to Vauk on the sofa. He still looked dazed and completely confused. "I think some introductions are in order. Christoff, you obviously recognize Vauk." The resemblance between the two satyrs was striking; it was obvious they were related. "This is Trent Walters."

Vauk spoke up for the first time. "He's my friend and lover." Vauk's face was firm, almost like he was daring Christoff to say something.

Instead Christoff smiled. "I'm glad Vauk has someone to love." Vauk smiled in return.

"You said you'd been looking for me for a long time. How did you find me?"

Christoff looked sheepish, but Vauk held his gaze. "I started to sense your dreams about six months ago and I was able to sense you more and more as time passed. Sometimes I'd dream of you, and eventually, I was able to track you down, with the help of others in the village." Christoff's face became earnest, "Everyone's been looking for you for a long time, but there was no trace of you until about six or eight months ago."

Vauk nodded. That coincided with when he was starting to get control of himself again. "How's my... I mean, our father?" Vauk's voice was soft, almost like he was afraid of the answer.

"He's with the gods."

"How long ago?" His voice almost broke, and he kept himself under control by sheer will. Trent put his arm around him, maintaining physical contact.

"He left us five years ago last spring." Vauk blinked back tears. The one person, after Miki, whom he'd really hoped to see again was his father. "After you disappeared, the village was in chaos. With no clear heir, our father's position as baccharist was being challenged by some who never liked him."

"But I was never going to take over for him."

Christoff continued. "It didn't seem to matter. According to father, everyone really loved you and truly wanted you as baccharist, but with you gone, the line of succession was broken. So he married my mother and they had me."

"Where is she?" Vauk seemed to be overcoming his surprise.

"Still in the village. She loved him dearly and still feels his loss. They were very happy and loved each other. From what they both said, what started out as a marriage of convenience grew into a love match that neither expected."

"So when our father passed away...."

"I became baccharist. Lucky for me, Uncle Vasha and Uncle Sasha have been really helpful." Vauk smiled. Those could only be his childhood friends, and memories came flooding back.

Travis stood up. "Why don't you show Christoff around the farm?"

Trent whispered, "Do you want me to go with you?"

"We'll watch Luka for you." Travis was already squatting down to pet the terrier.

Vauk nodded slowly. "Yes, please." Trent and Vauk got up and led the way to the door with Christoff following. Travis was already rolling about on the floor, playing with Luka.

"Love, let's visit Mika." Vauk nodded and led the way to the young doe's enclosure. Trent opened the gate and Vauk went inside, followed by Christoff and finally Trent.

The doe cautiously walked to Vauk, keeping a close eye on Christoff. "How's my little girl?" The doe nuzzled Vauk's leg, wanting some attention. Vauk made cooing noises as he gently rubbed her back.

"She's lovely, Vauk. But why does she let you get so close?"

"It's my talent. Animals seem to trust me. I can almost read their minds, know what they need. What's your talent, Christoff?"

"I don't know. I've always been good with others, our father taught me well, but if I had to guess, I'd say I have a special talent for music."

The fawn chose that moment to start running. "She wants to play." Vauk took off after the doe, playing chase. Trent joined in as Vauk tired, with Christoff watching the entire scene, laughing and calling encouragement to both of them as well as the doe.

Once the doe had had enough of the game, the brothers and Trent walked together through the farm. The more they talked, Trent could see Vauk becoming more comfortable with his brother. Trent was pleased, but cautious. He was glad that Vauk seemed to be hitting it off with his brother, but he was also wary—the timing of the visit was suspect, along with the fact that something just wasn't right. It was only a feeling, and he had no intention of mentioning it to Vauk, but....

"Tapfer, it's a nice day. Let's go to the lake." Trent looked over at a laughing Vauk and smiled to himself.

"Yes. Let's get Luka and take him with us." Trent was grinning as Vauk smiled. "I'll be right back." Trent walked quickly back to the house.

Cembran and Travis were sitting together when Trent came in. Luka had been sitting next to Cembran, but he perked up and raced to meet Trent. "We're going to the lake and I thought he might like a swim."

Travis patted Cembran's knee and then stood up. "I know Vauk is probably taken with his brother, and Christoff seems genuine to me."

"But...?"

"When he first arrived, I had the strangest feeling; even the animals were quiet."

"I noticed that when we got here as well."

"You remember that day at the lake when Vauk first felt Miki, and I said I felt something malevolent, almost evil?"

Trent nodded. "I remember."

"When Christoff arrived, I felt the same thing again. I'm not sure if it originates from him or not, but be careful."

"Should I tell Vauk?" Trent hated keeping secrets, but he didn't want to upset him needlessly, particularly if Christoff wasn't involved in what had happened to Vauk.

"You can if you feel you have to, but I'm not really sure. And keep in mind, Christoff was born after Vauk was captured. I don't know if he's involved now or what. Just keep a close watch on him and I'll do the same."

"I will. I'm just worried about Vauk. He's had so many shocks and surprises, and I want Christoff to be as nice as he seems... for Vauk's sake."

Cembran patted Trent's shoulder. "We know. Now, go on down to the lake before this one," Cembran pointed to a tail-wagging little terrier who was bounding across the furniture, "tears the whole place apart." Cembran was almost laughing as Trent opened the door and Luka jumped outside, turning around to wait for Trent, tail wagging his entire backside.

Luka followed behind Trent as he headed down the path to the lake. Occasionally he'd veer off to smell something interesting, but he'd quickly catch up, his tail going as he sniffed around.

Reaching the tree line around the lake, Trent stopped. Vauk and Christoff were sitting together on the sand. Christoff had a small "pan" flute and he was playing a soft, slow melody, Vauk swaying gently, completely engrossed in the music. The tune wasn't one Trent was familiar with, but Vauk obviously was, because even from where he was standing, he could see Vauk's lips moving, mouthing the words. Not wanting to disturb them, Trent sat down, leaning against a tree, and Luka jumped into his lap.

Watching them together, Trent was surprised how much alike they both were, particularly uncloaked, like they were now. Both were large satyrs, with such similar facial features and horns that if he met Christoff on the street, he'd wonder if he were related to Vauk. They were even reacting to the music in the same way, swaying gently and each tapping their left foot, wearing divots in the sand.

The song ended and the music faded away. Vauk looked around and saw Trent sitting in the shade. He smiled and waved as Christoff started playing again. Getting up, Vauk walked to the shady area, sitting next to Trent. "I remember these songs."

"I could tell." Trent leaned against Vauk, listening to the music.

As they watched together, Christoff got up, and the music changed to a bright, spirited melody. Vauk's brother started to dance and skip around the water's edge, looking very much the quintessential mischievous, happy, romping satyr.

"This brings back so many memories."

Trent shifted his gaze from Christoff's dancing to Vauk. "Happy ones, I hope."

"Mostly, yes." Vauk was smiling as Trent kissed him. "Want you, Tapfer."

"I know, Love. The music seems to be affecting me too." Trent deepened the kiss, and then gentled it with great effort. "Unfortunately, we need to wait until later, I think." Trent cocked his head to indicate that they had an audience.

Christoff was still playing and dancing, but they'd been joined by Jeremy, Phillip, and Dovino, who'd come to the lake for their afternoon swim.

"Who's that?" Dovino tilted his head in Christoff's direction.

"My brother, Christoff."

"Wow. Cool. I didn't know you had a brother." The three young satyrs sat down to listen.

"Neither did I. We just met this afternoon."

Christoff stopped his playing, joining the group in the shade. Introductions were made, and they made small talk until the boys excused themselves, undressed, and raced naked into the water, splashing and playing together.

"Let's give them some privacy." Trent nudged Vauk, who nudged him back. "Their swimming will escalate into the usual satyr activity pretty soon." Christoff smiled knowingly. The three of them got up and headed into the woods as the boys in the lake started kissing.

By the time they had completed their tour of the farm and got back to the house, it was dinnertime. Travis and Cembran invited Christoff to join them. Dinner was pleasant and convivial, everyone getting along and laughing together.

After dinner, Cembran cleared away the dishes. "You're welcome to stay with us. We have an extra bedroom."

The laughter died on Christoff's lips and his eyes got dark. Luka, who'd been curled up beneath the table, growled.

"I have a hotel room in town. Thank you, but I should be going." Christoff said goodbye to everyone, thanked them for their hospitality, and got up abruptly. "Is it okay if I come again tomorrow?"

Travis nodded. "Certainly."

With a final good night, Christoff made what seemed like a hasty exit.

Vauk looked stunned. "What happened?" Everyone looked around at one another, confused. Pushing back his chair, Vauk excused himself and disappeared into his room, quietly shutting the door.

"Did you feel that?" Trent was whispering.

Travis nodded. "It's the same thing I felt earlier. Weird, isn't it?" Trent silently agreed. "But this time I know it was coming from him."

"Yeah, but only for a few seconds." Luka jumped against Trent's legs, wanting to be held. "I spent most of the day with him and didn't feel anything like that at all. He actually seemed lighthearted and happy, thrilled to have found Vauk. I just don't get it."

"I don't either. Cembran, any ideas?"

Shaking his head, Cembran said, "No."

"He'll be back tomorrow. We'll keep a close eye on him and see what happens then." Travis looked to Vauk's closed door.

"I'll see you in the morning." Trent hugged both Travis and Cembran good night.

Chapter Twenty

T rent entered the bedroom, seeing a large, familiar figure curled into a ball on the bed. "Vauk...." The figure shifted, turning to look at him. Trent knew Vauk was confused by Christoff's hasty departure—hell, they all were—but Vauk tended to take things to heart, and that worried Trent, because it left Vauk vulnerable. "Let's go for a walk." Vauk's large body shifted again, sitting on the edge of the bed before standing up and following Trent out of the room. Travis and Cembran were talking quietly as they passed through the living room. "We'll see you in the morning." Trent nodded gently in acknowledgment and they headed outside, turning in the direction of the lake.

Approaching the tree line around the lake, murmurs and gasps reached their ears. Stepping onto the edge of the sand, they saw the source of the soft sounds. A familiar pair of satyrs was curled together on the sand, their soft sounds of pleasure warming the last vestiges of twilight. "Must be Steven and Brock." Trent turned his eyes away from the couple.

Vauk nodded in agreement. "Definitely." Quietly, so they wouldn't disturb the couple's lovemaking, they stepped back into the trees. "Maybe we should go back to the house."

As they walked, Trent gestured to one of the shelters and they headed toward it. Vauk entered the small shelter and started to get comfortable, but Trent indicated that this wasn't their destination. "Grab a blanket and a couple pillows." Vauk complied, and Trent got a blanket as well, and a lantern. "Let's go."

Slowly, in the darkness, Trent led the way along the familiar path and across the farm fields to the doe's enclosure. Mika approached as he opened the gate. "Why are we here?"

Vauk followed Trent into the enclosure and closed the gate behind them. Slowly, Trent walked to the far corner of the enclosure, spreading a thick blanket on the ground, laying out the two pillows and the other blanket. "I think Mika will share her home with us for the night." He couldn't make out Vauk's expression in the soft lamplight, but he hoped he was pleased. The night was pleasant, but a little chilly as he slipped out of his clothes and climbed beneath the blankets.

The lamp cast just enough light for him to see Vauk removing his clothes as well, and then a large, warm body joined him in the blankets, arms pulling them close together, their lips touching in a strong kiss. From the first touch of their lips, Trent could feel the uncertainty and energy coursing through his lover. Trent had expected this reaction and the thought of a wild, primal lovemaking session made his own blood race. "I can feel the wildness." Vauk's eyes glowed in the lamplight, locking onto Trent's. "Don't hold it back; let me feel it, release it." Trent deepened their kissing, tugging on Vauk's lips. "I want it!" He saw Vauk blink at the force in his voice and then their lips crashed together, all attempts to hold back the frenzy whirling inside his lover dropping away as Vauk rolled Trent onto his back, pressing him against the ground with his weight.

Arms, strong and vise-like, pulled them close, skin against skin. Vauk's kisses were hard and insistent and Trent met each tug of Vauk's lips, each thrust of his tongue, each scrape of his teeth. He could taste a hint of blood as Vauk continued his bruising, needy, unflagging kiss. The weight on his body felt solid, hard, almost overpowering, and Trent went with it, knowing that Vauk's wildness would only be satisfied if he allowed his own inner wildness to run free. Vauk didn't want submission, not this time; the wild portion of his being craved conquest, needed to fight and win, to replace the uncertainty with power, stability, and hard-won love. Something deep inside Trent told him with absolute certainty exactly what Vauk needed. "What do you want?"

Trent could feel Vauk's knees forcing his legs apart. "I want you, need you! Can barely control it!" Vauk's teeth were grinding together, the need was so strong.

"Then don't. Take what you need!" Trent pulled on Vauk's lips, ramping up his own desire, knowing Vauk's hold was tenuous at best. Vauk's weight was gone and Trent felt his legs being lifted, his knees pushed to his chest. He'd forgotten to bring anything, but there was no way he'd deny Vauk now.

"Jesus!" A hot, hard, probing tongue stabbed at his opening, driving deep, opening him up. "What are you... ahhhh!" The tongue probed him again, hot and wet, setting him on fire while strong fingers kneaded his skin.

"You like my tongue in you?" Vauk blew gently against the hot skin. Trent threw his head back as the lantern went out, casting them into complete darkness, shutting off his sense of sight, heightening his other senses. Each of Vauk's touches sent him flying, fingers gently teasing his skin, tongue probing, lips sucking and kissing his most tender, private places, each sensation a surprise, happening without warning, outside of his control.

"Vauk, that feels so good. Please... don't stop." Trent heard a soft growl as the tongue answered the soft plea, reassuring that he had no intention of stopping. "Gonna...."

Everything stopped. "Not yet. Not 'til I'm inside you, until we're together."

Trent was panting for breath, hoping desperately that Vauk didn't take too long. His entire body was vibrating with excitement. "Please, Vauk. Hurry, please."

Then Vauk was pushing into him, filling him, joining them together, and he kept filling him, stretching him. Trent sighed and gasped as he felt Vauk's hips rest against him. Then he was moving, driving into his body, and all Trent could do was feel and hear. Gasps, grunts, and whines reached his ears as Vauk thrust deeply. Trent met each thrust, whimpering as Vauk hit the sweet spot with each downward movement. Trent looked in Vauk's direction. All he could see was a pair of eyes, but feel, oh, he could feel each and every movement Vauk made. Each twitch, each muscle contraction, each thrust sent waves of pleasure through Trent's body and he wanted to come, he wanted to come very badly, but he was determined to wait for Vauk. He could tell by the way Vauk was breathing that Vauk was close. "Tapfer, come for me, come for me now...."

That was all Trent needed, and a groan built deep in his chest, his own climax starting in his toes and working up his body. He was shaking and cried out, screaming his release across the fields, with Vauk following seconds later, filling him with hot, molten pleasure, calling his love to anyone within shouting distance.

"Vauk... love you." Trent felt Vauk withdraw from him, a hitched breath, and then a warm weight settled on his body as they held each other, their breathing evening out gradually while they kissed between heaving breaths.

"I love you, Tapfer." Vauk settled on the blanket next to Trent, pulling them close together.

Their kisses were soft, gentle, the passion spent, the wildness in both of them satisfied. Trent shifted slightly, pulling the blanket over both of them, then settled next to Vauk, curling against the big satyr's body as sleep took them both.

In the morning, Trent was bathed in warmth. The air was cool, but he could feel the warmth of Vauk's naked body pressed against his back. Opening his eyes, he smiled when he saw the doe curled on the blanket in front of him, her back pressed to his stomach. Trent gently stroked the young doe's side, watching as her eyes slid open. Raising herself onto her feet, she slowly ambled away and started her morning grazing. Trent shifted closer to Vauk and let his eyes slide closed again.

"Hey, boys."

Trent cracked his eyes open to see Cembran standing on the other side of the fence. Trent yawned and quickly covered his mouth with his hand. "Morning, Cembran." Trent had the decency to look slightly embarrassed.

Cembran smiled. "Everywhere I go this morning, I find sleeping satyrs curled together." Trent looked puzzled, and Cembran continued. "You and Vauk, Steven and Brock sprawled together by the beach, and I found Jeremy, Phillip, and Dovino in the hayloft." Cembran was practically grinning.

Trent wasn't quite sure if Cembran was driving at something. "I'm sorry. Maybe we should have stayed at the house." Trent was starting to wonder if they'd offended Cembran somehow.

"Don't be silly. Sex outside, close to nature, is in our blood, part of being a satyr. It allows both parts of us to be happy and whole."

"Oh." Trent looked relieved. "I always fantasized about having sex outside. I just thought it was a kink of mine."

Cembran chuckled as Vauk squirmed next to Trent. "Nah. As Travis says, 'It's a satyr thing.'" With those final words, he turned and headed across the field to the sheep barn to continue his chores.

Trent nudged the warm, sleeping satyr next to him. "Vauk… Love… we should probably get up." Sitting up, Trent stretched, only to be pulled back against Vauk's warmth as a pair of lips captured his. Their kisses deepened, and Trent moaned softly into Vauk's mouth as a tawny head nudged his cheek and a long tongue slurped against Vauk's cheek. Trent pulled his head back and laughed. "Looks like somebody's ready for her breakfast." Vauk humphed softly at being interrupted, but Trent knew it was all show.

Standing up, Trent danced slightly in the cool air as he pulled on his clothes. Vauk chuckled as he watched Trent shiver in the cool morning air. "Come on; it's not that cold."

"As I remember, you were worried about boiling your bits in the hot tub. Well, I don't want mine all cold and shriveled." Trent pulled on his pants and tugged his shirt over his head.

Vauk stood up, the blankets pooling at his feet, the morning sun shining on his naked glory. Trent's body reacted immediately, and he was about to undress and throw himself at Vauk when he saw a figure step from the path near the house, heading for the front door.

Both of them stopped and looked at each other. The farm became quiet: no sheep bleating, no birds singing, nothing but complete stillness. Vauk furrowed his brow, looking around. Trent turned his head. Mika was standing in the middle of the pen, eyes wide, sniffing the air, ears perked, her body hunched, ready for and expecting danger. "What's going on?"

Trent turned to Vauk, shrugging. "I don't know, but the same thing happened yesterday when we arrived." Just as suddenly as it started, the farm returned to normal. Birds sang, and the animals went back to eating. Even Mika relaxed and went back to her grazing. "Yesterday, I thought I could have imagined it, but not twice." Trent stopped, focusing all his attention on Vauk. "I'm afraid that what I felt yesterday was coming from Christoff, and this morning…?"

"I was afraid of that. His appearance was just too coincidental. What do we do?" Vauk started pulling on his clothes.

"I'm not sure, but no one should be alone with him, just in case." Vauk agreed. "Especially you, Love." Trent squeezed Vauk's hand gently, and after making sure Mika was fed and watered, they gathered up the blankets and Vauk headed toward the farmhouse while Trent returned the blankets to the shelter, mulling the events of the last day or so through his mind. After putting away the bedding, Trent headed back to the farm, meeting Brock and Steven along the way.

Brock looked serious. "Travis told us that Vauk's brother showed up yesterday."

"You mean the half-brother he didn't know he had, yeah." Trent knew he sounded a little bitter, but he couldn't help it. "Christoff arrived a few minutes ago. Would you like to meet him?"

Steven jumped to answer. "We'd love to." While they walked, Trent told them what he could about Christoff.

In Travis and Cembran's living room, Trent made introductions, after which the lawyer in Brock took over. "How long have you been in town?"

Christoff squirmed a little. "I got here two days ago and met Vauk yesterday."

"Where have you been staying?" Brock tried to keep his expression bland, but it was apparent to Trent that Brock was on to something.

"We… I'm staying at a hotel in town." Both Trent and Vauk could hear a touch of annoyance in Christoff's voice.

Steven came to the rescue. "Brock." Steven patted Brock's knee, his expression one of mock exasperation before turning his attention to Christoff. "You'll have to forgive him. He's a lawyer and sometimes he forgets he's not badgering witnesses."

Brock feigned indignation. "I'll badger you." His fingers ran across Steven's ribs, and the smaller satyr squirmed away, laughing.

Trent looked around the living room and gave Cembran a questioning look, wondering where Luka was. Cembran signaled Trent and the two of them stepped outside. Cembran pointed toward one of the fields, where Cembran's dog, Sham, was playing with Luka. "They've been romping together for hours." Trent watched as the two dogs ran together, jumping and chasing after each other. With a glance and a smile, they went back inside and rejoined the conversation.

Steven used the interruption as an opportunity to change the subject, and they spent the next few hours chatting about general topics. As lunchtime approached, Steven and Brock excused themselves and said their goodbyes, with Brock motioning to Trent. Christoff and Vauk were talking quietly, and Trent slipped out behind them, walking with Steven and Brock toward the lake.

Brock didn't mince words. "I don't know what Christoff is playing at, but I saw him in town last week when we were eating at Faye's."

Trent wondered out loud. "Why would he lie about something like that?"

"I don't know, but there's something not quite right about him. He seems nice. In fact, he's quite personable, and I don't know why I feel this way. I can't quite put my finger on it, but...."

"I know," Trent agreed. "I can't put my finger on it either, but a few times I've felt something very strange. Most of the time I don't feel anything out of the ordinary. I just don't get it."

Steven leaned close, whispering, "You could follow him." Both Brock and Trent looked at Steven like he'd grown a second head, but Steven continued. "When he leaves tonight, follow him, see where he goes, who he sees, what he does. There's a reason he lied about how long he's been in town."

"You know, that's not a bad idea." Trent stopped to think, but Steven was way ahead of him.

"When he leaves tonight, call us. We'll pick you up and follow him into town."

Trent nodded as he thought it over, making a reluctant decision. "Okay."

Brock quipped gently, "My Steven, the detective."

Steven smacked Brock's butt gently. "Be nice."

"I'm always nice." Brock slipped an arm around Steven's waist. "Especially to you." Trent smiled as he watched the two of them walk toward home, hands gently caressing, their affection for each other apparent. With a deep sigh, he turned and went back inside.

Trent noticed Vauk and Christoff sitting together in the living area, speaking softly. He couldn't make out what Christoff was saying, but his hands were gesturing like mad and Vauk sat rigid and stiff, clearly agitated. When Christoff noticed Trent, he said a few more words and then sat back in his chair, relaxing.

Trent went into the kitchen area to help Cembran, catching his friend's eye. "How long were they talking like that?"

"Most of the time you were gone."

Trent whispered under his breath, "Shit." What was Christoff up to? As he watched Vauk's reaction to what Christoff had said to him, Trent's resolve firmed. *I'm going to figure out what he's up to.*

Chapter Twenty-one

Vauk sat staring into space, seeing nothing. After a few seconds, he again became aware of his surroundings. Trent was helping Cembran with the dishes, his eyes glancing Vauk's way every few seconds. Christoff was relaxing, sitting back in his chair, with a satisfied look on his face that Vauk wanted to slap off him. Confusion, conflict, and a little anger whirled within him, and whenever his eyes met Trent's, he could tell he saw it too.

The room was quiet; only the soft clinking of the dishes and the occasional question about where something went marred the stillness that to Vauk felt uneasy. Most of all, he needed to talk to Trent, and he needed to talk to him alone, but Christoff had been staying close since he arrived and wasn't giving him time alone.

"Christoff, would you help me with a few of the chores? I've got a ewe that's been feeling poorly. Your music might help her." Thank god Cembran was incredibly perceptive. How could Christoff refuse?

"Sure." Christoff smiled, thoughts of playing his music changing his facial expression to one of happiness. Lifting himself out of the chair, Christoff looked to Trent and Vauk before following Cembran outside.

As soon as the door closed, Trent settled himself on the sofa, next to Vauk. "What is it, Love?" They heard the door open again as Travis came in from outside. He saw the earnest, concerned look on Trent's face and quietly went into his and Cembran's bedroom, staying close, but giving them some privacy.

"Christoff wants me to come back with him. He says he wants me to share the baccharist role with him. He says that the village and our family need me."

Trent felt a twist in his stomach, but he managed to keep his voice level. "What did you tell him?" Trent feared what the answer would be as he took Vauk's hand in his.

"Nothing. I didn't know what to say." His voice rang with doubt and confusion. "So much has happened lately."

"What do you want to do?"

"I don't know." Vauk held his head in his hands. "I'm so confused." He turned away, looking at the wall, anyplace where he wouldn't have to see the disappointment he knew he'd see in Trent's eyes. "Part of me wants to go home, see those I remember, those who loved me." Vauk stopped, turned to Trent, forcing himself to face him, face the look he knew he'd see. But it wasn't there. To his surprise, he saw only patience and understanding. Yes, there was a touch of hurt in Trent's eyes, but he also saw love. "Part of me, the happy, un-scared part, wants to stay here with you. Loyalty pulls me back, but love keeps me here. I can't figure out what I should do." Vauk gestured with his hands, imitating a scale.

"You don't need to decide right away." Trent's hand slid along a bearded cheek.

Misunderstanding, Vauk shot to his feet. "Don't you want me to stay?" His voice was filled with hurt and anger.

"Yes, Love." Trent remained calm, his voice level and soft, the same tone he used to soothe one of his frustrated students. "Sit down." Trent patted the sofa next to him and Vauk complied, tension stiffening his body. "I'm not telling you to go. I... this isn't fair... to you. I could tell you what I want and you'd probably do it to make me happy." Trent looked into those chocolate eyes he loved. "But you need to be happy." Trent's voice almost broke; only sheer will kept him under control. "This is a decision you need to make and no one can make it for you."

"It's so hard...."

"I know, but know this as well: I'll love you always, no matter what. But, please, whatever you do, take your time. Things may work out."

"But he's my brother, my family." Vauk was still so caring, so trusting sometimes, even after all he'd been through. It was one of the things Trent loved most.

"I know, but there are still many things we don't know... yet. Remember, someone tried to have you captured again and someone's been messing with your dreams and thoughts. We don't know who it is."

Vauk's eyes became hard. "You think my own brother, a man raised by my father, would do this to me?" His voice got louder and the door opened and closed to Travis's bedroom.

Trent was becoming frustrated, but he tried not to let it show. In truth, he'd do just about anything to keep Vauk here with him, but that was selfish and he knew he wouldn't stop him if Vauk truly wanted to leave. "I don't know and neither do you, but I think it's time we found out."

Vauk nodded slowly. "Yeah, I guess it is." Vauk scooted closer. "I'm sorry for getting angry." Trent caressed Vauk's leg with his hand, signaling his forgiveness without words as he looked into Vauk's eyes. "I promise I won't make a decision until we know something."

Trent breathed a sigh of relief. "Thank you," he said, and leaned forward, his forehead gently resting against Vauk's. "If it's okay with you, I'm going to try to see if we can find out something."

Vauk's forehead crinkled, but he didn't pull back. "What are you going to do, Tapfer?" The voice imitated an indulgent parent.

"I'm tired of waiting to see what will happen next, so we're going to take some action of our own."

"What are you going to do and who is we?"

Trent kissed Vauk's lips gently before confessing the plan. "Steven, Brock, and I are going to follow Christoff when he leaves tonight, see where he goes."

"Why?"

"Brock said he's been in town for longer than he told us, so we're going to see if we can figure out why."

Vauk pulled his head back. "Then I'm going too."

"No!" Vauk stiffened at the force in Trent's voice. He saw it and softened his tone. "I need you safe. I need you to stay here with Travis and Cembran."

Vauk crossed his arms, looking partly menacing and partly like a petulant child. "I don't think so." Trent almost laughed, except Vauk looked so serious.

Trent huffed out his breath. "Please, Love. There's someone out there that tried to cage you. I just want you safe."

Vauk's expression changed and Trent knew he'd do what he wanted. "I know you don't like Christoff...."

Trent kissed Vauk softly, smiling. "It's not that I don't like him. I actually do, but something's just not right and I don't trust him. Not when it comes to you and your safety."

"I guess. But be careful tonight," Vauk acquiesced.

"I will, I promise." Trent shifted and picked up his cell from the table. "I need to make some calls and then we can go outside." Trent lifted his eyebrows suggestively. Vauk smiled and sat back.

Vauk sat quietly with a hand on Trent's thigh as Trent made a few phone calls, freeing his schedule for the next few days by rescheduling his tutoring sessions to later in the week. Once he was done, they went outside, making a direct line to Mika's enclosure. Both were surprised to see Arthur inside, playing chase with the young doe.

A slightly winded Arthur met them at the gate. "Who's the stranger with Uncle Cembran?" Turning to Vauk, he said, "He looks sort of like you."

"He's my half-brother, Christoff. He came here to find me."

Arthur smiled his usual, bright smile. "Cool." Arthur whirled around as the doe butted her head against him. Arthur took the hint and returned to their game.

Trent looked around the farm; everything looked quiet. Listening intently, he could hear notes from Christoff's pipe floating from the sheep barn. "Come on." Trent pulled Vauk toward the forest and the start of the path to Vauk's clearing. "Cembran will keep Christoff occupied for a while. Besides, what satyr could resist those sheep of his anyway?"

Trent grinned and Vauk grunted softly, hoping he knew what Trent was getting at. "I think it's time we were alone for a while."

"Alone?"

"Yeah, alone. Alone. Want you to make me scream."

"Oh… that kind of alone." Vauk's eyes turned dark, his voice going low. "I can definitely do that."

"I know you can." Since Vauk might be considering Christoff's offer, Trent figured he'd give him something to compare it to. He knew he probably wasn't playing fair, but if Vauk was considering leaving, he'd make damn sure he knew what he was leaving.

With Vauk leading, they stepped into the forest surrounding the pastures, the cool, dappled shade a stark contrast to the direct warmth of the sun. Trent watched Vauk's strong backside as they wound their way along the now-familiar path to the clearing, which stood quiet and a little forlorn. The small hutches and the enclosure that had been Mika's home were empty. "It doesn't feel the same."

"It wouldn't; you're not the same." Vauk looked puzzled. "This was your home when you needed to be alone, to find yourself again after you were rescued. You don't need it anymore."

"I don't understand." Vauk stood at the edge of the clearing, looking around.

"This isn't your home anymore. You've made a home at the farm with your friends, people who care about you." Vauk nodded, a little sad. Trent stood in front of him, arms around his neck. "That doesn't mean that it can't be a special place, a place for love." Trent tilted his head, bringing their lips together in a kiss with promise and a touch of reassurance, and Trent felt Vauk shiver just a little.

"Love that, Tapfer," Vauk moaned into Trent's mouth before taking the offered lips again. "Our special place." They stood together in the sunshine, arms around each other, bodies pressed together, lips kissing, eyes closed, each lost in the pleasure and closeness given by the other.

"Let's go inside." Reluctantly, they parted, however briefly, and went inside the small shelter that had been Vauk's home for almost a year. The sleeping pallet was still there and Vauk retrieved the bedding from the storage box, making them a soft, comfy bed. "What do you want?"

"Lie down, Vauk." Trent used his hands to coax the big satyr onto the bed. Kneeling next to the large body, he kissed his satyr lover as his fingers worked the buttons of Vauk's shirt. "Let me make love to you." Vauk raised his head, eyes questioning. "You always take care of me, make me feel so special. I want to do that for you." Vauk's eyes closed and his head rested on the bed as Trent undid the last buttons, letting Vauk's shirt fall open, his powerful chest bare to Trent's view. "Love how strong you are." Trent leaned forward, capturing a nipple between his lips, sucking gently and whirling his tongue around the fleshy nub.

"Love that, Tapfer." Moans and whimpers continued as Trent worked one nipple and then the other, alternating as his hand stroked in small circles over Vauk's stomach, each circle becoming larger. Fingers slid beneath the waist of Vauk's pants before retreating again. Trent let his fingers ghost over the skin just above Vauk's manhood, teasing the shaft as they passed, eliciting a soft whimper.

Trent could barely contain his desire, but knew he had to, needed to make this special for Vauk. The taste of Vauk's skin as he kissed his way down Vauk's stomach was making his head spin. Opening Vauk's pants, Trent continued kissing down the hard, flat stomach, parting the flaps of fabric, kissing down into the V. "Trent," Vauk whined softly, "don't tease me so."

Trent continued kissing and tasting as his fingers again slid along Vauk's skin, up his chest to lightly pinch the hard nipples.

Vauk's hips undulated slowly into Trent's touch. Deciding to be merciful, Trent slid his hands along Vauk's hips, pushing the pants lower, freeing Vauk's erection from the confines of its fabric prison. He continued pushing the fabric down the satyr's thickly haired legs. Shifting his body, Trent removed Vauk's pants and knelt back, looking at his naked satyr laid out on the bed. "So handsome... so sexy."

Trent captured Vauk's lips with his while long fingers curled around the base of Vauk's shaft, squeezing and releasing, but not stroking. "Vauk, have you ever?" Trent let his fingers swirl behind Vauk's balls, ghosting over his most private opening. Vauk rocked his head slowly on the bedding. "Oh."

"But, I want you to love me." Trent looked into Vauk's deep chocolate eyes, searching for doubt, seeing none. "Please make love to me." Vauk opened himself to Trent to accentuate his meaning.

Trent kissed Vauk hard before whispering, "I'd love nothing more than to love you." The complete meaning of what Vauk was offering was not lost on him. Vauk was offering himself in a way he never had before, not to anyone, not even Miki. A small tear pooled in his eye and rolled down his cheek before he could blink it back. Standing, Trent shed his clothes, his eyes never turning from Vauk's.

Once naked, Trent crawled up Vauk's body, his big satyr's legs parting for him invitingly.

As Trent kissed his lover, Vauk's legs curled around his waist and Trent slid his hands across Vauk's skin, cupping his firm butt. "Love you, Vauk." Trent's fingers skimmed over Vauk's puckered flesh.

"I love you too." Vauk's arms wrapped around Trent, pulling them close together as they kissed. Trent could feel Vauk shift slightly beneath his as his cloak fell away. He could feel the occasional wisps of Vauk's tail as he kneaded Vauk's butt. In response, Trent released his own cloak, wanting to make love to Vauk as his true self.

"I want you, Tapfer."

Trent lifted his head, his eyes gleaming. "I need to get you ready first." With another kiss, he slid down Vauk's body, lifting and spreading the long beefy legs. His hand wrapped around Vauk's shaft, tongue swirling around the head, lips then sliding down the hard shaft and across the balls. Trent smiled as the large body vibrated with excitement.

"Trent, what are you... oh!" Vauk cried out as Trent's tongue circled the tight, puckered flesh of his opening, lips nipping at his skin.

"Like that?"

"Uh-huh." Vauk arched his back into the sensation.

Trent licked his way up over Vauk's balls and along his shaft, taking him into his mouth, retreated, and licked his way down to Vauk's opening. He continued this routine, each time spending more and more time opening Vauk, preparing his lover for what was to come with tongue and fingers.

"Please, need you."

Trent knelt between Vauk's legs, positioning them on his shoulders before slowly and carefully pressing into Vauk's body. Vauk hissed softly as his muscle was breached for the first time. Trent stopped, making sure he wasn't hurting him. "It burns a little."

"Is it okay? Do you want me to stop?"

"No, please don't stop." Vauk's eyes were clouded with need as Trent pressed deep inside and stopped. Slowly, he retreated, and Vauk moaned softly. Setting a slow, easy pace, Trent started moving inside his lover, locking his eyes on Vauk's.

"Look at me, Love." Vauk's eyes had drifted closed and they rolled open, locking onto Trent's. "You're so hot, so good." Trent ran his hand along Vauk's stomach, taking his shaft and stroking in time to his thrusts.

"Trent... harder, please." Complying with the moaned request, Trent picked up the pace, careful not to hurt his lover. Vauk's body started to shake beneath him. "Close... so close...." He cried out Trent's name as he came, shooting white ropes onto his stomach. Vauk's climax pushed Trent over the edge and he emptied himself deep into Vauk's body as he cried out his love.

Regaining his breath, Trent withdrew slowly before resting on top of Vauk, kissing him deeply. "You were wonderful, Love."

"So were you, Tapfer." Vauk knew he'd be sore, but it would be a new and good kind of sore that would remind him of Trent.

They held each other close before dozing off, Trent still lying on top of Vauk. When Trent woke, Vauk's eyes were still closed, their bodies sticking together slightly. "Love, we should get up. Christoff and Cembran are going to be wondering where we are."

A soft growl echoed from the chest beneath him, followed by arms pulling him back down. Vauk's eyes didn't even open, his breathing even.

Trying to be gentle, Trent slid off Vauk and cleaned himself as best he could before pulling on his clothes. Once dressed, he nudged the dozing Vauk awake and watched as the big satyr dressed, his pants sliding over his round, firm butt. Together they put the bedding away.

Satisfied and smiling, they left the shelter, shutting the door tightly, and headed down the path back toward the farm. When they stepped from the forest, they saw Christoff and Arthur sitting on one of the pasture fences, Arthur listening as Christoff played his pipe to the gathered sheep. The dichotomy in Christoff's behavior wasn't lost on Trent. How could someone so innocent and earthy, playing his pipe with such unbridled joy, be the source for the malicious feelings he'd sensed on previous occasions? Granted, Trent knew that these feelings he was having were new to him and he could be wrong. There were so many things that didn't feel right. Trent wasn't sure what to make of them, but he hoped he'd be able to find out something soon.

They made their way toward the music. Christoff stopped playing as they approached. "Please, don't stop. It's lovely." Trent leaned against Vauk as Christoff resumed his serenade. When he stopped playing, the look on his face was abject joy, like he'd transcended himself somehow.

Trent smiled and the small group dispersed, going back to the farm and their respective chores. Trent worked in the vegetable garden with Travis, while Vauk, Cembran, Christoff, and Arthur spent the rest of the afternoon working with the animals.

As chores were finished, everyone congregated back at the house, with Travis and Cembran starting dinner.

Trent felt the same cold, almost evil feeling he'd felt previously, as he expected, and Christoff immediately stood up, looking almost blankly at them. "I've got to go. Thank you for your hospitality." Like the previous evening, he said good night to everyone and made a hasty retreat.

The door had barely closed behind Christoff before Trent was on the phone.

Steven answered.

"He just left."

"We'll pick you up in two minutes." Trent could hear Steven moving about. "We're getting in the car now."

"I'll be here." Trent hung up the phone, kissed Vauk, and raced out the door, knowing Vauk would explain what was going on. Trent raced down the path, emerging near the road just as Brock's car pulled up to him. Trent jumped into the backseat and they took off toward town.

Chapter Twenty-two

The car flew down the road toward town, Brock driving like a bat out of hell, Trent holding tightly to the chicken straps for dear life. Maybe this wasn't such a good idea; every time the car went over a bump he swore the car left the road. "What type of car was Christoff driving?" Brock asked from the front seat without turning around.

Brock went over another bump and Trent squeaked before answering, "It was a red sedan." The car went over another small rise and Trent knew that they'd left the ground.

Steven turned around, looking into the backseat. "Brock, Trent isn't used to your driving; I think he's turning green." Brock grunted but didn't slow down. "It took me awhile to get used to Brock's maniac driving."

"I thought you always liked my driving."

Steven squealed as Brock took one hand off the wheel and goosed his butt. "I love your driving in the bedroom," Steven turned around, protecting his butt from Brock's hands, "but on the road you're a total menace."

Brock shook his head in mock annoyance. "Sorry, Trent, but we need to catch up to him so we don't—" A car appeared ahead of them, and Brock finally—to Trent's great relief—eased off the gas. "Is that him?"

Trent leaned forward, peering between the seats. "Yeah... I think so." Brock slowed further and they maintained a safe distance behind. Christoff drove directly through town and pulled into the parking lot of a small, inexpensive motel on the far edge of town. The motel had seen better days, but it appeared to be clean and the building well kept, the yard planted with bright flowers.

Christoff pulled up to one of the units farthest from the office and went inside. Brock pulled his car into the parking lot and shut off the engine. "We need a cover. There's no way the manager's going to allow us to snoop around Christoff's room. Steven, go inside and see if they have a room available. If they do, get one for tonight and try to distract them if you can."

Steven opened the car door. "What are you going to do?"

Brock answered like someone who'd done this before. "We're going to park in front of the room door and try to snoop around." Steven nodded in agreement and walked toward the office, while Brock parked his car.

Surprisingly, the car provided a reasonable amount of cover, especially from the motel office. Trent got out of the car and crouched low, looking at the room Christoff had entered. The door was closed and the curtains had been pulled closed. Getting closer, Trent crouched beneath the window. When the curtains closed, they'd caught on something, creating a small wedge in the drapes. Cautiously, Trent lifted his head and peeked through the small part in the curtains.

Christoff, satyr features visible, was lying on the bed with another man who Trent didn't know. Christoff had his head in the man's lap and Trent watched as the older man looked around him. He could tell he was talking, but he couldn't hear what was being said. Christoff appeared to be relaxing and falling asleep.

"What can you see?" Trent jumped and pulled away from the window, relaxing when he realized it was Brock.

"Christoff and another, older satyr are on the bed together." Trent peered through the window again. "I wish I could hear what they're saying."

"I'll keep watch." Brock scurried away, back to the cover of the car, while Trent continued to watch through the window. Unfortunately, there was nothing to see, except two satyrs lying on a bed together. Trent was curious who this other satyr was, but other than that, there was nothing of interest and Trent knew that the longer he stayed where he was, the more likely he'd be caught, so he stepped away from the window and got back in the car.

"Well?" Brock questioned as Steven got in the car.

"There's nothing to see."

Steven twisted around. "There was one room left for tonight. I got it if you want to use it. It's one away from Christoff's room."

Trent looked alternately at Brock and then Steven, unsure of what they should do. "I'm really not sure what staying will accomplish. I mean, the only thing we found out was that he's staying with someone, someone older." Trent sat back in the seat, thinking. "Shit... I keep thinking like a human." That got their attention and both Steven and Brock twisted in their seats. "A satyr's appearance ages based upon life experiences, like having children or grandchildren, right?" Both Steven and Brock nodded. "So the satyr with Christoff looks older because he's had children, not necessarily because he is older."

Brock thought for a minute. "Yeah, that's true, but what does it tell us?"

Trent grinned and started to laugh. "Nothing at all."

"They could be lovers," Steven observed as he thought.

"I don't think so. There was no tenderness in the way the older satyr held Christoff, at least not the type a lover would exhibit. It looked almost business-like—and strange." Trent puzzled, trying to think if he'd missed anything, and he concluded he hadn't. "We may as well go."

"We have the room for the night. Why don't we go there for a while and check on them again later, see if we can see anything else?" Brock didn't really sound convinced that they'd have better luck later.

"It's worth a try." Trent got out of the car and followed Steven into the room he'd rented.

"Jesus!" Trent grabbed his head with his hands, looking like he was in pain.

Steven was right there, helping him into the room, "What's wrong?" Steven helped Trent to the bed. "Are you hurt?"

Trent could barely talk; he just motioned for Steven to wait as he reclined back on the bed. Brock entered the room, closing the door behind him. "What's going on?" Steven shrugged and looked at Trent.

"I don't know." Trent grabbed a pillow, putting it over his eyes, shutting out the light. "Go see if you can see anything." Trent heard the door open and close again just before he covered his ears with his hands. "It feels like my brain's melting." Trent moaned into the pillow. Then, slowly, what Trent was feeling started to make some sort of sense—well, maybe. "He's yelling, screaming." Trent lifted the pillow so whoever was still in the room could hear him. "The anger is overpowering." Trent took a deep breath, trying to block some of what he was feeling. "You have to do more. You have to convince him."

"Do more of what? Convince who?" Steven sat on the edge of the bed, holding Trent's hand, becoming more and more concerned by the second. The door to the motel room opened and closed again. "Brock, we have to get him out of here, now!"

The next thing Trent knew, he was being lifted off the bed, pillow still over his eyes, carried outside, and laid on the backseat of the car.

"Hey, what's going on?" a strange voice called.

Trent heard Brock answer what must have been the manager. "He's not feeling well; we're taking him to the hospital." Trent barely heard the car doors close and the engine start before the car began to move.

Slowly, with each passing second, Trent started to feel better. His head began to feel normal and the pressure inside lessened. Breathing deeply, he willed his body to relax. Finally, he opened his eyes and looked around. Steven was crouched on the floor of the backseat, hovering over him, stroking his forehead. "Are you feeling better?"

"Yeah, but I've got one hell of a headache." Trent started to sit up, but felt dizzy. "I feel like I've been drinking for days with a hell of a hangover."

"Jesus, you scared me." Steven helped him sit up slowly as the car continued through town.

"I think I scared myself." Trent found he could breathe much easier now and his head was really starting to clear, the dizziness fading. "Where are we going? I don't need the hospital."

Brock answered from the driver's seat. "I'm taking you back to the farm."

Trent held his head as the car went over some bumps. "Thanks. And Brock...."

"Yeah?"

"You can slow down now; we left the hounds of hell behind us two miles ago." Trent heard a grunt from the front seat and felt the car slowing. "Steven, call Travis, and tell him we're on our way back and we need to talk. I don't quite know what's going on, but one of them might be able to help." Steven nodded and took out his phone to make the calls as he shifted from the floor of the car to the seat.

Trent spent the rest of the ride half-listening to Steven talk on the phone. Most of his concentration was on all the things going through his head. Finally, Steven hung up his phone. "I called Travis and he'll get everyone there." Trent nodded, keeping his eyes closed as the car sped toward the farm. Hopefully someone could make sense of what had just happened to him, because he sure as hell couldn't.

The rest of the ride was quiet. Trent kept his eyes closed and tried to relax in the backseat. Steven hovered like a mother hen while Brock drove, slowly... well, slowly for Brock. After what seemed like forever, Brock pulled into Travis's parking area. Trent didn't move as he heard the car doors open. Slowly, he cracked his eyes open. "Can you walk?" Steven was still hovering, but now it was somehow comforting.

"The world stopped spinning, so I think so." Tentatively, Trent put his feet on the ground and raised himself onto his feet, taking a few tentative steps. Steven shut the car door and the three of them made their way to the farm.

Brock opened the farmhouse door and held it for Trent, who stepped inside. Travis was sitting on the sofa talking on the phone while Vauk looked like he'd been pacing the floor. The big satyr turned as soon as Trent walked inside, and two seconds later he was being crushed against a large, warm body with huge arms wrapped around his back, while Luka whimpered and bounded around his legs. "You had me so worried." Trent managed to lift his head as two lips crashed into his, kissing the life out of him. Vauk pulled out of the kiss. "Don't ever do that again!" Then he kissed him again, softer this time, the anger and frustration draining out of him once he had Trent in his arms.

"He's okay, Vauk." Brock patted the big satyr on the shoulder and sat on the sofa as Travis finished his call and hung up the phone. Vauk didn't release his grip one bit. They just stood together, or rather, Vauk stood there holding Trent who couldn't have moved one inch if he wanted to.

"Love, can we sit down?" Vauk eased his hold and they walked to the living room. Vauk sat in one of the chairs and pulled Trent onto his lap, reestablishing the bear-hug grip on his lover. Rather than fight it, Trent leaned back against Vauk's chest, truly relaxing for the first time since they'd arrived at the motel. Once he was settled, Luka jumped on his lap, licking his face, his tail going a mile a minute.

"Gathod and Doug will be here in a few minutes." Travis got up and helped Cembran in the kitchen, returning a few minutes later with mugs of hot, sweet tea.

The front door opened and Arthur raced inside, bursting with energy, which quickly evaporated when he saw the dour, nervous faces. "What's going on?"

"We need to have an important talk." Brock motioned for Arthur to come close.

"Oh." Arthur looked perturbed. "One of those talks you don't think I'm old enough to hear." Arthur crossed his arms, definitely looking put out.

Brock tried to keep his cool. "Why don't you go back to the house and when we're done here, Steven and I will go swimming with you before it gets dark."

To give Arthur credit, he didn't fuss, but he did stare Brock down until the experienced, high-powered lawyer started to look uncomfortable, blinked, and looked away. Then Arthur turned and headed for the door.

"Arthur, wait." Travis turned to Brock. "Don't you think it's time he learned about our world, the good as well as the bad? He's about to go away to college and he needs to know how things really work."

Brock looked about to argue, but stopped and nodded his head, saying something under his breath that sounded like "My parents are going to kill me." Cembran handed Arthur a cup of tea and Brock indicated for him to sit next to him on the sofa. As soon as he was seated,

Luka jumped from Trent's lap, racing across the floor to launch himself at Arthur. The young satyr caught him mid-leap, laughing and accepting kisses. "Where'd you learn to do that?"

"Do what?" Arthur sipped from his mug as Luka settled on his lap.

"Stare me down like that."

"From you." Brock had the decency to look surprised, while Steven hooted and snickered. "Whenever I've done something where you think I'm wrong, you try to stare me down. I just used it against you this time." The near glee in Arthur's voice was barely contained. Brock leaned back on the sofa, unsure if he should be offended by the remark, or pleased that Arthur tried to emulate him. Brock decided on pleased and smiled.

A soft knock on the door announced Gathod and Doug's arrival as the door opened and the sheriff and his partner entered the room. The usual banter that would accompany their arrival was immediately cut short by the tense expressions and general mood in the room. Gathod looked from person to person, finally focusing his attention on Cembran. "What's going on? Did someone die?" Gathod meant it as a joke, but no one smiled. "Sorry."

Cembran handed both of them a mug of tea. "Don't worry about it. We're a little tense." Cembran hugged his oldest friend and one-time lover. "We're glad you're here. I think we could use your expertise." Cembran motioned them to chairs.

Gathod and Doug took their seats, with Doug getting curious. "So what's the problem and how can we help?"

Travis looked at Trent, and then began. "Yesterday morning, Vauk's brother Christoff appeared at my door looking for Vauk. He seemed like a nice guy and he appeared genuinely happy to have found Vauk after all these years."

Vauk interrupted. "Before yesterday, I didn't know I had a brother." That got Doug and Gathod's attention. "He's obviously my brother. He looks sort of like me, but he really looks like my father."

Trent was getting impatient. "Whenever Christoff would show up, I'd get this feeling, sort of cold and malicious. The animals felt it too; the entire farm would get quiet. Then late in the evening I'd feel it again and he'd bid a hasty retreat."

Gathod was listening intently. "Did anyone else feel it?" Travis and Cembran both nodded, Steven and Brock shook their heads, and Vauk nodded slowly.

"We got curious and decided to follow Christoff to see where he went and if he was seeing anyone, particularly since he lied about how long he'd been in town." Doug raised his eyebrows, but said nothing. "We followed him to the Rose Motel and watched him enter a room."

The cop in Doug was taking over. "What did you see?"

Trent answered the question. "I saw Christoff with another satyr I didn't recognize. They were lying on the bed together, but they didn't appear to be lovers." Trent saw Doug nod but he said nothing. The others in the room were hanging on every word. "Basically, there was nothing to see, but Steven had gotten a room, so we decided to wait awhile and check later." Trent felt Vauk's arms around him tighten and Luka jumped off Arthur's lap, settling at Trent's feet. "We'd just gotten into the room, when it hit me."

Vauk spoke softly as he stroked Trent's cheek. "What happened?"

"I'm really not sure. I started to hear someone else in my head, someone really angry, yelling and screaming."

"Was it Christoff?"

Trent shook his head. "No, it was the other satyr, and he was screaming and berating Christoff. The things he was saying to him."

Doug looked confused. "You could hear what he was yelling in your room?"

"No, I could hear his thoughts."

Brock interjected. "Trent had me peek in the room and all I saw was two satyrs lying together on the bed, with Christoff asleep, tossing and turning."

"The things I was hearing in my head were dreadful and they were all directed at Christoff. He kept telling Christoff that he had to get him here, had to do more, had to convince him. He was being absolutely cruel to him and there was nothing he could do to get away." Trent snuggled close to Vauk, needing his reassurance. "One thing is very clear: the things we were feeling weren't coming from Christoff, but from this other satyr."

"So what we felt…." Travis was thinking out loud.

"In the mornings was probably Christoff trying to vent and get rid of what was being forced into him, and at night was the other satyr calling him back again."

"Was it like what happened at the gardens?" Vauk asked softly.

"No, I could hear his thoughts, but I didn't enter his mind." Trent turned to the group. "Steven and Brock got me out of there and headed back here. As we got farther away, I could hear fewer and fewer of his thoughts until they finally faded away completely."

"Did either of you feel anything?" Gathod asked Brock and Steven and each answered that they hadn't. "So only you could read his thoughts."

"They weren't his thoughts so much as what was driving the intense emotions. It's hard to explain, but mostly I was feeling things. The words I got were carried on those negative feelings and they were intensely hurtful and filled with hate, jealousy, and fear." Trent looked at them, worried and confused. "What I want to know is why I'm the only one who felt anything."

Everyone looked at Gathod, waiting. "My initial explanation is that you have some sort of connection to him."

"How?" Trent was becoming agitated and Vauk tried to soothe him. "I've never seen this person before."

"The other possibility is that you're sensitive to the emotions he was putting out and you were able to pick up on them."

Vauk rubbed his hand gently along Trent's spine. "That would explain what happened at the gardens as well. You could be picking up on intense negative emotions." Trent nodded and reclined against Vauk, enjoying his touch. "I bet this goes along with your unique dream-weaving abilities."

Trent let his nervousness fade away. "Yeah, that could be. At least we know your brother isn't behind all this, but we're not much closer to finding out who is."

Doug smiled. "Maybe we are. What room are they in at the Rose?"

"Number five. Why?"

"I want a picture of this mystery satyr. The two men who took Vauk are still sitting in my jail. They haven't made bail and their trial isn't for another month. Maybe they'll recognize him, and if they do know him, it just might shake them up enough to tell us something."

"Then what do we do?"

Travis leaned forward, his confidence reassuring. "We lure him here where we're strongest. How, I don't know how yet, but we'll work on that after we hear from Doug."

Everyone seemed content with the plan and the group started to break up. Steven, Brock, and Arthur headed down to the lake to catch a quick swim in the last light of the day. Gathod and Doug said their good nights and headed home, holding hands as they left.

Cembran got out of his chair, picking up the dirty cups and placing them in the sink. "Trent, do you need something to eat? You didn't get much dinner."

"Thank you, yes. That would be very nice. I'll help you." Trent shifted off Vauk's lap.

"I've got it. You just relax for a while. You've had a rough few hours."

Before Trent knew what was happening, Vauk had tugged him back on his lap. "Not going to let you out of my sight for a while. You really scared me, you know."

"I know." Trent tilted his head, looking up at Vauk. "I love you." Their lips met in a soft, tender kiss.

"I love you too."

A few minutes later, Cembran had a snack ready and the four of them sat at the table.

"I hate to bring this up again, but I didn't want to say this in front of everyone." Trent put down his fork as he waited for Travis to continue. "Sometimes I get these feelings and usually I know what someone's gifts are, and I hate to say it, but I have a feeling that you do have some sort of connection to our mystery satyr. Maybe it's through your feelings for Vauk, but there is a connection of some type. That, combined with your natural abilities, is probably the reason for why you felt what you did at the hotel."

Trent shuddered. "I'm not sure I like this."

Cembran patted Trent on the shoulder to reassure him. "We know, but part of this is because of the strength of your love for Vauk. Without that, this probably wouldn't be happening." Trent looked confused and a little overwhelmed. "You've already formed a connection to him and a need to protect him, and this is probably a manifestation of that need."

"So you're saying this may be a good thing."

Cembran nodded and Travis changed the conversation to more pleasant topics.

Cembran got up and started clearing the dishes, and Trent tried to stop himself from yawning without much success. "Why don't you go to bed? I'll clean this up." Trent yawned again, and they said their good nights and headed off to bed. Travis and Cembran both watched, a little concerned, as they entered the bedroom with Luka following at their heels, the door closing softly behind them.

Chapter Twenty-three

The bedroom was quiet, like a small sanctuary away from everything else. Trent cleaned up quickly, slipped out of his clothes, and silently climbed into bed. As soon as he was settled, Luka jumped on the bed, nestling next to him. Trent heard Vauk cleaning up and he waited for him to join him. Closing his eyes, he let his hands stroke the small terrier, trying to forget, at least for a while, the events of the day. The opposite side of the bed dipped as Vauk lay down next to him. "Are you okay, Tapfer?"

Trent rolled onto his side, curling against Vauk's large body. "I am now." His hands carding through the dark hair on Vauk's chest, head resting on the big satyr's shoulder, he said, "Love you."

Vauk's head turned to the side, their lips meeting in a gentle kiss. "Love you too."

Trent shifted his body, climbing on top of Vauk. "Make love to me, please."

Vauk growled as he flipped them over, kissing the life out of him. Trent heard a muffled yip and then Luka managed to extricate himself from the covers and jumped down from the bed, curling up on the rug. Not that Vauk or Trent noticed—they were way too wrapped up in each other. Their kisses continued until they both needed to breathe, and they stopped just long enough to gasp for air and then their lips crashed together again.

"Vauk, Love…. Please, I need you so bad." Trent wrapped his legs around Vauk's waist, exposing himself to his lover's touch.

Vauk reached to the nightstand, retrieving the small bottle and lubing his fingers before pressing two inside his lover. As the fingers breached the guardian muscle, Trent moaned loudly, then grabbed Vauk's head and pulled him down into a hot, passionate kiss.

Vauk's fingers moved and explored. "God, do that again." Vauk massaged Trent's prostate until the man beneath him was vibrating with excitement. "Vauk, please, I'm so close." Trent's hips were pressing up against Vauk, trying to get purchase; all he needed was just a little more. Then the fingers were gone, and Vauk's hands gentled his hips onto the bed.

"Relax, Tapfer. This isn't a race, but a long, slow ride." Vauk raised his body slightly, his hands soothing Trent's skin, letting the smaller man cool down a bit. "Settle, Tapfer. Settle back on the bed." Vauk grabbed a pillow and raised Trent's legs. The smaller satyr started to vibrate again, this time in anticipation.

"Need you." Vauk placed a pillow beneath Trent's hips and placed himself at Trent's entrance, slowly sinking into his lover while Trent let out a long, low moan. "Yes!" Vauk started to move, and Trent met each thrust, driving Vauk deep inside him. He'd had lovers before, but never had he felt such a driving need to be joined with someone, both physically and spiritually. "More... want more."

Vauk picked up the pace, driving himself deep into his lover. "You're so sexy, Tapfer." Trent stroked himself, but Vauk gently batted his hand away. "No... only me. Grab the headboard." Trent complied and Vauk kept up his merciless pace with Trent calling out his encouragement.

"That's it, Tapfer... come for me. You're so hot, so sexy laid out on my bed. Come for me." Trent could feel a climax building, but he wasn't quite there.

"Love you, Vauk."

"Then show me how much... come for me." That did it. The pressure inside was overwhelming and Trent came hard, whimpering as he shot on his stomach without touching himself.

Vauk felt Trent tighten around him as he came and that sent him over the edge. He called out his release in monosyllabic, nonsensical sounds.

Trent pulled Vauk down on top of him, kissing his lover hard and moaning softly as he slipped from his body. "Love you so much."

"Love you too."

"Please don't leave." In his moment of weakness, Trent had finally given voice to his main fear, and he waited to see what Vauk's reaction would be.

Vauk pulled up, looking down at Trent. "Who says I'm leaving?"

"I'm afraid you'll go back with Christoff." Trent leaned forward, putting his arms around Vauk's neck. "I don't want you to go."

"How long have you been keeping this inside?" Vauk leaned forward, settling Trent back on the bed.

"Since this morning when you told me he'd asked you to go back with him."

"Look at me, Trent." Trent turned his head, looking Vauk in the eye. "I'm not going anywhere unless you go with me." Vauk captured Trent's lips, kissing him hard to accentuate his point. "I'd be incomplete without you." Vauk let out a deep sigh. "I still think you should be with a satyr who you can share your Triuwe with, but if you've got your heart set on me, I won't deny you anything, because I love you with everything I am."

"I won't leave you either; you make me happier than I ever thought possible." Trent caressed Vauk's cheeks as they kissed again, holding each other tight.

Releasing Trent from his embrace, Vauk slipped from beneath the light covers, returning a few minutes later with a warm cloth and a towel. Trent shifted on the bed, but Vauk stilled him with his soft tone. "Let me."

Trent relaxed on the bed as Vauk gently ran the cloth over his still-tingling skin. Vauk then used the towel to pat Trent dry before returning the cloth and towel to the bathroom, and climbing into bed. Trent curled against Vauk's prone body, head resting on his shoulder, hands languidly stroking the strong chest, occasionally plucking at a still-perky nipple. No words were spoken. None were needed now; instead, they let their hands and bodies do the talking, stroking and caressing, loving and kissing through the warm, pleasant afterglow.

As soon as they settled down, Luka jumped on the bed, slinking up to their pillows. After receiving a few scratches and imparting dog kisses, he padded to the foot of the bed, curling into a ball, and promptly fell asleep. "He's something else, isn't he?"

Vauk hummed his agreement as Trent's fingers stroked his cheek before gently caressing the scalp at the base of his horns. The skin was very sensitive, and stroking a satyr there or at the base of the tail was one of the most intimate forms of satyr-touch possible. Vauk's eyes closed as Trent carded his fingers through Vauk's hair, gently massaging the big satyr's scalp.

Trent could feel Vauk relaxing into sleep, and he tried to relax himself, but found it difficult—his mind didn't want to turn off. Finally, his exhaustion caught up with him and he fell asleep with Vauk's arms around him and Luka snuggling to his feet with the cool night air blowing in through the windows.

Morning came really early for Trent. He woke when Vauk got out of bed. "Go back to sleep." Vauk sat on the edge of the bed, rubbing his lover's back until he dropped off again, only waking later when he heard voices outside the door.

Forcing himself out of the comfortable bed, Trent quickly cleaned up and dressed.

"Morning, Trent." Doug, in his uniform, was sitting in one of the living room chairs, speaking with a concerned, jittery Vauk. "I was just filling Vauk in on what I found out." Trent sat on the sofa next to Vauk, waiting for Doug to continue. "After I left last night, I got one of my deputies to pay a visit to Christoff's hotel room. Another deputy was across the parking lot with a high-powered night-vision camera and we were able to get a picture of this other person with Christoff, which we showed to our two friends in custody."

Vauk shifted. "Can I see the picture?"

"I'm having another printed; for some reason the camera lab only printed one. I'll have a copy brought by this afternoon. Anyway, they obviously recognized the person in the photo, and after some prodding, finally confessed that he put them up to capturing you in exchange for airfare and some money to come to this country."

Vauk huffed and sat back. "So now we know for sure that someone is definitely behind what's happened to me, but who? And what do we do now?"

"We lure him here." Travis's tone was definite. "We need to deal with him so he doesn't do this to anyone else, and I think I know how to get him here."

"How?" Vauk and Trent said in unison.

Travis's reply was one word. "Christoff."

Everyone was quiet as they waited for Trent to continue. "I'm hoping that Christoff isn't a willing participant, and from what you described last night, I doubt he is, but we have to be sure."

"Then what?" Trent was a little anxious, but he thought he could see where Travis was going.

"If Christoff isn't a willing participant, then we might be able to get him to help us once he realizes what's been happening to him." Travis zeroed in on Vauk. "You need to talk to him, see if you can feel him out."

"I'll try, but I don't know how successful I can be." Vauk looked to Trent for support.

"Just be yourself, Love. He's your brother. Approach him as someone who cares for him and cares about him." Trent held Vauk's hand. "You have an enormous capacity to love. Let him see and feel that, and he'll respond." Trent nipped Vauk's ear. "I know I have."

Cembran chimed in, "Do I have to separate you two?" His voice humorously mocked Trent's "teacher voice."

Trent pulled back in mock horror, raising his hands in the air. "No, Mr. Cembran, we'll be good." The five of them broke down in peals of laughter, releasing the tension that had crept in. Doug said his goodbyes, still laughing as he closed the door behind him.

Still chuckling himself, Trent stood up and pulled Vauk to his feet. "Let's take Luka outside and see if we can help with some of the chores."

Vauk nodded, and then asked, "When do you have to go back for work?"

"My schedule is free until Thursday."

Vauk leered. "That's what you think." Then he grabbed Trent's butt.

"Get out of here before I throw cold water on you. Geez, these youngsters." Cembran was shaking his head in mock frustration, trying to keep from grinning.

Trent started chucking again. "Aw, Cembran, you're not that old." Trent dodged a dish towel on his way to the door, he and Vauk hurrying outside. Turning back, they saw Travis circle his arms around Cembran's waist. Travis winked at him just before the door closed. "Cembran is definitely not too old."

"What?" Vauk turned, noticing that Trent had stopped, staring at the closed door, talking to himself.

"Nothing." Trent knew that Cembran was in fact quite old by human standards. "Those two are such an inspiration, like proof that anything's possible."

Vauk took Trent's hand, pulling him toward the garden. "Anything is possible. After all, you somehow found me, even when I wasn't sure I wanted to be found." After a few playful grabs, Trent started his weeding. The two of them worked together until the farm went still and Trent felt the now-familiar angry feeling that announced Christoff's arrival as loudly and clearly as a bullhorn.

Without looking up, Trent called, "Christoff, we're in the garden!" They both continued their work until they saw a pair of legs walking along the rows.

"I wasn't out of the woods yet when you called. How'd you see me?"

Trent rested back on his legs, taking off his gloves. "I didn't. I felt you," he said, his tone matter-of-fact.

"What?"

Vauk answered, taking control with a deep breath. "We need to talk, Christoff." Vauk slipped off his gloves, placing them next to Trent's before getting up and helping Trent to his feet. He wanted to talk where they wouldn't be disturbed. "Let's go to the lake; we can talk there."

Vauk headed toward the lake without another word, expecting Christoff to follow, which he did. Trent stayed put, not sure whether he should follow. His question was answered when Vauk turned around and gave Trent a look that clearly said, "What are you waiting for?" Trent caught up, and the three of them walked to the lake in near silence.

Vauk sat on the sand with Trent next to him, while Christoff remained standing, looking confused. "Sit down so we can talk."

Christoff complied, sitting on the sand across from them. "Are you going to tell me what you meant when you said you felt me?" Christoff glowered at Trent with confusion and disbelief.

Trent glanced at Vauk, wondering if he should say something, but Vauk shook his head slowly and Trent kept quiet. Then Vauk explained. "Each morning when you arrive, the farm gets quiet and we can sense something very dark and cold." Vauk carefully chose his words. He knew Trent had always described the feeling as malevolent, but he didn't want to give too much away. "It was that same feeling that alerted us to your arrival this morning, and we were wondering if you were all right." Vauk thought it best to get Christoff talking, and he thought expressing concern would get him started. He really hoped he was handling this right, but he was going to give it a try, and the twinkle in Trent's eyes was encouraging.

"I've been having these really intense nightmares for a while." Trent watched for signs of deception. "Almost as soon as I fall asleep, I start having these really intense dreams, people yelling at me, wanting me to do things for them that I can't do, and telling me they're unhappy with me. Lately, my dreams have centered on you." Vauk listened intently, but said nothing. "That it's very important that you come home to your family, and that the village will suffer if you don't return." Trent watched Christoff's body language, face, and eyes intently, looking for any signs of deception, but saw none. Just the open, honest, genuine satyr he'd seen playing his pipe for the sheep. "I guess that the energy from my nightmares might be lingering when I arrive." Christoff lowered his eyes, cheeks coloring in embarrassment. "I'm sorry. I didn't mean to cause anyone any trouble or discomfort." His voice was so childlike that Trent didn't know what to think, and Vauk looked completely lost. This definitely wasn't going the way they'd expected at all.

Christoff noticed the perplexed looks on their faces. "Is something wrong? Did I do something…?"

"No, not at all." Trent patted Christoff on the shoulder as he got to his feet. "I'll be right back."

Trent headed toward the farmhouse, Christoff's reaction running through his head. As he emerged from the trees, he saw Travis coming from the goat barn. "Travis!" Trent motioned for him to wait and he caught up with him.

"Is there a problem?"

"A bit of something unexpected."

"How so?" Travis's curiosity was piqued.

"Christoff has no idea about what's been happening to him. He thinks he's been having nightmares."

"You believe him?" Travis seemed skeptical.

Trent nodded. "Either he's the world's best liar, or completely unaware of what this other satyr's been doing."

Travis whistled. "That's possible. If he's really strong, he may be able to put Christoff to sleep, control his dreams, and then make Christoff forget he was ever there. That would explain his reaction. But Trent… be careful. This guy's dangerous, particularly since you can feel him too—that gives him the ability to hurt you."

"I know, but what do we do about Christoff? We need to help him."

"Try to get him to remember some part of what's been happening to him. If he remembers something that was suppressed, that might have a cascade effect."

"Thanks, Travis." Trent turned to go back to the lake.

"You're welcome. Call right away if you need help."

Trent smiled. "I will, I promise." He raced back to the lake.

Vauk and Christoff were still sitting together, talking. As Trent approached he heard Vauk's deep laugh.

"Hey, Tapfer. We were just talking about Dad." It was good, really good for Vauk to have someone to share his stories with.

"Hey." Trent sat next to Vauk and listened as Vauk finished his story. He really didn't want to throw cold water on them, so he decided to wait and see where the conversation led.

"Christoff," Vauk looked at Trent, "we have something that we need to talk to you about." He indicated that Trent should take it from here.

"I know we just met and you have no real reason to trust me, but that's just what I'm going to ask you to do." Christoff looked at him and waited, obviously curious. "I want you to think back to last evening when you left here." Christoff nodded slowly. "Tell us what you remember."

Christoff scrunched his face. "What I remember about what?"

Trent kept his voice light, trying to cover his excitement and hope. "Just humor me and tell me what you did after you left the farm."

"I got in my rental car and drove back to the hotel."

"Which room did you go to?"

Christoff squinted in suspicion, but answered, "My room."

"What was the room number?" Trent knew he had to get Christoff to delve into the details.

"Seventeen," Christoff continued. "I spent the evening watching television." Trent kept himself from showing a reaction because Christoff had in fact gone into room twenty.

"Are you sure of the room number?"

Christoff squinted, his voice becoming tentative. "I think so...." The first hint of doubt crept into his voice.

"Were you alone?" Trent watched Christoff closely.

"Yes. I lay on the bed, falling asleep in front of the television. Why are you asking these questions?" Christoff's confusion seemed genuine.

"Christoff... brother...." Vauk leaned forward, gripping Christoff's shoulder in reassurance. "I just met you two days ago, but you're my brother and I love you. Just think carefully and try to remember."

"What is it that I'm supposed to remember?"

Trent shook his head. "I can't tell you. It's something you need to remember on your own." Trent continued. "What did you watch on television?"

"I can't remember...." Christoff's voice trailed off. "I should be able to... but I can't." *Because there's nothing to remember.*

Trent thought this might be the first chink in the armor. "Was there someone with you?" Trent kept his voice soft. "You weren't alone, were you?"

Confusion and disbelief colored Christoff's face and Trent could tell when things didn't quite fit for Christoff. "No... yes.... I mean, I'm not sure now."

Vauk leaned forward, touching his brother's arm. "You weren't alone."

"No, there was someone there." Christoff's voice was very soft, and he was murmuring to himself as though he couldn't believe what he was remembering. "There was... but it seems like it's someone else's memory."

"It's not; it's your true memory," Trent added to Christoff's sighed words. "Trust yourself."

"Who was it? Who was with you?" Vauk asked excitedly.

Christoff opened his mouth, but he didn't get a chance to answer.

"I was with him!" All heads snapped toward the trees.

Chapter Twenty-four

"Sasha!" Vauk called out in joy, happy to see his old friend. Then his smile faded as the ramifications of Sasha's appearance occurred to him. "Sasha, how could you?" Damn, Trent would have done just about anything to keep that hurt, dejected look off Vauk's face.

Sasha just laughed as he watched the agony on Vauk's face, reveling in the pain and hurt of another. What a bastard.

"Uncle Sasha, I remember what you've been doing." Christoff's voice was dripping with hurt and confusion. "Since Dad died I thought you were helping me, and instead you've been trying to control me." The betrayal hit the young satyr hard.

"So what." The huge satyr laughed. "There's nothing you can do about it." Christoff immediately fell on the ground, holding his head and whimpering in pain. "I can hurt you anytime I want, simply by thinking about it."

Trent could feel Sasha's attack on Christoff. In fact, it was taking all his energy and concentration to keep from falling on the ground as well. He grabbed Vauk's arm to steady himself, trying not to let Sasha know how he was being affected. Trent whispered to Vauk through gritted teeth, "Help him," knowing he'd also be helping himself.

"Kadje Alexander, stop this!" Vauk shouted at Sasha as he glared at his former friend.

Sasha laughed again. "Anything you want." Christoff stopped squirming, his hands moving away from his head. Vauk knelt down, making sure his brother was all right without taking his eyes off his former friend. "What the hell's happened to you?" Vauk's anger was pushed aside by the hurt and pain of betrayal. "We've been friends since we were kids." Vauk helped an exhausted Christoff get to his feet as Trent relaxed after Sasha's onslaught.

"You were just a means to an end. I was never really your friend, just a kid from the poor side of the village you took pity on." The spite was palpable.

"That's not true! You were my friend. That didn't matter to me and you know it. It only seemed to matter to you." Vauk tried to keep his voice level and calm, and Trent could hear the pain just below the surface.

Sasha's eyes softened. "It really mattered, especially when you and Miki started spending more time together. When he was gone, fighting in the human war, we spent all our time together. But then he came back and you never had time for me anymore!" Sasha was practically shouting as he vented the hurt he'd built up over the decades.

Trent leaned close, his mind clearing from the attack on Christoff. "He was in love with you."

"That's right. Even he gets it, but you never did!" Sasha was shaking, his anger overflowing. "It wasn't until you and Miki became Truists that I really figured it out."

Vauk was staring at Sasha in horror. "Figured what out?" He was afraid of what Sasha was going to say next.

"That I needed to get rid of Miki. Then you'd return to me and it'd be like it was before. We could be together and you'd be baccharist, and I'd be your mate." Vauk was too stunned to interrupt. "So I found some men from the circus and I arranged to have Miki captured, but they took you instead. At first I was heartbroken, but then I stumbled on something even better. I realized that I could feel your Triuwe bond with Miki, but not his to you, so I blocked it." The bastard actually smiled. "He thought you were dead." Vauk rushed at Sasha. "Don't!" Vauk stopped as Trent and Christoff held him back. "I'll kill Christoff without ever touching him!" The threat stopped him in his tracks and he glared at Sasha, who looked wickedly triumphant. "Miki died a month or so later."

"But you didn't have what you wanted."

The smile on Sasha's face sent chills through both Trent and Vauk. "But I did. Miki was gone, you were gone, and I played the grieving friend to the hilt. Your father even took me under his wing. It was perfect. But then he decided he needed to have another child and he married," Sasha pointed, "his mother, and they had him."

Trent interrupted. "Is that when you decided you needed to find Vauk? You needed him, and he didn't know you'd had Miki captured. So about twenty-seven years ago," Vauk's head swung around in surprise, "you decided you had to find Vauk, and if you found him he'd be grateful. Hell, he might have fallen for you, and since he was the oldest, he'd be the heir and you could still get everything you wanted." Trent's tone was dripping with disdain.

Sasha ignored Trent's tone. "Yes, but I couldn't find him, so I went home and waited. Christoff grew up, revering his Uncle Sasha, and as he grew older, I figured out how to control him. When your father died, he became baccharist and I told him what to do. It was ideal." He almost giggled with glee.

Trent sneered. "You'd have everything you wanted, but let me guess: about a year ago, you felt Vauk again and you knew he was a threat to your plans. So you tried to lure him home so you could eliminate the threat."

Sasha's sneer was back. "Exactly, but he wouldn't be lured, so I brought Christoff to help me finish the job." Sasha reached into his pocket, pulling out a small gun. "Now I'm going to finish you off once and for all." Without thinking, Trent stepped in front of Vauk, putting himself between him and Sasha. His instinct was to protect his lover. "Get out of the way. I'll shoot you too!"

Now it was Trent's turn to smile. "Don't you want to know the hitch in your plans?"

"Sure," Sasha mocked, "why don't you tell me?"

"When you looked for Vauk, you met Claire and stayed with her while you searched, didn't you?" Trent used his "I know what you did" teacher expression.

"Are you the result of my dalliance with her?" God, this guy was completely self-absorbed and heartless.

"Yes. You're my father." Trent's enthusiasm was underwhelming.

"Well, well... let me guess. My son and my so-called childhood friend are now lovers. Well, isn't that convenient." Sasha raised the gun.

Trent's thoughts were on hyperdrive. Sasha didn't get it. As Sasha's son, Trent would inherit some of his father's abilities and have a connection to him, and maybe he could use that to his advantage. Trent felt a surge of adrenaline and he knew what he had to try. Concentrating, he wound his way along the energy Sasha was projecting back to the source. He could almost see it as well as feel it: the hurt, the irrational hate, the bitterness of love spurned for another, all created a path that Trent could follow. The next thing he knew, Trent was looking at himself, Vauk, and Christoff at the end of a gun in his own hand. "Put the gun down." Trent could feel Sasha's thoughts assailing him, but this time he knew what to expect and he was able to block most of them. "Put it down!" But the strongest of Sasha's thoughts and emotions kept assailing him, pushing and weakening him.

The gun lowered and then dropped to the ground. Christoff rushed forward, but Vauk stopped him, not realizing that Trent was in control, at least temporarily. "Don't. He can still hurt you." Christoff stepped back, watching.

Sasha's thoughts kept assailing Trent and he couldn't hold them back much longer. He had to get out... but he had an idea. *"Just a few more seconds...."* Then Trent's world went black....

"Are you okay, Tapfer?" Trent opened his eyes; Vauk was kneeling over him, looking worried and haggard.

Trent's head felt like it was going to explode. Slowly he tried to get up, but the world started spinning and he closed his eyes to stop it. "Where's Sasha? Don't let him hurt you."

"Shhh. It's okay. He's lying on the sand, not moving." Vauk's voice was blank, devoid of emotion when he spoke of his childhood friend.

"Is he dead?" Trent opened his eyes again. Things were still spinning, really spinning, and he snapped his eyes closed again. He tried to move, but felt too weak and gave up.

"No. He collapsed when you did." Vauk's fingers stroked Trent's forehead and cheek. Trent leaned into the touch, needing the connection to his lover. "I sent Christoff to get Travis." Trent relaxed against Vauk's body, breathing deeply, all energy drained from him.

Footsteps and voices interrupted the quiet as Christoff burst through the trees with Travis and Cembran right behind him, each of them talking and asking questions.

"What happened?" Travis's voice carried over the others and silenced them as he stood next to Vauk, looking concerned.

Vauk looked at Sasha's still-prone body. "He was the one who had me captured." Vauk turned his attention back to Trent. "He did it again. He rushed to the rescue again, and this time he saved both of us." Vauk looked at Christoff and then to Trent, whose eyes were closed and his breathing shallow. Travis leaned to Trent, feeling his neck, making sure Vauk's Tapfer was okay before shaking his head.

Cembran and Christoff, who'd been checking on Sasha, left the big satyr where he lay, joining Vauk and Travis. "Travis. Can you help him?"

"No, he's beyond my help." Cembran rested his head on Travis's shoulder, crying softly against his lover. "There's nothing physically wrong with him that I can find." Trent was barely breathing and Travis put his ear to his chest. "He's barely breathing at all."

"Lemmle, why?" Cembran sniffed as he rested his head on Travis's shoulder, waiting and hoping.

Trent took a deep breath and then became still, deathly still. "Tapfer, don't leave me." Tears rolled down Vauk's face. "Please stay." The tears kept coming. After what seemed like an eternity, Trent took another breath and was still again. Vauk kept whispering words of love. "Stay with me, please." The time between each breath seemed like an eternity, like Trent's body couldn't determine whether to go on or not. Everyone watched and prayed as Trent's breathing remained intermittent. Then Trent took a breath, then another, and another. "Tapfer, come back to me."

"I'm here, Vauk." The words were faint, but they were there. Slowly, Trent's breathing evened out and his eyes fluttered open. "I'm here, Love." Vauk's tears were flowing freely as he leaned forward, kissing his Tapfer gently as everyone breathed a collective sigh of relief.

"Where's Sasha?" Trent's voice seemed labored.

Cembran answered softly. "He's over there and seems to be asleep."

Trent leaned to Vauk, taking comfort from his lover's embrace. "He is? Thank god it worked." He seemed to be speaking to himself. "He'll probably be asleep for a while."

Travis touched his shoulder. "Are you going to be okay?"

Trent nodded, "I will be. It just took more out of me than I expected."

Vauk held Trent close, his fear abating slowly. "You had me so scared. I thought I was going to lose you."

"I'm sorry." Trent stroked Vauk's bearded cheek. "I almost stayed too long." Trent buried his face in Vauk's shoulder, comforting his scared lover. "It's all right now. I'm fine and so are you."

"Do you want to tell us what happened?" It appeared that Travis had elected Trent as the spokesman.

Trent explained about helping Christoff recover the memories that Sasha had suppressed in order to control him, Sasha's appearance, and his explanation for what he'd done over the years.

"How on earth did you disarm him?" Cembran interjected.

"He's my father and I was able to use that connection to jump into his mind and take control of him for a few minutes."

Cembran continued. "But how did you put him to sleep?"

Trent snickered. "Just before leaving his mind, I implanted a vision of a puzzle, telling him the solution would reveal the way to everything he ever wanted, but that the puzzle could only be solved in his dreams."

Vauk laughed a hearty laugh, tightening his grip on Trent. "You mean he'll sleep until he solves the puzzle?"

Trent smiled a wicked smile. "Not exactly, but it should keep him busy until we can figure out what to do with him. His dream will keep him occupied for a while."

"Is it the same puzzle you gave us in class?" Arthur had joined the group, a curious look on his face as the young satyr wondered what he'd missed.

"The same one."

"That's so cool." Arthur looked at Sasha, lying on the sand, a smile on his sleeping face. "But what are you going to do with him?"

Trent took his phone out of his pocket and a minute later he was speaking with the sheriff. "Doug's on his way."

Travis looked conflicted, his eyes darting from Vauk then to Sasha's sleeping form. If he allowed Doug to take Sasha, he'd be jailed and caged, something that ran counter to everything he felt. No satyr should be caged, no matter what they'd done. And allowing Doug to take Sasha would make him no better than the person who'd had Vauk captured all those years ago. Making up his mind, Travis turned and stepped to the edge of the water, looking toward the sky and speaking softly. "What's he doing?" Trent muttered as he settled into Vauk's embrace.

Vauk shrugged, but Christoff leaned close, whispering, "He's communicating with Bacchus," his voice filled with awe and wonder. "I saw Dad do it once."

Travis nodded his head and muttered a few last words before turning back to the group. "Let's go back to the house." No one questioned or argued; they just followed Travis as he led the way down the path. Vauk got to his feet and helped Trent stand. Together, they too headed down the path with Vauk turning just as they entered the trees to see a mist forming around where Sasha was laying.

Vauk shook his head slowly. "Bye, Sasha. Hope it was worth it." Then he stepped down the path, his arm around Trent.

When they got to the farmhouse, Doug was waiting for them, with Gathod arriving a few minutes later. Vauk and Trent brought everyone up to speed on what had happened by the lake.

"I'd better go see to Sasha." Doug was out the door before anyone could stop him.

Once the story had been told again, Gathod's curiosity got the best of him. "What I don't understand is how you knew what to do once you entered Sasha's mind?"

"Something similar happened a few days ago when we were at the gardens. Some kids were chasing Luka." At the mention of his name, the terrier jumped into Trent's lap, licking his face. "They threatened us with a knife and I found myself looking out his eyes."

"But how did you know how to enter Sasha?"

"I figured that since I could feel him so strongly, I could trace those feelings back to their source, which I was able to do. Besides, I now know that there was indeed a connection with him: he's my father."

Gathod sat back, grinning. "So my first thought was right."

Trent grinned back. "Yes. We'll never doubt you again." Trent wasn't sure how he really felt about all this. His father had been the one trying to hurt Vauk. All his life he'd wondered who his father was and the reality was a real disappointment.

The door opened and closed, interrupting Trent's thoughts. "He's gone!" Doug stood in the doorway looking upset and angry.

"It's okay." Travis calmed his old friend. "He's been taken care of." All the satyrs nodded their heads slowly, including Arthur.

"But how?"

Arthur got this wicked, mischievous look on his face. "It's a satyr thing, Uncle Doug." The room burst into peals of laughter as Doug grumped for a second and then laughed as well. When they calmed down, everyone had more questions, and Trent did his best to answer them.

Finally, it was Cembran who finally put an end to the third degree. "I think most of us have chores to do, and these two need some time alone." Cembran started handing out chores to everyone like a drill sergeant. Doug bade a hasty retreat before Cembran gave him chores too. After all, he was still on duty. Christoff was the last to leave. "I'm going back to my hotel."

Cembran gave Christoff a big hug, holding the young baccharist tight. "Go get your things and check out; you'll stay here for the rest of your visit."

"I don't want to be a bother."

Cembran scowled for a second and then smiled. "You're family; you'll stay with us."

Christoff smiled and returned Cembran's hug before racing out the door and then popping his head back inside. "Thanks. I'll be back."

Cembran grabbed Travis's hand and started pulling him outside. "We'll talk later," Travis managed to say as he was dragged out of the house, leaving Trent and Vauk alone.

Trent felt himself encircled in a pair of strong arms. "You did it again, Tapfer."

"Did what?" Vauk's lips were close; Trent could feel the warmth and he could barely think.

Vauk smiled, his lips meeting Trent's. "My Tapfer, coming to the rescue again." Trent was trying to think of something, but Vauk was kissing him again, hard and insistent... and oh, what the hell, thinking's overrated. Trent let go, kissing Vauk back as their bodies pressed together. "Bedroom?"

"Uh-huh." Yes, thinking was definitely overrated and Trent couldn't move; his body had been short-circuited by Vauk's lips. That was remedied when he was lifted off his feet and carried into the bedroom. "Going caveman on me?"

"Depends on if you like it." Vauk kicked the door closed before laying Trent on the bed, kissing him hard.

"Oh yeah, I like it, caveman." Trent's breath hitched as Vauk's shirt hit the floor, followed by his shoes and pants. "My naked satyr... the perfect view."

Trent's clothes were removed hastily. "Now that's the perfect view." Vauk gawked at the naked body on the bed. Then Vauk was with him, on him, lips pulling, tongue teasing. Nipples were nibbled and laved, abs feasted upon as Vauk made love to his rescuer, his hero. "Love you, Tapfer." Those lips, Vauk's lips feasted on the long, lean body beneath him, smiling as Trent's back arched into the touch, writhing against his kisses, and moaning as his tongue touched intimate, private places.

"Vauk," Trent moaned insistently just before they joined, their bodies moving together in love. Gentle, loving endearments fell from their lips like autumn leaves, sending them soaring together on currents of unrestrained pleasure as their combined release sent them flying.

Chapter Twenty-five

The sound of a pipe playing happily drifted through the bedroom window. A happy, sated Trent smiled as he opened his eyes, a softly snoring lover lying next to him, an arm across his chest. Trent shifted slowly, not wanting to disturb his sexy, hunky lover. The arm around him tightened, pulling him against Vauk's big body.

"We should get up, Love." A low groan was followed by a tightened grip that had Vauk spooning against his back, a hard shaft pressed to his butt. Trent smiled as Vauk mumbled softly in his sleep. He could still hear Christoff playing his pipe along with what were fast becoming the normal, comforting sounds of the farm. *What am I going to do?*

Trent knew he had to go home, go back to work, but he hated leaving Vauk and his friends. Granted, he'd be back in a few days, but being with Vauk only on weekends wasn't going to cut it. He wanted this, what he had right now, Vauk's body pressed to his, arms holding him close, each and every night. Trent loved his job and he loved his students, but he also loved the satyr who'd captured his heart. The problem was that he couldn't figure out how to reconcile the two. A small sigh escaped him as he pondered his options. He could probably get a job teaching here, but it was unlikely they'd have the resources to offer the classes he really liked to teach. He already had his dream job teaching bright, sometimes gifted students, preparing them for college and beyond.

A deep breath whooshed out of Trent as he asked himself, *what do you really want? What's important?* The answers to those questions, when put that way, were very simple: he wanted the satyr who was currently holding him close. Rolling over, Trent stroked Vauk's bearded cheek. "Wake up, Love." Trent kissed the full lips as he wound his arms around Vauk's neck. His lover's eyes didn't open, but the big body shifted, pinning Trent beneath him, knees spreading his legs apart. "Vauk."

"Shhh... no talking." Vauk brought their lips together as he pressed himself to Trent's opening and slowly entered his lover's hot, slick body. Vauk's eyes didn't open and Trent followed his lover's lead, letting himself just feel: the stretch of his body being filled, Vauk's lips on his, hot hands stroking his hips and chest, while his own hands gripped Vauk's shoulders and back.

Vauk's movements were agonizingly slow, so slow Trent could feel every contour, every vein, every twitch as Vauk moved within his body. His skin seemed hypersensitive; everywhere Vauk touched tingled. Low moans and whimpers were their only sounds as they moved together, communicating their pleasure through touch and taste without words to get in the way. The sounds continued, passion building slowly, steadily, no rushing, no hurrying. They were both enjoying the journey they were taking together.

Trent arched his back, his head shaking from side to side on the pillow as Vauk hit his pleasure center each and every time. Mouth open, pleasure transcending sound, Trent climaxed, his body throbbing and thrumming as Vauk came deep inside him, filling him with love.

Trent remained still beneath Vauk's comforting weight as he waited, before slowly opening his eyes to Vauk's smiling face and dancing eyes, and then his lips were taken in a loving, tender kiss. A small whimper escaped as Vauk withdrew from his body and he relaxed against the sheets. "Do you want to get up?"

Trent shook his head. "We'll just lay here 'til you're ready to do that again." Slowly, reluctantly, they did get out of bed, kissing and touching as they cleaned up and dressed before finally leaving the room. Luka was waiting for them, curled on one end of the sofa, his ears perking up when the door opened.

Trent called the dog, asking him if he wanted to go out as they headed for the door. As soon as the door opened, the small terrier raced outside, ears flapping as he ran in excited circles chasing grasshoppers before racing back to them.

Christoff and Arthur waved from the door of the sheep barn before disappearing inside, each returning with a lamb and a bottle. Vauk and

Trent walked to where they sat on the grass feeding the lambs. "Hey, Mr. Vauk, Trent. Feeling better?" Arthur looked up, but quickly returned his attention to the lamb when he started sucking on his fingers instead of the bottle.

"Hey, guys." Trent sat next to Arthur, but Vauk remained standing.

"Christoff, could I talk to you?" Vauk seemed suddenly serious. Christoff nodded and handed his lamb to Trent, who looked a little lost, but took the lamb anyway and watched Arthur as he started bottle-feeding the small animal.

Vauk and Christoff wandered away, talking softly. Trent watched them together, wondering just they were talking about, but from Vauk's stance, the conversation seemed relatively relaxed, so Trent concentrated on the warm, cuddly little bundle in his arms.

The lamb finished her bottle, then curled up on Trent's lap and promptly fell asleep. The simple pleasure of feeding a small, delicate creature reinforced the decision he'd come to earlier. "She's so precious."

Arthur smiled as his lamb finished his bottle and curled up in Arthur's lap. "They really are."

"Now I understand why you love them so much."

Arthur chuckled. "It's a part of all of us. For me, it touched something deep inside." His hand stroked the sleeping lamb's soft wool. "I just want to help them."

Trent could understand wanting to help others. That's why he became a teacher. "Are you ready for college?"

Arthur nodded thoughtfully. "I leave in two weeks. Brock and Steven are going to take me."

"Isn't that a little early?"

"Yeah, but I've got two weeks of testing and I'm hoping I can test out of a lot of the basic freshman classes. We have to pay for the credits, but it'll put me on a fast track."

"Not too fast, I hope. You need to enjoy the experience," Trent replied earnestly. He'd loved his college years and he hoped Arthur would too.

"I intend to, but I'll also work hard so I can come back and make a contribution to our world."

Trent grinned at his former student. He had no doubt Arthur would make a difference to all of them. Hearing footsteps, Trent looked away and saw Vauk and Christoff. They sat down on the grass, both looking happy and content. Slowly Arthur got up and took his lamb into the barn, returning to pick up Trent's lamb and taking her into the barn as well. "Do you need help?" Christoff called inside.

Arthur's head popped around the doorframe. "No, they're all set. You want to go swimming?" Arthur's earnestness had Christoff laughing as he got to his feet. "Race you!" The two satyrs took off at a run toward the lake.

Luka, who'd been playing in the grass, bounded over to Trent, leaping onto his lap. "What were you and Christoff talking about?"

Vauk laughed indulgently. "I was wondering how long it would be before your curiosity took over." Trent chuckled at the truthful assessment, leaning against his lover. Vauk took a deep breath. "He wants me to go back with him. Now that Sasha's gone, he's not sure what to do and he feels lost."

A knot formed in Trent's stomach and he pulled away, his attention turning to Luka, a tear running down his cheek. This was what he'd feared most, and after all this....

A hand on his chin gently lifted his head. "I told him to follow his heart and to remember what he learned from our father. He's the baccharist and it's time he stand on his own without Sasha or me."

Trent swallowed. "You told him no?' He sniffled, blinking his eyes in disbelief.

Vauk looked indignant. "Of course I told him no. I'm not going anywhere without you." Relief flooded through Trent as he again leaned against Vauk, arms wrapping around his chest as he tilted his head back for a kiss, which was gladly given.

"I see you two are finally up." Trent turned and saw Travis approaching. Vauk gave Trent another kiss and then started to get to his feet; there were chores to be done before it got too late. "Don't get up; I want to speak with both of you." Vauk settled back on the grass as Travis sat down. "The farm across the main road is for sale and I've had my eye on it for a while now. The pastures are perfect for raising sheep and we've been contemplating buying it to expand the farm so we wouldn't need to clear more land here. But another thought occurred to me, and both Cembran and I thought we should approach you to see if you'd like to buy it."

"It's been empty for a year or so, but the house has been cared for and maintained. The pastures will need some fence work, but they've been fallow for a while, so they'll be fresh. Cembran and I have been tightly controlling our breeding to keep the flock size under control, but we'll be able to provide enough sheep to get you started." Travis grinned. "Particularly since one of our rams got loose in one of the pastures last fall and we got a huge crop of lambs this year." Trent looked at Vauk, who looked back at him. Neither of them knew what to say, but the excitement on both their faces was evident. "Think about it, talk it over. You don't need to make a decision now." Travis got up and headed to the goat barn with a smile on his face.

"That was a surprise." Trent's eyes were glowing as he looked at Vauk. "Our own farm. What do you think?" Then Trent's face fell. "How can we ever afford it?"

Vauk thought he was going to get whiplash from the emotional changes alone. "We'll work it out, but money isn't a worry. Christoff told me that my father left some money for me that's still on deposit. He never stopped hoping that I'd return. But money isn't important." He looked earnestly at Trent. "Is this what you want?"

"What I want is to go to sleep next to you each night and wake up to you every morning. I want you to be happy and content… and I want a big garden so I can make things grow."

Vauk kissed him hard, adding a touch of passion. "That's what I want too. A place with friends, and animals, and you. A home… a real home."

Trent breathed deeply, smiling. "Let's arrange to look at the place and talk it over when I come back this weekend. That'll give us both a little time to think." Vauk nodded his agreement before kissing Trent again and getting to his feet. Trent followed suit and they walked back to the house together.

Dinner was quiet, just the four of them seated together around Travis and Cembran's table. Trent had insisted on cooking, and plates were being filled amidst the usual dinner conversation.

"Arthur said something interesting to me today," Trent commented between bites.

"How so?"

"We had a conversation about college and he told me that he was going to work hard so he could make a contribution to our world. I didn't think anything of it at the time, but the more I thought about it, the more I'm wondering what he meant."

Travis put down his fork and looked at Cembran. "He's feeling it already," he said, surprise evident in his voice.

Trent stopped eating. "Feeling what already?"

Travis became very serious. "Cembran and I were brought together for a reason, and so were you and Vauk, Brock and Steven, Doug and Gathod, even Jeremy, Phillip, and Dovino."

"That seems farfetched."

"It's not. We were all brought together because we have a part to play in a greater destiny—Arthur's destiny." Everyone stopped eating; forks clattered on plates and three sets of eyes watched Travis, waiting for his explanation. "I don't know what his destiny is, but this place and each of us have a part to play." Travis picked up his fork and started eating again. "What surprises me is that he's already feeling its pull."

"Does Brock know?"

"Yes, he does. He figured it out awhile ago, but he knows no more than we do."

"What do we do?" Trent started eating again.

Travis's eyebrows rose. "Nothing. Whatever it is will unfold when the time is right."

"Wow. I've never been a part of someone's destiny before." Trent sounded sort of honored.

Vauk ran his finger gently over Trent's bottom lip. "Yes, you have, Tapfer. You've been a part of mine, the best part of mine."

Epilogue

The path was dark, yet familiar, a large, dancing fire visible through the trees. Their satyr friends gathered, waiting for the start of the bacchanal. Trent and Vauk stepped from the trees together, looking around at the now-familiar scene that still got their blood racing with anticipation. They'd barely emerged from the trees before Trent was embraced in a big hug. "Arthur, I wasn't expecting to see you."

The young satyr stepped back, smiling at his former teacher before greeting Vauk. "Uncle Travis called early this week and asked if I could attend, so Brock picked me up at school last night," he explained with his usual enthusiasm.

The excitement in the air was palpable; they could feel it to their toes. Greetings were exchanged in hushed tones and returned with everyone gathered.

"So are you excited?" Brock startled them as he approached from behind.

The smile on their faces was almost answer enough. "Yeah. We closed on the farm late last month. Vauk's been living there, getting things ready for the sheep."

"How much longer will you have to commute?"

"I've given notice that I'll be leaving as of the end of the semester." Trent looked at Vauk, eyes dancing. "So by January, I'll be living here full time. The house in town has been sold."

Vauk interrupted. "But we kept the hot tub." He playfully nibbled Trent's ear.

"Yes." Trent's smile was mischievous. "We kept the hot tub." Trent returned his attention to Brock, "I've got a job teaching at the high school here."

"What'll you teach?" Steven laughed as Brock pulled him into the conversation, literally, by wrapping his arms around his lover.

"It's intriguing how things work out: the high school was interested in starting an advance placement humanities program and with my experience, they hired me to design and teach it."

Brock smiled sheepishly, nuzzling Steven's neck.

That look answered a nagging question that had been lingering in Trent's mind for a while. "Did you have anything to do with this?"

Brock feigned innocence. "Me? No...." Brock threw his hands up in mock exasperation and then whisked Steven away. Trent had suspected that somehow Travis and Brock had had something to do with the new program's creation at the school, but neither was 'fessing up. All he knew for sure was that his classes were full next semester with some of the brightest kids from the area.

Vauk leaned close, whispering, "Don't question your good fortune."

Trent snaked his arms around Vauk's neck, pulling him into a kiss. "I don't intend to." Things were working out and they were happy; that's what mattered.

"Welcome, friends, to our November bacchanal!" Trent released Vauk and turned around to face Travis and Cembran. "Tonight is a special evening with a very special guest." Everyone looked around to see the new face as Travis turned his gaze to the lake. "You are welcome. Please join us!" The clearing got quiet as a mist formed on the calm surface of the water, coalescing into two figures that floated above the surface until they reached the shore.

Trent recognized Bacchus instantly. The tall, imposing satyr was hard not to recognize, but his companion mystified him.

"Miki." Vauk's voice was barely above a whisper as he stepped forward, barely able to believe his eyes.

Bacchus stepped onto the shore, smiling brightly, and then approached Travis and Cembran, speaking softly and touching them like old friends. He greeted each person in attendance, sharing a thought or gesture with each individual. When Bacchus approached Arthur, the young satyr was awestruck. Bacchus smiled, and with a sweeping gesture, gathered him into his arms, hugging him warmly.

Trent watched as Bacchus spoke softly with his former student. Most of those gathered seemed surprised, but as Trent looked at Travis, he saw a bright, knowing smile.

Finally, Bacchus approached Trent and Vauk. "Trent, I'm so happy to see that you've found your way back to us."

Trent took Vauk's hand. "I did… we did."

"Vauk, I brought someone for you." Bacchus motioned for Miki to join them. "You had a long road back to us." Miki approached but didn't speak. Vauk stepped forward, but Bacchus stopped him with a gentle touch. "He's not really here; he's between worlds right now. He can see you just like you can see him, but unfortunately he can't speak and he can't hear or touch you." Slowly Miki raised his hand, palm out, and Vauk did the same thing, establishing a connection across dimensions. "He wanted me to deliver a message and a gift. The message is that he wishes you happiness and love—above all else, love." Bacchus looked at Miki, who nodded slowly. "He wants me to tell both of you to be happy with his blessing." A tear rolled down Vauk's cheek and Trent could feel his throat constricting.

Bacchus stepped back to Miki and slowly touched the figure's chest. A small ball of warm light pulled away from Miki, staying on Bacchus's hand. "Miki asked me to give you this, and tell you that what you freely gave is given back to you, so you can give it to another." Bacchus touched the light to Vauk's chest and it disappeared into him.

Tears streamed down Vauk's cheeks as he lifted his fingers to his lips, kissing them, and raising his palm. The now-fading figure repeated back the gesture, holding his palm toward Vauk as he slowly faded away.

"He's gone," Trent murmured softly.

"He could only come as far as he did because of his Triuwe bond with Vauk, but once he returned Vauk's Triuwe, the bond faded." Bacchus gently tugged both of them close, their heads touching. "Be happy and love each other. You've both had a long way to go, but you're home with your family and with each other." With a final touch, Bacchus pulled back and stepped to the edge of the lake before bidding everyone farewell and then fading into the mist.

Everyone was quiet, and then, softly, the music started. Joyful, happy music that filled the space and touched everyone and slowly, one by one, they began to dance.

Trent, Vauk, and Arthur stood together, each of them watching, but not moving, lost in their own thoughts. Then Trent took Vauk's hand. "Dance with me." Vauk nodded and together they whirled and leaped around the fire. Trent watched as Arthur looked on, fascinated. On their next approach, Trent grabbed Arthur's hand, pulling him toward the fire. "Come on, Arthur. It's time you learned how satyrs express joy!"

"Huh?" Arthur grunted as he was pulled into the circle of whirling dancers.

"It's time you learned how to dance!"

Andrew Grey grew up in western Michigan with a father who loved to tell stories and a mother who loved to read them. Since then he has lived throughout the country and traveled throughout the world. He has a master's degree from the University of Wisconsin-Milwaukee and works in information systems for a large corporation. Andrew's hobbies include collecting antiques, gardening, and leaving his dirty dishes anywhere but in the sink (particularly when writing). He considers himself blessed with an accepting family, fantastic friends, and the world's most supportive and loving partner. Andrew currently lives in beautiful historic Carlisle, Pennsylvania.

Read other titles by Andrew…

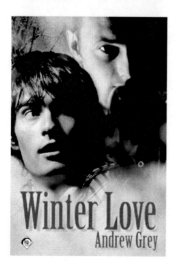

Other Fantasy titles from Dreamspinner Press

Lightning Source UK Ltd.
Milton Keynes UK
UKOW030228301011

181178UK00002B/13/P